Dear Bob

Dear Bob

Annie Porthouse

© Annie Porthouse 2003
First published 2003
Reprinted 2004

ISBN 1 85999 633 7

Scripture Union, 207–209 Queensway, Bletchley, Milton Keynes, MK2 2EB, United Kingdom
Email: info@scriptureunion.org.uk
Website: www.scriptureunion.org.uk

Scripture Union Australia, Locked Bag 2, Central Coast Business Centre, NSW 2252, Australia
Website: www.su.org.au

Scripture Union USA,
P.O. Box 987, Valley Forge, PA 19482.
Website: www.scriptureunion.org

British Library Cataloguing-in-Publication Data
A catalogue record of this book is available from the British Library.

Cover design by Phil Grundy
Printed and bound in Great Britain by Creative Print and Design (Wales) Ebbw Vale

Scripture Union is an international Christian charity working with churches in more than 130 countries, providing resources to bring the good news about Jesus Christ to children, young people and families – and to encourage them to develop spiritually through the Bible and prayer.
As well as our network of volunteers, staff and associates who run holidays, church-based events and school Christian groups, we produce a wide range of publications and support those who use resources through training programmes.

For my nan, whom I miss.

A freaky start

Fri 17 Sept

Dear Bob

Arrggghhhhh!! Just come round after v freaky dream – scared the pants off me (not that tend to wear undergarments in… sorry, too much info, swipe that).

Dream took me to youth group, where Jim (leader) was giving farewell chat (was deserting us to work for Geriatric Goats for God Ltd in Uganda, or whatever). He began like this:

'God isn't real…'

In true dream-like fashion the church hall began to sway – everything drifting into slow motion. Wanted to scream/cry/hide.

He went on to apologise for 'misleading' us over the past couple of years (hey – no probs Jim). Said he'd changed his mind about Uganda – was now off to spend year at 'New-Holistic-Enlightening-Centre' to 'find himself'.

Am having MAJOR freak-out. Like… think of it from my angle, Bob – there I was… the (almost) perfect Cn (Christian) girl (woman?) knowing exactly what (whom) I believed in (God) and what it meant for me in my life… church, lots of Cn pals, reading Bible every day (almost), knowing all Matt's songs off by heart (Redman)… even the guitar cords, and don't even PLAY the thing (amazing what you pick up being a page-turner)… and then, in a matter of seconds, someone I'd respected big time announces is all off coz:

'God isn't real'

in a dream! A stupid, insignificant dream (prob due to over-heating in sleep, due to dodgy radiator that can't suss out… always have nightmares when get too hot and sweaty… or is it that always get hot and sweaty due to nightmares…? hmmm…).

8:22 pm Not that am sweaty person in general, please note.

8:30 pm Apart from when do extreme amounts of aerobic exercise… which (fortunately) is about as often as bother to have eyebrows 'tidied' (never).

Sat 18 Sept

5:47 am

Dear Bob,

No, is not insignificant (the dream).

Arrgghhh... brain hurts now as used multi-syllabic words before breakfast... nooooooo... did it again! How come am even up at this time of... day/night?

Has sunk in deep: Jim... Mr Ace-Cn,
Mr Happy-to-lead-the-worship,
Mr Moving-in-the-gifts,
Mr Cool-youth-group-leader...
denied the existence of God,
albeit (good word) in a dream.

Has caused me to doubt/question/pace up and down (doesn't take long in here... am convinced humans were never designed to live in such TEENY spaces).

Not sure what's going on – am v messed up. HELP! Need emotional (and spiritual?) 1st aid.

Am lost.

8:45 am Just had ½ packet Pringles for breakfast (SC&Onion).
Great. Now lost... AND obese.

Sun 19 Sept

3:32 pm

Dear Bob

Another freaky dream last night. Not as profound as last one tho. This time was Pooh (Winnie the) in story where he gets stuck in entrance to Rabbit's den coz he's eaten too much honey. Except in MY case, Pooh (me) had eaten too many Pringles.

Was stuck tight, buttocks wedged in den and head poking out in the sun... a multitude of friends/family gathered around and started lecturing me (Pooh) on dangers of eating too many Pringles. But THEY were munching away on pack after pack (of varying flavours).

'Give them up Judith darling,' said Mum in ghost (+ball+chain) like voice. 'You'll only get addicted and have to be delivered from the Spirit of... the Pringle...' she sang whilst stuffing a large handful (SC&O) down her own gob.

Arrgggghhhhh! Felt a billion times fatter.

Couldn't even pray for comfort in hour of need as not sure what to think about God.

Tweenies usually does the trick when am blue (for a bunch of pre-schoolers, their sense of harmony is pretty fab)... it's on now... but failing to turn me into a less depressing colour.

Last day of Freshers' Week today. Shame. Has been v cool. Quite forgotten am here to study... 3 years of Freshers' Weeks would surely be more fun.

Mon 20 Sept

6:12 pm

Dear Bob

1st ever lecture today. Should you learn details, you'd spontaneously combust (love that phrase!) due to boredom overload, so won't share them.

Really did have high expectations re lectures. They always sounded so grown-up... much more sophisticated than 'lessons'. Are nothing to write home about tho (saying that, included all details in last email to Mum, who'll find them riveting, no doubt).

Got quite distracted (not unusual) thinking how it would be real cool to BE a Tweenie. As in someone who prances around in loud costume and solves moral dilemmas in under 20 mins.

Would be Fizz... or Jake... tho Milo's quite fun... not Bella for sure... who'd want to be THAT bossy cow? Wonder what they get paid... perhaps will enquire if whole degree thing doesn't work out.

Don't ask why I chose psychology – am not too sure of reason. Need psycho-analysis/counselling/general help myself at the mo. To be honest, am scared.

11:45 pm Actually, not Fizz, as doubt could get voice to go that high... unless in extreme pain... like in style of having legs waxed...

Wed 22 Sept

10:13 pm

Dear Bob

Just seen *Silence of the Lambs* with Libs (someone she knows got it out on video) – did NOT contribute in a positive way to current state of mind. (Libs = Liberty Young, lives: floor above me, studying: psychology, same as me, but she's good at it, status: single, and non-Cn.)

Always been scared of scary stuff, like scary films. You know, the ones with baddies, killing, torture, war, torture…

esp torture.

Was always me who was convinced (on fairly regular basis) there was evil burglar downstairs in early hours of morning. Would wake up Mum – send her down to check. Reasons for this:

1] *Waking Dad would take all night, and most of following day, and*
2] *one glimpse of Mum in flowery 70s nightie would scare Mr Burglar away, pronto…
trust me.*

Was me who spent hours surfing net for info re nuclear bombs/biological warfare, and after effects, so would know what to do (esp since 9/11).

But pre-JimDream, could talk to God about such stuff, and read a multitude of comforting verses to regain 'my peace'. Could chat with Jim – have him pray for me… but has all vanished now… down drain like manky washing-up water.

Bit of a bummer this should happen in 1st week of uni.

Things aren't exactly going to plan.

Thur 23 Sept

2 pm

Dear Bob

Just back from another yawnyawn lecture. Interesting bit: watching Prof Carr's wig slip further and further backwards off head each time he got over-excited (which he did A LOT). Was willing it to fall off altogether… for him to be revealed for baldie that he is, but twas not to be.

11:32 pm Just been for drink at Fir and Ferret with Libs. Told her what was on mind re dream and God and all that. Her reply:

'Jude honey… stop farting around with all this God crap… come and have some FUN… hick… live the life… go on the pull… get wrecked… hey babe, it works for me… hick!'

(After 4 pints Dry Blackthorn – I was counting.)

It does too (work for her). She seems happy with who she is and with life, yet has no faith in God to account for it.

Lost her just after last orders – she went up for ANOTHER pint Dry B (how DOES she do it… my legs and brain go jelly-like after just I). Went looking for her after a bit. Found her chatting to this guy… well, eating his ear. He looked all smug and slimy AND blew smoke directly in my face. Left without her.

Haven't heard her come back yet. Guess she'll be out for few more hours… if she comes back at all tonight.

Mum wouldn't approve of Libs. Can hear her now:

'Darling, you mustn't spend too much time with…
with the…
those who…
NON-Christians.

They might lead you astray.'

Lead me astray from WHAT? To WHAT? Huh.

Is it poss that I'd never really believed in God in the 1st place?

Yeah, course I'd believed in God… well, think so… hmmmm. Maybe. Probably. Oh… sorry… goodnight.

12:07 am Can't sleep. Getting quite cross (understatement of the millennium) with several people, all at once. Going to invent some emails to help me… errr… organise my thoughts (vent my anger)…

```
To: ma&pa@cityofboredom.com
Subject: Brainwashing
Mum & Dad why did you brainwash me into becoming
a Cn¬ and not let me decide for myself?
```

```
To: jim@indrivingseat.com
Subject: Dictating
Jim why did you dictate my feelings and beliefs
to me¬ without letting me stop to think it all
```

through?

To: homechurch@wackyland.com
Subject: HUH?
Pastor Vic all that leaping up and down and speaking in tongues and stuff you encouraged me to participate in what was that all about? God? Me? The church? Loonies Anonymous?

To: libs@wildchild.com
Subject: Chucking up & chucking in
Libs why are you expecting me to chuck it all in and follow you in your quest for lads and liquor? How do you expect me to cope with more than 1 Dry B per evening?

To: profcarr@baldiesanon.com
Subject: Lack of hair
Yo Prof why do you wear that stupid wig? Why do you get excited about the selfish gene theory? NO ONE gets excited about that. Get some help mate.

Am going to eat just 1 Pringle (BBQ) for medicinal purposes (to induce sleep)…

12:15am Well, maybe just a couple more, now tube's been opened…

V v late! Almost asleep when sudden extreme banging at door… twas Libs, who'd clearly been leaning v hard on door, coz when I opened it she fell right into me, mumbling,

'Shooo-d… wassupshooodbabe… wannasleepienowshoood… nightie nightie… hick… shooooood!' etc.

Steered her in direction of HER room – tucked her in her bed, as she slipped into a blessed state of unconsciousness.

Honestly… should charge for such a service.

Fri 24 Sept

10:32 am

Dear Bob

Questions:

1] *Who broke into room last night and finished off* ALL *BBQ Pringles? Couldn't POS-SIBLY have been moi.*

2] WHY *are curtains waterproof? Remind me of Nat's w proof sheet under his regular one, in case he pees in his sleep* (Nat = *my nephew, he's* 2).

3] *Do they think we're gonna* PEE *on said curtains? Guess Libs might find it a tad hard to locate loo after trillionth Dry B, but even SHE would prob avoid curtains.*

Just gonna check what wrote to you last night.

Ah, yeah, sorry bout that. Feel guilty now. Do actually love parents v much, and Jim and Libs (tho only known her a week)… but hold fast to feelings re Prof Carr.

Ought to be starting essay today:

'To what extent can evolutionary theories account for human behaviour?
Critically discuss with reference to Darwin's theory of evolution by natural selection and Dawkins' selfish gene theory.'

But will leave til tomorrow, when 'peeing on curtains' query has eased off a bit.

Hope Libs has elephant-sized hangover today and feels v guilty about last night… but doubt this to be the case. Do her parents even KNOW what she's like? (One thing have noticed – she never talks about her parents… always changes the subject… odd.)

Have banned myself from Pringles.
Felt like huuuuuuge BBQ monster, all day.

Mon 27 Sept

3:40 pm

Dear Bob

1st ever driving lesson just over. A snippet for you:

Him: Now, Miss Singleton, I actually just requested that you turn left at the next junction. Do you mind telling me what your indicator lights are currently suggesting to the surrounding traffic?
Me (in head): Yes I do mind, you stupid snotty instructor-guy who insists Christian names are obsolete.
ME (out loud): Errr… oh, yeah, right, I'll just change it to… there we go.

(Head): Why didn't you just SAY I was indicating the wrong way, like any normal human being?

Him: That's better. We don't want any nasty accidents now do we?

Me: Nooooo, we don't.

(Head): How OLD do you take me for – 5? Don't patronise me you old git!

(Swearing was not part of upbringing, and is not part of my nature, but generously allow myself to use certain semi-swear/slang words… 'git' is one of them.)

He has a tendency to tap his pencil on his clipboard – does it every time he tells me off. Guess is sort of threat… 'You do that one more time Miss Singleton and I'll ram this pencil up your nose… REALLY HARD.' (Or could just be nervous habit.)

Not sure if I was cut out to drive. Never even seen *Top Gear*.

So here's me – 18, still a virgin (this is no lie) and have never even experienced *Top Gear*… is this normal?

6:03 pm Haven't had any Pringles all day – am cured, hurrah!

Might just pop to kitchen tho, to see what other snack can devour – a healthy fat-and-calorie-free one if at all poss… like juicy lettuce leaf/stick of crispy crunchy celery…

6:14 pm Arrrrggghhhhhhhh!! Entered kitchen and some guys were sat around table, tucking into PRINGLES (Cheese&Onion/S&Vinegar). Don't they KNOW it's my weakness? Can't they see how HIPPO-like those things are making me every time see/smell them? They offered me some – couldn't refuse – would have looked odd, and want to 'fit in' as much as poss. (Had to go for C&O… even tho they make breath sim to that of d instructor, who has stilton breath, they are surely far better than nasty old S&V.)

Not sure who I was trying to kid… don't even HAVE above mentioned green salad-type food-stuffs in my cupboard, that is white, and has a lock (in case that is in any way relevant).

Also… MISS… SINGLETON… LOVES… PRINGLES!!
There. Said it. Feel better now.

10:56 Yeah, tis an unfortunate surname to own… feel free to have a chuckle at my expense… everyone else does. Was bad enough already, but made 3 million times worse when old Bridget Jones showed up and decided it was the name belonging to ALL those who were without partners. Have considered changing my name to something more sexy, like Law (get it?!) or Halliwell (as in Geri). Course, if you turn up in the not too distant future, and we tie the knot, will be rid of it forever, AND won't be single... hurrah!

Huh... ought to sue Ms Jones for damages.

Hmmmmm, there's an idea... will rally round all those in country who share my surname, and start class action suit against her... yeah... that's a comforting thought... might help me sleep tonight. (Lib's HorrorMovie-Pal is doing law, and I read one of her textbooks during worst bits of *Silence of the Lambs*... thus my unlikely knowledge of such things as 'class action suits'.)

Tue 28 Sept

10:47 pm

Dear Bob

Didn't do much today.

Listened to Libs drone on about bloke she went out with last night:

'He was soooooooooo DULL. Duller than dull, like the dullest person you could imagine... like duller than Carol Vorderman.'

Couldn't help thinking twas ME who was by far dullest person on planet... I blame the 'borrrrrrrrring' genes inherited from Ma&Pa... can't even roll my tongue! Why is she hanging around with ME?

What's WRONG with Carol anyway?

'He kept on and on about his BEEEP Audi TT convertible – how it does 0 to 60 in 6.5 seconds... who cares? Not ME babe, that's for sure... he didn't even PAY for my BEEEP Big Mac... I had to cough up myself!'

A tough cookie she sure is... a feminist she is not.

Felt it was a good time to tell her about my longing/yearning/deep-rooted desire for a bloke. She seemed vaguely interested, so explained how was after more than just ANY old bloke, but one of the marrying sort. Can hear myself now...

Me: Ummm... I just wanna find Mr Right. Mr Divinely-chosen-just-for-Jude Right. I long to tell 'him'... well, what's on my mind – my deepest thoughts. Not just that though... all the stupid mundane stuff too, like what really pees me off, and what my fave food is, and... yeah... so I've started writing to him, sort of like a diary I guess, but just for him.

Libs: Uh-huh? And then, when you finally meet your hubbie-to-be, you'll lock him in a cell and force him to READ all these BEEEP letters, filled with your deep thoughts, your boring thoughts... and your dietary requirements?!

She always makes my plans look feeble. It's a special gifting she has. If she belonged to my home-church she'd be known as 'the girl blessed with the gift of discouragement'.

Wed 29 Sept

11:23 am

Dear Bob

Am really hoping you're into food shopping in a big way, as think have just made 1st and last visit to local Tesco:

TillGirl 'Keri': (*Sounding bored with her job, and life in general.*) That'll be twenty-two pounds fifty-nine please.

Me: (*Panicking as had planned to spend £5 on extra/yummy food a week – max.*) Errr... really?

Keri: (*Wondering what possessed the Planet Dork to let me out for the day.*) Yeah, really.

Me: Ummm... but I thought that... twenty-two fifty-nine? You don't mean FIVE fifty-nine do you... per chance?

Keri: (*Now super-unimpressed.*) NO, I don't. Look at your receipt if you like, it's all there.

Me: Oh, no, it's OK... I'm sure you're right...

Keri: (*Getting pee-ed off.*) Yeah, people generally think so, as a rule.

Me: Well, can I pay by Visa card then, as I don't have that much cash?

Keri: (*Relieved we were getting somewhere at last.*) Yes. Do you want cashback?

Me: Huh?

Keri: (*Back to Planet-Dork-type-thinking.*) It's a debit card... DO-YOU-WANT-CASHBACK?!

Me: Urrr... no, probably not. (*Made mental note to ask Libs what 'cashback' was.*)

Keri: And do you have a clubcard?

Me: (*Help - more foreign Tesco-ese.*) Well, no... should I? Do I need one? How much are they?

Keri: (*Taking pity at this point, fortunately.*) Errrrrrrr… no worries – but ask at Customer Services if you want one.
Me: Oh, yeah, thanks, I will. (*A Mount Everest-sized lie… was going to LEG IT out of there as soon as was through.*)

Bob, please don't write me off as hideously immature and useless. Is just that had only ever used my Visa card a couple of times before, and knew NOTHING about cashback, and as for a clubcard… Mum always shopped at Asda, and never took me (as never wanted to go… surprise surprise) so tis not my fault, honest. Ah well… it can only get easier. Can't it? Please say yes.

Felt a bit panicked re Keri. (Why not 'Kerry'? what's so evil about the letter Y all of a sudden?) Made me worry again about coping in big wide world (of uni). Hadn't thought it'd be a doddle, but then had initially been thinking that God and his angels would be looking out pour moi, stopping my feet trampling on stones, or whatever that bit in Psalm 91 says (know you'll have good Bible knowledge, Bob, so won't insult you by looking it up to put in correct verse).

9:14 pm Or WILL you have any knowledge of the Bible at all? Here's me, doubting my faith, when am weirdly still assuming you will hold the Super-Cn-of-the-decade award… hmmm. But, if…

God isn't real (Arrrgghhhh… there it is again!),

then his angels are about as real as Santa (come on – a big boy like you should know he's your Dad + 2 cushions + cotton-wool beard, by now)… so how am I gonna cope with things even HARDER than shopping in Tesco, like drugs and errr… other dangerous stuff people say happens at uni?

Oh Bob – come and take me away from all this… soon.

Fri 1 Oct

8:42 pm

Dear Bob

Another smelly d lesson today.

Times told, 'The mirror is your friend!' – 7

Times told to turn one way and managed to indicate the other – 4

Times told, 'Miss Singleton, what does the speedometer say?' – 5

Times thought that if speedometer could 'say' anything it would be a darn sight MORE interesting than StiltonBreath – 3,000,000

Doesn't he know he's dealing with someone who got 33 out of 35 for their theory test? (Passed it today – whoo-hoo!)

In case you were wondering, was being chastised for driving too slow, not too fast. Thing is, if have to drive past a granny walking on pavement, can't help but imagine her suddenly deciding to leap into road, shopping trolley and all… so automatically slow down, just in case.

My emergency stops could currently be described as maybe-will-just-bring-the-car-to-a-gradual-halt stops.

So tis clearly safer for me to drive slowly, but StiltonBreath can't see it that way… insists I do 30 in 30 zone, not 20. If EVERYONE drove at 20, world would be a safer place… fewer horrible accidents, tho might take ages to travel long distances… motorway would become car park… hmmmmm-mm…

As pavements fairly chocka with people (inc aforementioned grannies) sense is only right to go slowly. The one who mings of stilton doesn't care about people like I do – obviously not a Cn.

But then am I really a…

and there I go again.

Sat 2 Oct

11:34 pm

Dear Bob

CU today (why is on Sat when I will be at parties etc?). Twas 'an introductory informal drink' at F&Ferret… is called BURP (Bymouth Uni Revival Plan – whoever christened it that needs SERIOUS help).

Know what you're thinking Bob: 'Why is she going to that, when she's not even sure he's really there (God)?' Thing is, knew 1st question all pals back home would ask, after: 'How's the talent?' (or 'How often does your room get cleaned?' from Mum) would be: 'How's the CU?'

Could hardly say, 'Dunno, don't go… not sure I believe in all that any more.'

Had got to know quite a few of them in Freshers' Week – about 100 of them in total... 100 WHAT? Cns? Believers? Losers? Nutters? Hmmm. Anyway, am pretending to be one of them until suss it out (life, God etc). Shouldn't be too difficult... have been one pretty much all my life, til now.

Had heard so much about CUs from student friends, so had really looked forward to going, being in the centre of things, and even... wait for it... getting on the committee... the ultimate goal for every Cn student... well, it was in my case. Huh.

They're a mixed bunch. At CU at old school, we were all sort of from the same mould... same type of church (raving charismatic) same style of clothes, same taste in music etc. But here... didn't know you could get Cn chess-playing geeks, Cn goths with multiple piercings, Cn hippies, Cn designer-clothes freaks...

Oh yeah... REALLY hot bloke at BURP called Reuben. Is in a class all of his own. V cool, like at least as cool as naked chef (watched every show and not even HINT of nakedness... shame).

Is just my type... long blonde hair (tied back in ponytail, but in manly-stud fashion, as opposed to girlie-Barbie). Sort of hippy/surfer dresser, bound to be fab Cn... perfect... Reuben... If he doesn't turn out to be you, will edit this bit, if you see what I mean (Reuben that is, not old Jamie). Reuben... the man who saved his bro from death... Reuben... come and save me from my miserable eternal state of being a Singleton. Hmmmmmm... R...E...U...B...E...N...

Mon 4 Oct

8:46 pm

Dear Bob

Hmmmm... how shall I describe myself? Well, picture this (just in case we meet over internet and I have to email these letters to you, and only actually meet you on day of wedding, or something bizarre like that).

5 ft, 6.
Female-star-of-Friends-style figure.
Long brown curly-ish hair, shampoo-ad-style.
A cute face, dead symmetrical.
Not a blackhead in sight.

OK, the girl you are picturing... is my sister... and I look NOTHING like her.

Actually, people say we do look alike, so I smile and say, 'Oh, do you think so?' then add under my breath, 'Yeah, right, if I was slimmer, taller, prettier, had great hair and no zits and all, we'd be twins for sure.'

Anyway, am thinking about my sister because visited her today (she's about 20 mins away on bus). She is pregnant.

Remind me not to get pregnant, or at least not to be seen in PUBLIC when am pregnant – couldn't cope with feeling/looking any huger than already am (size 14/height 5 ft, ½ inch)... in case that means anything to you, or you thought I had trouble squeezing into lifts.

Abby reminds me of Monica off *Friends*, lost in Obsessive-Compulsive Disorderland. Don't get me wrong, do love her, in a sisterly sort of way, but find it difficult to be HER sister.

Was pondering on this thought earlier today, as watched Nat use a yellow crayon to add Laa-Laa to the lounge wallpaper design. Recalled once overhearing Mum say to her: 'Abigail, you're a clever girl... you can do ANYTHING you put your mind to.' She's never said that to me.

Laa-Laa clones were appearing all over the wall when Abby came in the lounge, shrieked (in a controlled fashion) and set to work on their elimination. No wonder she never asks me to babysit.

Oh, she's also married to a perfect guy – Amos. They're one of those couples that you assume were matched at birth – Abby n Amos. Like Romeo n Juliet (without the tragic ending of course) or Posh n Becks (would kill to look like Posh). Went to their church once (Abby and Amos's, not Posh and Becks's) and it was instantly clear that they were loved by all, as was Nat. The perfect family. The perfect Cn family. Huh.

He is Kenyan... she met him over there when she was... oh, enuf of them... got to go, meeting Libs@F&Ferret at 9 pm, which now observe was 9 whole minutes ago!

Tue 5 Oct

9:38 am

Bob

Just had hour long shower. Bliss! (Room is en-suite – whoo-hoo!) Feeling the need to make the most of new freedom... at home, showers involved setting timer for 10 mins!

Got d lesson later – at least one of us will smell fresh!

10:15 am Oh. Just remembered. A weird and disturbing thing occurred during yesterday's visit to Abby's. Was using upstairs loo, as downstairs loo occupied by Nat, who is coming to terms with using the toilet instead of the potty (aren't you glad you get all these details?!) and overheard phone convo of Amos's:

'Hi – it's me... how's you? Uh-huh... no, I haven't told her yet... it's not the right time... I know I said I would... sorry... (*Pause.*) Not sure, maybe... maybe next week... Look, (*Voice raised slightly.*) look Kate (*Voice lowered again, don't think he wanted to be heard from downstairs.*) this means a lot to me – it's got to be done right, my life won't be the same again, give me TIME to... no... yes... no... uh-huh... OK... yeah... I know... yeah... OK. Must go – dinner's ready... yeah... bye.'

He's quite a hot guy really, for a bro-in-law. He and Abby could well model together on the front of *Happy Clappy Families* or some such yet-to-be-published magazine. But he's NOT kind of guy to mess around with other women. No doubt he prays loads, loves every man/woman/crawling insect... knows the Bible so well you'd think he was involved with the editing in some former life (not that believe in former lives... do I?).

Hmmmm. A bit worrying. Perhaps is nothing though. Yeah, like Kate could be... err... his... long lost identical twin sister... and... she has just come to this country... but he can't tell Abby coz... coz... she would be freaked out by it... and he doesn't want this to upset her as she's pregnant... and...

Hmmm... OD'ing on *Hollyoaks* has polluted my mind – many apologies.

Wed 6 Oct

12:04 pm

Bob

Do you ever feel that no one understands you? Am feeling like this right now. Maybe this is reason am writing all this to you, in this bizarre probably-need-to-see-shrink-rather-than-become-one way.

Right, am going to stop waffling and start essay... RIGHT NOW!

12:15 pm Well, got as far as lining up books on bed, all THIRTEEN of them... how on earth am I gonna SKIM through that lot and extract exact info needed? Come back A levels… all is forgiven.

Anyhow, just been distracted by another thought…

In the past, have seen pals 'lose their faith' due to something dramatic in their lives (death in family, getting ill themselves, whatever). Had sometimes wondered if something like that would do the same to me, but doubted it. Held fast to the many (many many) books that tell the story of Cns who find an even deeper faith through tragedy. But never thought that something as stupid as a DREAM would knock me so hard. Suddenly feel more lost than before.

On that bright note, will leave you alone and go WRITE THAT ESSAY!

4:46 pm OK… know what you're thinking… the slacker hasn't done a single thing re essay… well that's where you'd be wrong, my dear Bob… had written all of 29 words… (errrrr, including title) when Libs materialised. Decided to share above 'lost' feelings with her… big mistake. She laughed in a way that enabled her to shower me with the Big Mac she was in the process of consuming, and congratulated me on my discovery that each and every one of us is 'well-lost'.

She practically lives on Big Macs… if the diet of personkind was reduced to only Big Macs and Dry Bs, she'd be a happy bunny.

6:03 pm Am beginning to think the Big-Mac-gal might just be right. Are we ALL lost? IS God real?

If he's not, then what are we here for anyway? To enjoy ourselves and have a laf? Maybe. Why not do whatever pleases ME, instead of what I feel I OUGHT to do? Wow… never had such non-Cn thoughts.

Have notched up a good few hours over several years at church, 'serving', 'doing', 'helping' for no money (and often no thanks whatsoever). Was ready to start that all over again here, at BURP… but not sure if can be arsed now (sorry, correct spelling of 'arsed' currently unknown…).

So is it OK now to go out with/sleep with guys – a whole ARMY of Bobs, and some Marks, Grahams and Jons – just for fun…?

Please reply: 'Whoooah there Jude… this is getting WAY out of control!' Thing is, do I care enough about God (or the possibility of him existing) or myself, or others, to stay all squeaky-clean and… boring?

Are you following all this?

Will probably edit out such trash before you read this, but will leave in for now – getting all my thoughts down is kinda helping… and, to date, you're a good listener.

Now, where are my Pringles?

Views Tate

Fri 8 Oct

9:31 pm

Hmmmmm… to wear or not to wear? That, oh Bob, is the question. Am referring to WWJD wristband (purple) that has faithfully graced my wrist for donkey's years… well, a couple at least. Why would I take it off? Coz Libs just informed me we're off out tonight, as in 'going out' as in… to a club! Have now got a whole 29 mins to make myself look sim to Posh/Britney/Kylie, etc. Thus, unsure what to wear, esp in relation to fashion accessory that is sooooooo Cn…

9:45 pm OK, have settled on slightly tarty skirt and v v tarty top (that makes mini-boobs appear medium-sized, tho still more Kate Moss than Jordan). Would never have worn said skirt and top together before, but feel like being someone else tonight… 'Jude the Tart'… hmmm, has a kind of ring to it.

Am taking (ripping) wristband off right now… feel like a priest de-robing himself of holy garments, before committing some deadly crime.

9:56 pm Off to Libs' room now… hope I look hot/cool enuf for her to be seen out with me.

Sorry… that should be 'feel like a priest de-robing him/HERself…' Do they wear holy garments, like robes and weird hats, or am I thinking of bishops?

OK, de-focus on clerical wardrobe, re-focus on dancing like Miss Minogue, and on holding my booze so as not to appear like mega lightweight…

Sat 9 Oct

10:54 am

I AM world's supreme lightweight champion… still have thumper of headache to prove it. How I currently feel:

Spiritually: if there wasn't a God before last night, there def isn't one now.
Physically: like a piece of poo.

Mentally/emotionally: in a state of PAAAAANNNNNNICCC!!

Oh, you wanna know what am gassing on about? Right, will start where left off on Fri eve…

So I go up to Libs' room (I'm on 1st floor, she's on 2nd) expecting her to be ready, as she'd said to come at 10, but had to wait further 20 mins for her to complete her 'prep-for-clubbing' rituals. Much of this involved the de-hairing of her legs. Think it took so long due to her supposedly 'disposable' razor looking at least 6 months old. Is this an early sign of student poverty?

Anyhow, so we eventually leave campus and arrive at Fusion. Had hardly flashed our NUS cards at the door (twas student night so got in cheaper – woo-hoo!) when Libs begins to work her magic, and before I knew it she was off strutting her funky stuff on the dance floor with some hip lookin dude, and I was alone, propping up the bar, alone, nursing my 1st ½ pint Dry B of the evening, alone, until…

Geek: (*Looking rather like Jim Carey, but in a bad way.*) So, haven't seen you at Fusion before… you a fresher?
Me: (*In my best 'leave-me-alone' voice.*) Yeah…
Geek: (*This was obviously good news.*) Ahhhhhhh… a fresher, eh?
Me: Yeah.
Geek: So, you don't know much about Bymouth then – where all the cool shops are, the best places to eat, who not to sleep with…
Me: Nope.
Geek: Well, that won't do, I'll have to give you a tour sometime… what ya doin tomorrow… don't worry you'll be in safe hands… we could meet at McDs and take it from there… 1 o'clock any good for you?
Me: Nope, and I don't need a tour thank you, I have a map.
Geek: Ah, maps of Bymouth must be really up-to-date these days… if they even tell you who not to sleep with, I mean, that's a quality map – must have cost ya.
Me: (*Already certain of ONE person I wasn't going to sleep with, map or no map.*) Go away.
Geek: Ahhhhh… a frisky fresher, eh? I know your sort. You're not interested in any guided tour of Bymouth, you want a guided tour of my room, and then some! Well, I wouldn't normally do this babe, but for you I'll make an exception.
Me: Go away!
Geek: Come on darlin, get ya coat, you've pulled…

Me: G-O A-W-A-Y!!!!!!

Geek: Oooohh… playing hard to get, eh? Like I'm supposed to believe you're not BEEEP gagging for it you little frisky fresher you…

And before I had a chance to throw remainder of Dry B over him (which would have been so cool, had I thought of doing it at the time), he grabbed my KateMoss boobs… one in each hand, and leaned right into me, and I mean RIGHT into me… an unbelievably grim experience. Could smell vast amount of drink on his breath – surprised he managed to make as much 'normal' sounding convo as he did. He then declared he needed the bog, adding:

'Don't move from this spot darlin… I'm kerrrrmin back for ya…'

Knocked back remainder of Dry B, and walked off, aiming to get as far away from FriskyGeek as poss. Only few metres away from bar, when felt tap on my back… swung round ready to punch his lights out (or perhaps just to say something v nasty) but twas not him. Seriously, THIS guy was no geek… and I was in love!

'Tate' had witnessed my harassment, was concerned for my well-being, and offered to buy me a drink (accepted – had a red wine, as that's what he was having, and he seemed kinda classy).

From then on he treated me well, made excellent convo and made me feel… ummm… special and, dare I say it… sexy. He was v opposite to FriskyGeek, in so many ways (looked more like Brad Pitt). Wondered if he were you, Bob, if you see what I mean.

Tate, a cool name… a cool guy… wasn't sure what he was doing spending time with me! Didn't care.

Right, so we chat for a good hour (well, yelled over the 'in-yer-face' music) and then he suggests we go to a party at his mate's house. Go along with this… not as if I was likely to catch up with Libs again anyway – assumed her to be back in some bloke's room already.

On leaving Fusion, he explains further that it's more of a 'gathering' than a party. 'A group of like-minded people coming together to share and to grow,' or something like that. Had avoided saying it up til this point, but asked if it was a church meeting – said that I went to church sometimes (tried to sound v non-committed). He brightened up and said I'd fit in well… started to talk about the insight the Bible provides the 'group' and such talk.

Couldn't BELIEVE it – how ironic to be chatted up by a Cn... had just turned my back on God – didn't make any sense, but went with it as Tate well worth it.

So (sorry this is so long, but really need to tell someone about this), we get to his friend's house – quite a grand old Victorian semi in the posh part of Bymouth. He walks on in as if it's his house, no knocking or doorbell or anything. It was like these people (about 15 of them, mainly 2nd and 3rd years, some weren't students) were 'family'... really cared about each other, and about lots of stuff, like the state of the planet, the education of children and the rise in crime, and all that. Most impressive.

Even more impressive was Ethan, the man whose house it was. I say 'man' as he had to be at least 30 – some kind of artist I think. He was... hard to describe, but he oozed niceness, knew and loved everyone, and seemed to be the leader of the group, in a v informal way tho. Still wasn't sure what kind of group they were tho... Methodist, C of E, Catholic... there just weren't enuf clues. That weird whale-song-type (New Age?) music could just be detected, making the whole room feel like it was 'alive' in some way.

Then, it started. 'It'? Yeah... Ethan began by reading from the Bible, and saying how we should all be like Jesus. Everyone agreed wholeheartedly. Ethan had that kind of voice that made you want to agree with everything. It was like he knew stuff, and when he spoke you wanted to listen and learn. So far so good. Then came the freaky bit. Freaky beyond all freakiness... 'freak-a-rooney' (as Milo the Tweenie would say).

Ethan said that Jesus had returned again to earth, 30 odd years ago, in the form of... him! Yeah... the guy really believed he was 'the chosen one', Jesus – part 2, Jesus – the sequel...

Even more amazing was that his announcement was not greeted with mass wetting-of-pants-style laughter... they all just nodded their heads and agreed with everything he said. Some of them looked as if it'd all just fallen into place: 'Of course Ethan is divine. Why didn't we notice this before... duurrrrrr... silly us!'

THEN he started to talk about unions between his 'followers', those he could trust to help him with his work. Such unions needed to be strong and built on trust and love. He said the rest of the evening would involve strengthening such unions.

THEN he beckoned to him a babe-like girl (2nd yr?), sitting right near me. She obeyed, he took her hand, and LED HER OFF UPSTAIRS, looking v much like they weren't about to get down to some more Bible study, if you catch my drift.

THEN, during the next 10 mins or so, others paired off, and headed in the direction of upstairs, eventually leaving me, Tate and another potential 'pair'.

Not sure what Tate had planned, but v sure that wanted out of Ethan's house pronto. Leant over toward Tate and said I ought to be getting back. Almost instantly realised that was a tres dumb thing to say – what student 'ought to be getting back', esp on a Fri eve?! He looked ½ disappointed and ½ annoyed, but could prob see I was itching to go, so we left.

Ah, forgot to mention that there was endless supply of booze at Ethan's abode and had several glasses of... alcohol of some sort – no idea what, but it went straight to head, along with the alc had consumed earlier at Fusion, and walking back to campus with Tate I was really feeling it.

Like REALLY feeling it. Recall a couple of things:

1] *Thinking how amazing it was that my legs were automatically working to make me walk, when had no idea how and no control over them whatsoever.*
2] *Thinking that being drunk is really cool and should do it more often.*
3] *Feeling v sick.*
4] *Thinking that being drunk is the pits and should never ever ever do it again.*
5] *Finally throwing up, over Tate's expensive Buffalo trainers, or were they Nikes? Sorry, trainers a complete blur – hard to see logo when buried in my puke (which seemed to whiff of BBQ Pringles, which had clearly come back to haunt and torment me in my hour of need, even tho were consumed a good couple of weeks ago).*

Sort of recall Tate 'trying it on' when we were nearing my room, and me pushing him away, then him doing it again, me not pushing him away (as brain and arms not making connection) and our lips meeting in a most agreeable fashion. He was so gentle. But then he got a bit more... errr... forceful.

Might have been sick again at this point – maybe it was just him making me feel sick...

And then I woke up... 9:43 am, today, Sat, in bed and UNDRESSED (= not good).

Haven't got up properly yet... still in daze, still panicking. Why? Coz have no idea what happened – how got into bed, how got undressed, if Tate put me here, if Tate was IN BED with me at any point...

.l I know is, was heavily under the influence, and he was keen. He wouldn't have, would he? Would I? Is it just that can't remember, or did I lose consciousness altogether? Have checked my body for tattoo saying 'freaky-cult-member' but am clean. Not sure how to check for evidence of… errrr… sex. Would I know if I had? Wish I knew stuff like this.

Plan to stay in room for rest of the day, sipping my warm water (yuk) and trying to recover and remember… yuk yuk yuk.

Sun 10 Oct

10:01 am

BURPers will be on their way to church about now – not tempted to join them. Well, am tempted to join Reuben in any activity, tho feeling a tad anti-blokes at the mo… going back to bed for a bit, head still throbbing… not gonna eat (must be bad).

11 am Arrgghhhhhhhhhhh… just thought of something…
I COULD BE PREGNANT!!!

11:05 am Taking short pause from panic-stricken pacing up and down room, mumbling, 'No, no, please not, no no no…'

11:12 am Pacing over now, but mumbling getting louder and more desperate…

11:15 am NO NO NO NO!!!
If Tate and I… ya-know-what… then I
Jude
could be…
with child.
Why didn't I think of this 1st thing on Sat am? What planet am I on? What am I supposed to do now? Nooooooo… this was not how my 1st few weeks at uni were supposed to be, not at all.
Great.
Super.
Fab.
Good old Tate…
Sneaky,
manipulative,
taking-advantage-of-drunk-females
Tate.

May God strike him down with multiple bolts of agonising, torturing and... very agonising lightning (if there is a God).

So, um, what to do? If I am, ya know, can't poss get rid of it, can I? To do so was wrong when I believed in God – would it be wrong now? Yeah, think so... can't poss imagine destroying a baby/potential baby.

A BABY!! That makes it sound soooo scary. Can't have a baby now, Mum would kill me, and even worse, Abby would support and help me – no no noooooo... will not be the black sheep of the family, not yet anyway. Maybe when I choose to be, but not like this.

Had several showers yesterday, in case it was poss to wash Fri eve away.

Think will have another now as feel all 'tainted' again... (or even 'Tate-ed'. Sorry, my 'jokes' currently affected by enormity of situation... not that they've ever been much better).

Wonder if any BURPers noticed I wasn't at BURP yesterday, or at church today. More specifically, wonder if Reuben noticed.

Mon 11 Oct

2:17 pm

Went to lecture this am... didn't hear a word ... something about some weird theory of Freud's (and believe me, he had many). Highly distracted by theory of my own meandering around my few remaining active brain cells, re Fri eve:

1] *I passed out somewhere near my halls/room,*
2] *Tate took me back to my room,*
3] *undressed me,*
4] *did whatever he wanted 'to' me,*
5] *left me tucked up in bed.*

But what did he do to me? Am I no longer a virgin? Am I with child? What if have scary STD?

Strange thing... feel v guilty. Big-time guilty, like in the nature of just having committed worst sin poss. And yet don't nec believe in God anymore, so shouldn't I feel like am free to do what I want? Surely tons of people (students esp) sleep around a whole lot. I do it once (and that's not even confirmed yet) and am contemplating turning myself in to cops.

Where does guilt come from? Have I done anything wrong? Is there such a g as 'right' and 'wrong'?

uestions, questions. Sorry, Bob, you're probably fed up with me by now, and rightly so. So wanted to be a virgin when I met you. Still do, God or no God. Sorry again. Sorry sorry sorry sorry.

If I did this kind of thing (clubbing/bringing lads back to my room) on a regular basis, would I get used to it, and not feel any guilt? Do I WANT to get used to it?

6:28 pm Am about to watch Friends to help take my mind off of me, my guilt and off Tate.

Sort of hungry, but so far even the smallest amount of food makes me want to puke over Tate's Buffaloes again (in fact, over all of Tate would be more satisfying).

6:33 pm Just threw myself violently in direction of TV and turned it off… too many references to drink, snogging, sex, babies, sex, guilt and yet more sex. Didn't want to see Jen (Aniston) as she reminded me of Tate, being married to Brad and all. Seemed so funny last time I watched it, but now just want them to go away – pick on some other friends, and LEAVE ME ALONE.

Wed 13 Oct

Head better overall, but still am finding quiet/dark surroundings preferable to 'thrash-metal/fluorescent bulb' surroundings (ie Libs' room).

D lesson – don't know who is more terrified for duration of lessons – me or StiltonBreath. Drove extra carefully due to poss extra passenger.

Am starring at j spud + cheese (that Libs just brought me, ahhh!) but can't stomach it. Will pop it in to bloke next door… am assuming he never got fed at home as all have seen him do since we got here is scoff his (plump) face.

Thur 14 Oct

Head almost settled… may yet pull through and live to get my BA hons (in 3 yrs time).

Guilt still lingering. Was it my fault? Did I/my tarty gear lead him on? Is just BEING at a club another way of saying 'sleep with me – I'm easy'?

Not too bothered about whole cult thing. Gives me the creeps when think about it, and is obviously wrong, if 'wrong' exists. Only went the once, and didn't sacrifice any children, to my knowledge, so don't think am going to hell for that (if there is a hell), am I?

Really don't like guilt. Not sure I carried round much/any of it before Fri eve. Is this a good or bad thing? Huh?

Attempted essay (that selfish Dawkins one that started couple of wks ago... no rush tho as not due in til beg of Dec!). Not easy, nay, impossible, to study when:

1] *stressed re whole 'lack of faith' in God thing,*
2] *might be with child,*
3] *head telling me to eat ½ tube SC&O Pringles under bed, but stomach arguing not yet ready for real food.*

Apologies for calling Mr NextDoor 'plump', which clearly is plumpist. He is plump, but then so am I, so not one to talk/accuse/judge etc.

Just before bed This hangover, which is just about over now, has lasted 6 days... is that a record? Not had a real hangover before so wouldn't know. Humm, perhaps is COZ have not had one before that this has lasted this long. Shall contact Guinness Book of Records in morning to enquire.

Fri 15 Oct

9:09 am
Decided to stop moping and start embark on some kind of 'self-help' plan. Have just rung 'student counsellor' (they're obviously well-prepared for us all to go loopy whilst here) — booked appointment for tomorrow. Yeah, think it will allow me to calm down a bit and think rationally. Yeah, am terrified (re seeing counsellor).

10:45 am Listening to Radio 2 in attempt to initiate 'operation calm' (60s music can be quite soothing, as long as it's Carpenters-style and not Rolling Stones-style).

Will she be nice? How old? Is she trained? How much do counsellors get paid? Could I be a counsellor? Must remember to slip in question re salary/company car/benefits/hols, whilst bearing my soul.

Sat 16 Oct

6:31 am

Yeah, stupid time to be awake. Am freaking out re thought of spilling guts to someone have never met.

4 hrs 29 mins till much dreaded app with shrink.

7:03 am Am reading *heat*… says that many big stars see shrink on almost daily basis, so maybe is not that bad, perhaps is quite acceptable, 'cool' even. Hmmmm.

7:52am Ahhh, just read back yesterday's letter – feel need to explain about Radio 2 (is on now). Thing is, am more into Radio 1 really. Well, on coming to uni DECIDED would be into Radio 1, as guessed it would give me a bit of street-cred (oooh – old-fashioned phrase = not good, will strike from vocab).

Radio 1 = good music (mainly) but think it should be re-named 'Innuendo 1' as that's just about all Chris Moyle's jokes are based on, bless 'im.

Anyhow, since JimDream, have been feeling a tad homesick. Not really for old room, or parents (as if, bless 'em) or church, or old pals… just for my old way of life and the simplicity of it – knowing where I was, with God and all. My parents are well-into Radio 2, and I continually had to walk around the house 'cleansing' various rooms of the sad noises/music/waffle.

Discovered that listening to Radio 2 in my room here reminds me of home and sort of knocks any homesickness on the head. Yeah, is naff station. Yeah, used to give my parents a hard time about it before, but now is my saviour.

Only prob is that have to launch myself across room (not far) to stereo, goalie-style, when anyone knocks (so they won't hear that am listening to such uncool vibes), hit my preset and hey presto, Innuendo 1 comes on… then can let them in.

If I knew any famous goalies, would have inserted name into above bit, but am completely unfamiliar with football, as can see no point in game what-soever. Only footballers I know are:

1] *Gazzer* (*coz he cried*)
2] *Gary Lineker* (*coz of Walkers adverts*)
3] *Becks* (*coz he's hitched to Posh, my hero*)

Perhaps you like football, and I'll have to learn to like it. Perhaps you will BE famous footballer… that's fine… if Posh can cope with it then so can I!

8:23 am Have wasted time writing above waffle. Actually 'getting into' Radio 2 (I really DO need professional help), so now only 2 hrs 37 mins till app.

Appetite back with a vengeance now, and need extra energy for emotional stress ahead of me… am scoffing family-size tiramisu for breaky… mmm-mmm (poss eating for 2 now).

10:45 am Time's up, am off now, wish me luck! (Not that I believe in luck, do I?)

Lunchtime Trying not to get grease on keyboard… grabbed chips and battered mushrooms (= scrumptious) on way home from app. They're nearly all gone and am already dreaming about some sort of pud that will complement them well… any ideas? If only you could talk back. Think having few days without much food has pushed system into over-drive… can't stuff food in my gob fast enuf…

Anyhow, 'How was the counsellor?' you rightly ask.

Well, 'Oscar' was a nightmare. Yes, a he. Had spoken to a female on the phone to arrange the app, so naturally expected this to be counsellor, but no. Let me give you a taster of our oh-so-special time together:

Oscar: (*In a voice sim to narrator from* Magic Roundabout.) So, Jane… tell me, in your own time, about your problems. Don't let anything in this room distract you, or anything you might be able to see out of the window, like those 2nd years playing hockey, for example. Don't let your fears keep you from releasing your inner worries, and, errrr… fears. We've got all the time in the world. Well, I have to lead an Indian Head Massage class in an hour's time, on the other side of the campus, but try to ignore that for now. Try to view this time as 'our' time or even just 'your' time. Jane, YOU are special… don't ever forget that. And I am here as your listening friend, who will… errr… listen to you. So take your time. Relax. Are you comfortable in that chair, or would you prefer the floor… some students seem to find the lotus position a good one in which to open one's soul… do you want to?
Me: Errr…no, the chair's fine, and it's Jude.
Oscar: (*Slowly and drawn out.*) Ahhhh, so you're calling my chair 'Jude', that's interesting. Making your environment seem safer by naming inanimate objects… hmmmm… must write that down…
Me: (*With unusual assertiveness.*) Look, do you want me to tell you my problems or not?
Oscar: Ooooh… now I'm sensing some locked-up anger. Interesting. But

it's OK, feel free to take it out on me, that's what I'm here for, to listen, not to judge... I promise I won't judge you... or 'Jude the Chair'...

Me: OK, let's just do this. Firstly, I'm not sure God exists any more, and it's freaking me out. Secondly, I think I slept with a guy last week, think I might be pregnant and, again, it's freaking me out. There. That's it. What should I do?

Oscar: Ahhhh... God. Now that's interesting. But who is God? Where is God? What is he, or she, like? God – yeeessssss. A classic case. (*Grabs notebook, spends couple of mins making notes, ignoring me, so I watch the hockey, or rather the sweaty hairy attractive legs of male players...*)

Me: Errrr... so, can you help?

Oscar: 'Help', now that's interesting Jane. Do you want to be helped? If so, why? Are you afraid of your own feelings? Are you afraid of yourself? Why do you need help, if, indeed, that is what you think you want?

Me: Right. OK. Moving on then, what about my sex problem? (*At this his little hippy eyes lit up like excited joss sticks, so quickly added...*) I mean, should I have done it, and what if I'm, ya know, pregnant and all?

Oscar: Sex. Yes, that's always interesting. You know Jane, it's never wrong to share special moments with others, even when those moments are of a physical nature. We are all free to 'join' with whomsoever we wish, just like the animals of the wild. Yes, animals, now they are interesting. I rather believe that in one of my past lives I was an octopus. Don't know why... just seem to have a strange, yet wonderful affinity with the creatures... (*Stares dreamily into space for good few mins with smile glued to his face – didn't seem to be aware I was in room.*)

Me: Are we done now?

Oscar: Jane, do you think we're done? Does your inner self feel content, or at war? Are you in tune with who you are? Can you honestly say that you are in a place of serenity and calm, or are you only just beginning on the voyage that all of us, one day, have to make? (*Dramatically, like there's an audience in the room other than me.*) Let me say again Jane – I'm here to listen, and not to judge or criticise. Just let it flow... release your knowledge about the way in which your Ying and Yang has become unbalanced, the reason your Zen is not connecting with your Feng Shui, tell me Jane... TELL ME NOW!! (*Checks watch.*) Errr... yeah, actually, save those thoughts Jane, and tell me... ummmm... (*Checks diary.*) Shall we say this time next week?

Me: Fine. (*Was easier than trying to explain reason why I hoped I'd never have to meet him ever ever ever again, unless it involved me 'releasing' several Rotwelers (Rottwelers?*

Rottweilers?) on him...)

Mmmm... think a Solero would go down nicely after chips (it's a tad sunny out, honest!) so will go and track one down. Cheers Bob.

Nearly bedtime Feeling down, which is odd as have just consumed 2 Soleros (Libs bought one too, but didn't like 'exotic' flavour, so ate hers in addition to mine).

Doesn't ANYONE care about my mission to find the truth about life? Is there a truth?

Is odd, but sort of impressed with Ethan's weird cult thing – they seemed to have been searching for the truth, and then they seemed to find it. Oscar thought that just about anything and everything could be truth, for any individual, if they wanted it to be.

OK, so let's say everything can be truth – 'the answer to life' etc. That doesn't make any sense. First you think about other religions and all... fine. But what about groups of Nazis and... other groups of such people that I don't know about but am convinced exist... ahhh... like those behind 9/11... are they truth/right/the answer??

Durrrr, 'Jane', course not.

So, on the flip side, is no one 'right', is there no truth to be found? Makes my search a bit pointless if so. Still, it keeps me busy and conveniently prevents me from studying, which, after all, is as boring as watching my Mum peel spuds.

To bed now...

Sun 17 Oct

Have just thrown up in basin, grim grim grim...
Oh... oh dear I... think I might be
Yeah, did it again, just reached loo in time – cleaning lady's gonna love me.
Why why why?
I'm usually so healthy and... not being sick.
Why does it... oh, hang on I
Yeah, you guessed it. Room starting to smell like BBQ Pringles (what is it with them?!).

Can't understand it.

Return of the hangover?
Going back to bed until normal again.
Forget church – who needs it when you're busy regurgitating?

Mon 18 Oct

Prof Carr not the best of sights 1st thing in morning, esp when still feeling puky (correct spelling?).

Lecture almost had life in it, but only almost.

Libs keeps saying I look the colour of pale snot, which only serves to make me feel puky-er.

Tue 19 Oct

Bob, is no good… am gonna tell Libs about

Sorry, didn't finish sentence as Libs at door. We had a chat. I told her. About Tate and stuff and poss preggie-ness. She was v helpful:

'Wanna test? Got one in my room, hang on a sec, poppet…'

A TEST? For pregnancy?! A pregnancy test?! Me?!

Aren't I supposed to spend ages deliberating over whether to buy one or not, then spend several v awkward visits to chemist, not knowing how to ask for one or worried that I'll be spotted by pals… and Libs has one IN HER ROOM – is that allowed?!

She's got a point tho – she commented that I could have been having morning sickness. It makes sense.
No no no. Please God (if you're there), NO!
Right, compose myself. Try to muster up some urine. Can hear her coming back…

Hairy tales

Fri 22 Oct

11:23 am

Am currently enjoying freshly fried mushrooms on toast, precariously balanced on lap. Yeah, tis a tad early for lunch – have always been one to start planning lunch from about 11.

Haven't written for couple of days… been rather 'off'.

Am not with child.

Libs' test told me so… major major relief! Still a child myself – def not ready to have one, let alone look after one.

S'pose sick bout was due to overeating (huge tiramisu, chips and battered mushrooms, 2 Soleros… all in 1 day… oops).

Am overjoyed, obviously, but still numb…

Did I sleep with Tate? When do I get to offload some of this major guilt, or has it moved in for good? If there is a God, have I blown any chances I had of reaching him?

Am homesick. Miss my room, my bed… and Mum.

Not in the sense of meaningful mother-daughter chats (which rarely had) but just the way she would be fussing round me now, knowing I was ill or down or whatever… she'd always fix my fave snack – fried mushrooms on toast, accompanied by a 'nice cup of tea'.

Strange how I spent couple of years longing to leave home, and am now ½ wishing I'd never left, barely a month down the line. Hmmmmmm.

Libs keeps saying to forget whole Tate/God/home thing and come out to Fusion this eve with her and pals, but said I had more important things to do (good job she didn't ask what they were as haven't thought them up yet).

5:32 pm Just got email from Oscar (counsellor)… shall copy n paste it for you:

```
Jane
I enjoyed our time together last week and was
```

```
privileged that you felt able to confide in me
about your sex problems. I have searched out
some useful books on the subject.

I also recall you saying something about faith
or religion. Bymouth University prides itself on
having representatives from all the major world
religions, any of which you would be able to see
by appointment.

Please contact my secretary if you would like to
get in touch with any of them.

See you tomorrow,

Oscar.
```

Great... he can't even remember I was talking about God, as in the Cn one. Huh. No way am I keeping that app with him tomorrow, he can read those 'useful' books on his own, him and his octopus.

Anyway, planning on going to BURP tomorrow... perhaps meeting with all those Cns will help pick me up, give me some sort of hope. Cns are supposed to be good at that, aren't they?

Mushroom-smeared plate still here – must return to kitchen and wash up (those with whom I share kitchen will get violent otherwise).

After all the hassle of actually buying some VEG, it didn't taste quite right somehow. Perhaps didn't use right oil...

perhaps is coz didn't have cuppa to go with it...

perhaps is just coz Mum didn't make it for me.

Sat 23 Oct

Bad bad BAD idea to START going to BURP a couple of weeks into semester. They'd all formed their own little groups of like-minded (like-dressed, like-denomination-ed etc) others. They all knew what to do, and when, and why... I just watched, alone, not in a group, feeling like a Solero in December... well out of place. (Darn it – now have made myself hungry.)

Cringed when 'prayer time' was announced at the end. Firstly, not comfortable praying to a God that am not sure exists, and not sure would want me even if he did. Secondly, scared of others spotting such fears and of me being revealed for the 'fake' that I am. Thirdly, terrified would be left out of little 'prayer circles' that were forming all around me, which I clearly wasn't going to feature in.

Just as I considered making a run for it, a lanky arm reached out from nearby circle/rugby huddle and dragged me in. When it was all over (worst 5 mins of today so far) the arm introduced me to its owner – Duncan.

Yuk yukkie yuk yuk. Duncan the geek fancies me! Wouldn't leave me alone, even when the meeting was clearly over. He is so geek-i-fied it's unreal. He's like King of all Geeks. Other geeks learn from him – he is their idol. OK, so in a way it was nice to have someone notice I was there and 'ungrouped', but why him?! Why oh why not someone else, like, say, for example… Reuben?

(He was there, but didn't get within 5 metres of him… will try harder next time, if can escape dear Duncs.)

Errrrr… just trying to think what other BURPers I can tell you about (Duncs introduced me to some… going to F&Ferret with them this eve actually). Yeah, now there's a gal called Lydia and she's the president (wow – what I would have done to be 'the president' of a CU, before JimDream). She seems cool. Not weird, not OTT (as Cns so often are) not tarty… just normal, and nice, and… yeah – nice.

Also there's Oren – quite a boring bloke, so not much to report. Another bloke called 'Fax'. Yeah, bizarre name, I thought so too. He didn't say much at all, so again, not much to report. Will keep you informed tho… perhaps will have something to tell you after tonight…

Sun 24 Oct

9:47 am

OK, am off to church now, with my new BURP pals… will fill you in on last night later.

4:32 pm Admittedly, they're not a bad bunch. Oh, alright, if you forced me into a corner and held a knife to my throat, I'd say they were cool – not as scary as had imagined.

Last night was great. First time 'out' since Tate evening, pretty much. Felt a lot safer with these guys than with him, Ethan etc. (Am excluding Duncs though, who continually makes me 100% freaked-out).

Turns out Lydia's ENGAGED! Yeah, like in style of soon-to-be-wed! Fax informed us that there are about 20 million more women than men living in Russia, working out to a ratio of 7 women for every 6 men (add 'never visit Russia' to my 'do' list).

Oren (who turns out to be vice-president) bought me ½ Dry B followed by can of Fanta (not intending to drink to excess for quite some time – also noted that Oren stuck to soft drinks all eve – how yawnyawn). He looked pee-ed off when he returned with my 2nd drink and found Reuben in his seat (NEXT TO ME!!!).

Twas fab for 1st few mins when Reuben 'took over' and told us all about Nazarene, the band he's starting up with some other BURPers (he's the singer… how cool is that?!). But then Saskia joined the table, and he spent the remainder of the evening very kindly making her feel part of the group.

Like me, Saskia's only just started at BURP… unlike me, she is skinny blonde sex goddess.

So, we all went to Bymouth Baptist Church this morning, just like good little Cns do (don't think they're on to me – a good sign). Was OK. Not as lively as church at home, but this a good thing as not sure could handle all that charisma flying around the place at this point in my life.

Reuben and Saskia sat together (she got a bit too close for my liking, the tart) while I was squeezed into an Oren and Duncs sandwich (Oren looked embarrassed… Duncs looked serene). Lydia and Fax were busy 'doing' churchy things… some people just can't help getting involved.

When I eventually reached the front of the coffee queue at end of the service, Fax, who was on 'pouring' duty, mentioned that if you squeezed out all the bacteria from your intestines, you could almost fill up a coffee mug (left coffee – grabbed a squash instead). Am beginning to see why he calls himself 'Fax'. Does he have a real name? Does he ever have anything normal to say? He's not bad looking… not a patch on Reuben. How could you have a relationship with someone who only has odd things to say?

Wed 27 Oct

'Miss Singleton – are you aware of when you last checked your wing mirror?'

StiltonBreath, are you aware of how much of a git you are… and who cares what's behind me anyway… it's what's in front of me that I'm concerned with… 'not killing anyone' is still my main objective, after all.

Ooooh... just got txt from Libs...

hwn pty sun eve 9pm at Un comin?

Hmmmm. Give me a mo.

Ahhh... got it. Halloween... mmmmmm... not really my thing... would make a great witch tho – the way my hair/skin looks today I wouldn't have to try too hard!

Occurred to me that Oscar might have a point (for a change). If there are reps of all world religions, then could talk to a Cn one, like a vicar or something. Perhaps they've got a hotline to the Pope.

Is Pope a Cn?

He's Catholic... is that allowed? Will ring his secretary (Oscar's, not Pope's) right now, before I chicken out...

Post-phone call Has NO ONE even heard of Christianity in this place?! Ms Secretary was thrilled that I wanted her assistance, but was convinced that I would get on better 'exploring' Buddhism, Sikhism, Islam, Hinduism, Hari Krishna, Zoroastrianism (huh?) or Jehovah's Witnesses (yeah, thanks, but not quite that desperate yet). ½ expected her to offer me a personal invitation to next mtg of Ethan/Jesus the 2nd, of which she and the Octopus are probably members.
'But surely everyone KNOWS what Christians believe, and to be honest, who, in this day and age, could think that 'God' could have anything to offer them?'

She eventually caved in and graciously allowed me to have app with the 'Chaplain' on Fri.

Chaplain...

Can't help but think of Charlie Chaplin. Will he look like him? C Chaplin himself once won 3rd prize in a C Chaplin look alike contest!! (Only know this coz Fax told me at Church on Sun, during 'Over the mountains'.)

Fri 29 Oct

Post-Charlie

Guess who's more scary... Libs in her Hannibal Lecter costume (she just called in to test it out for 'Hwn pty') or the uni Chaplain? Ya guessed it –

Ms Anna Harris was a walking Hannibal in her own right. A woman! What's happening to the world?!

Not sure how I coped. Put to her my probs re Tate/poss sex, and God/search for truth. Her reply:

'Ahhhh, Tate... a man. This is starting to make sense. You have had your life disturbed by... a man. You have had your body violated by... a man. You have been hurt and abused by... a man.'

With each mention of 'man' she kind of spat, and glanced over my shoulder, as if one were lurking behind me, ready to do some evil deed... like breathe. She went on in this fashion for some time.

Makes me wonder – has she been hurt badly by a man in the past and says this kind of thing by way of revenge? Or was she brought up by a man-hater, who, in turn, converted her into one?

OK, so blokes can be annoying, and often a bit thick... but they're not THAT bad, are they? Perhaps she knows stuff I don't. She hardly commented on my loss of faith... she mainly wanted to talk about men, and how they are in need of 'taming' by us women. Huh. Chance would be a fine thing.

Wondered if she was going to union 'do' on Sun... dressed as herself – 'Anna the man-catcher' who 1st catches her man, and then eats him alive, Hannibal-style. (Sorry, grim image.)

Sat 30 Oct

5:32 pm

Popped over to Sis Abby's today (had asked Libs to come too, but she mumbled something about being allergic to pregnant women, and scurried off).

Nat is sooooo cute! They've just taught him about opposites, like big/little, hot/cold etc (just in case you didn't know what opposites were). Today's quest was to master bumpy/smooth. So far, so cute. He ran his little hand across my jeans saying, 'smoooooove'. THEN he put his little toddler hand UP my jeans (v flared), ran his hand UP my leg, and pronounced it 'bumpeeee'. Technically he was correct, as haven't shaved in ages, but there was no need for him to embarrass me like that, in front of the *Tweenies* and all (on TV, not live in lounge).

Have just shaved as BURP mtg later, and who knows... someone may feel the need to put their hand up my jeans and stroke my leg! Keep catching myself singing, 'Hi-ho, hi-ho, it's off to BURP I go...' which is a tad worrying. Think am just happier since started going. Not that don't still feel confused/lost/bit lonely... but think these guys sort of care about me somehow... seems a shame to live a lie right in front of them... perhaps will tell them truth, when the time's right (like after graduating).

11:07 pm Arrrrgggghhhhh!! Most embarrassing thing of my LIFE so far just occurred. Can hardly bear to tell you. Promise me you'll forget this as soon as you've read it, and NEVER NEVER bring it up, throughout the duration of our married life, til the day you die... NEVER EVER EVER. Right, now you've promised, will continue...

Went to BURP – fine. They had a visiting speaker – fine. He was American – fine, like what speaker isn't these days?! (Apart from good old Nick Gumbel.) He got all enthusiastic and loud – fine, he's American – he's allowed. He got everyone else all enthusiastic and loud – fine, this is acceptable in England, if encouraged to do so by an American. So far, so fine.

Was feeling quite at home as lots of loud/loony preachers at home church. Also feeling rather smug, knowing how freshly shaved I was – wondered who else could claim such 'smooooove' legs!

So he's shouting away:

'Who belieeeeeves in Jesus?'
'Me/I do/us!' (*Say most of us – yeah, even pagan old me, just to fit in.*)
'Who LURRRRRRVES Jeeeeesus?!' (*Louder still.*)
'Me/yes/us!' (*Marginally louder, but still not matching him.*)
'OK then guys... hands up if you lurrrrrrrrve Jeeeeesus!!' (*As if not satisfied with our meek shouts, and in need of convincing.*)

Hands shot up all over the place... was just about to raise mine when it dawned on me... HELP! NO! Arghhhhh!
Had only shaved legs...
neglected armpits...
was wearing top with almost no sleeves
= potential nightmare.

Ironic thing was – I don't believe in Jesus (at least can't be 100% sure either way). So would have been lying if had raised hand, but desperately wanted to... knew would look such a prat if didn't.

So, all hands were now raised, except mine. All eyes were on me. Couldn't see all of them but could feel stares burning holes all over body – ouch!

No, couldn't do it. Was no way I was going to expose hairy pits to these lovely people... and Reuben was there!

Speaker glared at me too, while saying:

'Come on then, let's see those hands raised high to Gaad...' (Why do Americans say 'Gaad' and not 'God'... what version of the Bible do they GET over there?)

No, didn't budge. Pits wouldn't allow it.

Speaker then continued in sim fashion (for next HOUR) until aching arms were allowed down.

Why? Why why why? Why do these things happen to me, and not, for example, to pick a person completely at random... Saskia? Why couldn't it be HER with hairy unshowable pits? Huh. Bet she shaves them twice a day and thrice on Sundays.

Wonder if Reuben's the sort of guy to worry about hair, or if he just sees the person BEHIND the hair? Hmmmmmm. Poor bloke could hardly move during mtg due to Saskia practically sitting ON him. Still, he braved it out and even stayed after to talk to her – perhaps she needed prayer or something...

Mon 1 Nov

Ooooooohh... height of excitement... this just arrived in post for me, all for me...

Mr and Mrs Ford request the company of

Miss Jude Singleton and partner

at the marriage of their daughter

Lydia

to

Mr Jonathan Blake

at... blah blah blah

Is on 4th Dec – only 1 month away!

Plan of action… need to:

1| Find 'partner' to take, pref you – WHERE ARE YOU BOB?!
2| Lose weight.
3| Make dramatic alterations to appearance so am the hottest chick there.
4| Buy fab new outfit (which might involve not eating at all on all weekends til wedding, so can afford it).
5| Lose weight. Ah, already put that… but will leave on list as it's of paramount importance.

Fri 5 Nov

Tip for if you're learning to drive: don't have lesson on 5th Nov, after dark. Freaky whooosh-whooosh-bangs of fireworks can be quite distracting, to say the least.

Didn't distract StiltonBreath tho – he was on top form today…

Was suspicious from the start that something was up. Asked him if he'd put me in for my test without me knowing. He tapped his pencil extra-hard on his clipboard, and screwed up his face, but that was all – assumed it meant, 'No, Miss Singleton – you will NEVER be ready for your test.'

Drove around as normal (terrified, yet managing not to kill anyone) for duration of lesson, my hatred of fireworks/StiltonBreath festering within…

End of lesson, he says, with smug look on his face:

'And how often during this lesson, would you say, did you check your rear-view mirror?'

'Oh… loads of times,' I lied.

'Ahhhhh… that's strange,' he said.

'Huh?' said I.

He almost smiled.

This was when I knew something must be very VERY wrong. He reached over to the back seat and presented me with what he had obviously been leading up to for whole lesson…

…the rear-view mirror.

Huh, and double huh.

Sat 13 Nov

Whoops – over a wk = record gap in writing to you – please don't feel neglected… still love you!

Bit concerned Libs might be feeling neglected, since have been hanging around with BURPers lots. Mentioned this to Lydia last night… she suggested I invited Libs to BURP mtg. Laughed so hard I showered her with my Diet Coke (with lemon) then realised she was serious.

Lydia may be wise in general, but when it comes to Libs, the lass has got NO idea. Is not her fault, she's just never met her and thus doesn't know that Libs is the most un-convertable person in the history of the planet. She'd sooner give up Big Macs than hang out with Cns, let alone go to a Cn mtg!

Duncs is stalking me.

Everywhere I turn… there he is, asking if he can buy me a drink or carry my books (what corny 60s films has he been watching?) but, scarier than that… sometimes he's just THERE, in the background, looking my way, looking hopeful, looking geek-like. Please God, if you exist and are still interested in me, despite my mouthing you off rather, please don't make me marry him, kiss him, have his children etc. Ooooohhhhh… now feel pukey, will change subject…

Think will pop to Tesco and grab another of those tiramisu things – have you had one before? Sort of like trifle, but with more alcohol, and it has a sort of coffee taste = scrummy…

OK, so did that and just got 2/3 way through it, then remembered about getting slim for wedding, so will pop remainder of it to Mr NextDoor (have resorted to calling him this – not to his face – as don't know his name, and Nat calls his neighbours 'Mith-ter n Mith-ith nexth door'… it's too cute not to copy!).

He is sort of OK looking (Mr NextDoor) if a bit, ya know, not slim. Might be difficult to be married to him as he would finish his meals double quick and then start picking off my plate.

Ahhhh, but then I'd get thinner… so that would be good. Won't rule him out as a possible 'you' altogether then… guess he's not a Cn (unless listening to Marilyn Manson at full volume whilst smoking pot is part of some new outreach programme I don't yet know about).

Still not sure if you'll be a Cn or not Bob, as don't yet know whether I am one, or want to be one... still not sure if the big guy is real, or the biggest lie have ever been told.

Trip to laundrette long overdue... clothes starting to look 'shabby', as Mum would say.

11:34 pm Eardrums took a battering at BURP (even worse than M Manson!). Was sat next to one of those girls who always sings in 'harmony'. Translated, this means that whatever note we're supposed to be singing, she avoids like the plague. Why? It's not big and it's not clever... so why?

Down to F&Ferret after mtg... had good laf. Well, up til point when I commented that had expected uni to = being surrounded by those of different race/background/culture etc, to me ('to me' or 'than me'? Hmmm). As it was, had only made pals with people who were, dare I say it, almost exactly like me... no Chinese, no native Indian, no wheelchair users, no nothing. Reuben said he has a 2nd cousin who's ½ Welsh... Duncs added that he once lived in Spain... for a month... when he was 3. Not sure if that counts. Things were a bit dull for a while after this convo, as all feeling really boring and un-cosmopolitan (yeah, I thought this was just the name of a cool mag, but turns out to be the word for mixture of people, according to Oren). Then Fax, who'd added nothing up til this point, announced that orang-utans warn people to stay out of their territory by belching... and, for some strange reason, we all felt jolly again!

Am writing this pretty quick as guys will be here in a min. Invited them all back here at closing time... then raced on ahead by myself to check following:

1] *Radio set to 1 not 2.*
2] *Room reasonably tidy, so look like general tidy person (without appearing to be a scary cleanliness-freak, eg my sis).*
3] *All empty food packaging to bin/all uneaten junk food hidden in draw under bed, so as not to appear like total porker.*

Right... still some work needed re 2 & 3...

1:23 am Phew – they've just gone!

Managed to get room sorted in time... shame forgot about sad-looking underwear drying on radiator...

Guests were: Lydia, Oren, Fax, Duncs, Reuben... and NO Saskia... ha ha ha... what a shame!

Oren got talking about his gran, Maisie. Said she was quite lonely, could do with more visitors, and didn't live too far from here. After the rest of us had changed the subject several times, and he'd kept bringing it back to Maisie, he eventually asked if we'd be willing to come with him to see her tomorrow:

'To meet all you guys would really do her good... she doesn't get out much any more, being 82. It wouldn't have to be for long... and I kind of mentioned it to her already so she is sort of expecting you... you could see it as outreach...'

Turned out that Reuben is taking an ill friend to the doctors tomorrow (missing Nazarene jamming session) so couldn't come. He is so thoughtful. The rest of us agreed to go (Duncs only doing so after I had) and Oren looked perky for a change.

Hope Libs won't mind me deserting her tomorrow – don't want to think I've 'dumped' her.

Shortly after that, a knock at door – twas Mr NextDoor. Said that someone had dropped round a bag of books for me, but left them with him as I was out. Hadn't been expecting any books – bought all my textbooks at beg of term (cost me an arm, a leg and both kidneys). So asked what books they were...

Mr ND: Oh, ya know, just books...

Me: Yeah, but what books? (*Seemed quite impressive to have bloke visit me whilst others/Reuben there, so wanted to draw this out a bit...*)

Mr ND: Errrrr... like just a big pile... I'll go get 'em.

Me: No, I want to know what books they are – they might not even be mine – it might be a mistake.

Mr ND: Well, there's a sticker on the bag with your name on it – 'Jude Singleton', right? (*Heard a few sniggers from guys at this point, re surname, but let it go.*)

Me: Yeah, but what are the books about? I didn't order any books. Have you opened the bag?

Mr ND: Ummmm... sorta... yeah, didn't see the sticker at first, like. Actually they came, like, a couple of weeks ago...

Me: So, WHAT BOOKS ARE THEY? (*How hard could it be to answer?*)

Mr ND: Oh, like, is that the time?... I ought to go now, so...

Me: NOW... WHAT BOOKS... TELLLL MEEEEE!!!!

Mr ND: (*Takes deep breath.*) *The Kama Sutra, The Joy of Sex,* 101 *Ways to Please Your Partner Sexually, Sex and the Mind*… and errrr… *Sex Games for Beginners.* Or like, ya know, something like that… I haven't read them or anything. (*He said, going redder than I was.*)

Took me some time to explain to my amazed yet highly amused guests about Oscar, me, and my counselling needs (tho just said was homesick – didn't say about Tate/suspected pregnancy… guests prob left room confused as to why a counsellor would suggest such books to relieve homesickness).

Will return books asap. Will not open bag… unlike Joey and Chandler, am not into porn.

Do doctors work on a Sunday? Perhaps Reuben meant some sort of emergency clinic… his friend must be very ill…

Sun 14 Nov

After church, we piled into Oren's car and headed for Maisie's house. He casually mentioned she could be a bit cranky – we weren't to take it personally. Huh. 'How rude,' I thought. 'One shouldn't talk about one's gran in such a way.' Hoped he was nice to this poor lonely old lady and wasn't a granny-batterer in his spare time…

Could I have BEEN more wrong?! It was Oren that was being polite and Maisie that was… shall we say… the granny from hell. He was actually being quite kind/generous with the description of 'cranky'… she was intolerable. We were greeted with:

'Fought ere's s'posed a be 5 friens… this is only 4… kill one on the way an lock 'em in the boot, eh? I dunno – ya stoodents… fink yave got it all sorted. Back in my day we paid our way… oh yeah. None of this stoo-pid loan business. You fink you rule the world don't ya lovies? Well, I'm ere to tell ya tha ya DON'T an ya never will… you wiv ya fancy cloves… an wotchin ya fancy DVTs or wotever… huh…'

and so she went on,
and on,

and on… for the entire duration of our visit (1 hour and 23 minutes – I was counting). Anything we said, she complained about, and then complained about us (students… in fact anyone under about 60). Her teeny bungalow reeked of lavender, which, while a pleasant enough fragrance under normal circumstances, in this instance made one think of a dog who had swallowed a ton of the stuff, and then regurgitated it, many times over.

Lonely? Huh! She could talk the hind legs off a T-Rex… no wonder she's lonely – who'd want to spend more than 5 mins with her.

Hang on, make that 5 secs… not me for sure!

7.23 pm Libs just left room. She burst in a while ago with the line:

'I want you to be my friend!'

Was quite touched. Clearly she'd taken offence at how much time I've been spending with BURPers. I was obviously, in some way, important in her life… and she wanted me back.

Enquired as to why she was clutching a large catalogue…

'Er… Hello, Miss Durrbrain… like I said – I want you to be my friend.'

Turned out she wanted me to be her 'friend' in the sense that:

1] *She'd fill my details in on a form,*
2] *send it to catalogue,*
3] *they'd send me catalogue,*
4] *I'd then order from it,*
5] *we'd then share the £20 off voucher she'd receive (for introducing me to catalogue).*

(Bob – be thankful you're a bloke.) She had it all sussed – was v keen. She always seems sooooo desperate to save cash. Maybe she doesn't HAVE any parents, so no one is supporting her here
and she used to live on the streets
selling the Big Issue and…

hmmmmm.

Agreed to catalogue deal.

Asked if me spending so much time with BURPers upset her. She creased up, came over to where I was sitting on bed, gave me a huge hug and kissed me on forehead. If it'd been any other female, would have been scared silly, but this was Libs and was fast learning that with her, anything goes.

She said I was free to see who I wanted, as long as I made myself available to her now and then, for deep chats. With a slightly more serious look on her face she added that I was easier to talk to than some of her other friends, that she loved me, always would… and was hoping she'd turn out to be my Bob (knew she wouldn't stay serious for long).

Saw Saskia earlier… said she'd got flu, but was in 'good hands'.

Her faith in God must be super-strong… strange, seeing as she's such an annoying bimbo.

Must return Oscar's books… maybe will just have a little peek at one of them now that…

No No NO!! Not a good idea. Will sidetrack myself by tucking into giant bar of choc have just discovered under pile of half-rotting clothes (don't worry – it's a healthy one… packed with fruit and nuts!).

Slippery heat

Tue 16 Nov

Am in bed, wrapped in a white sexy see-through nightie-thing.

A couple of minutes ago, a bloke (quite hot) was paying a lot of attention to the big toe on my right foot.

No, it's not what you think…

I am, in fact, in Bymouth General Hospital.

Ah, hot nurse just been back at bedside, mumbling something about a change of dressing. I wish. This hosp nightie = v v hideous (lied about the 'sexy' bit).

So, why?

Why am I, healthy Jude, in hosp?

Let me transport you to the uni laundrette, where yesterday, my clothing and I paid a much-needed visit…

Put my 8 20ps in slot, mass of stinky clothes in w machine, and settled myself down with *heat* (Mr NextDoor had his clothes stolen from laund last week coz he failed to babysit them).

Just getting into article re Posh (details of kids' eating habits – fascinating, but at same time annoying as made me peckish – how can reading about organic fish fingers mashed with non-GM swede do that?), when in strolls Reuben.

'Wow – to be the w machine that washes his attire… what a privilege…' thought I. Then I realised I was staring right at him, and he was looking my way, so swiftly buried head in *heat*.

'Hey, Jude,' he said as he plonked his bag down by w machine next to mine. 'Oh… hi, Reuben,' said I, faking surprise at seeing him, which, with hind-sight, was a bit thick as he'd just seen me gawking at him.

He launched right into a very funny story about when Duncs came to the laund for the 1st time… he loaded up a w machine, couldn't suss out where to put the w liquid in, so threw a couple of lid-fulls straight into w machine, and set it going. After a bit, he wondered why he couldn't see any water sloshing around with his clothes, even tho they were spinning around. Confused, he enquired of a passing student how long he was gonna have to wait for the water... and got the answer:

'A very long time mate... that's a tumble drier!!'

Nearly wet myself with laughter... partly coz twas v rib-ticklin' story, partly coz wanted him to know that I appreciate his humour/storytelling abilities... and would be only to happy to marry him (enthusiasm even caused *heat* to slip off lap, onto floor). He then suggested we search for the drier in question, as he'd heard that you could still see the stains left by the liquid Duncs put in... despite him spending a good hour trying to scrub the thing clean. Literally LEAPT at the chance to share this special moment with my one true love... but, and here comes the icky bit... didn't take into account *heat* on floor not far from feet, and fact that floor was wet in patches, one of those being... under *heat*...

WHHHHHOOOOOOOOOOOOOOOSSSSSSHHHHHHHH!!!!!!!!!

Skidded along floor, past several w machines... and was stopped dramatically by a friendly Coke machine, that turned out to be not quite so friendly... seeing as it dented my head slightly, and broke my right toe.

And here's where the journey ends, still in the laund, with me clutching toe in agony (sure will laugh about this one day, but believe me, IT HURT!) and my hero, Reuben, ringing for help...

He told me help was on it's way... assumed he meant ambulance or sim. Within minutes Saskia turned up – it was HER he'd phoned... apparently she'd just started 1st aid module as part of her BEd.

Head and toe throbbing with pain pain pain by now... could see Reuben and Saskia beside me – him complimenting her on getting there so soon, her saying that he was so clever to think of ringing her,

him saying he liked her new top etc etc etc.

Then their words started to sound sorta fuzzy, then they looked sorta fuzzy... then...

Found myself lying in hosp bed in aforementioned un-sexy nightie.

Huh. Seem to be making habit of waking up in bed with no knowledge of how I got there... perhaps is something one should embrace as essential part of uni life.

Ouch and huh.

8:46pm Someone with a big gob (Libs?) has been letting entire world know am stuck in here... today's visiting schedule:

9:30 am – Duncs, with big bunch of flowers, chocs, grapes, huge card... stayed for an hour...

11:10 am – Oren, with his laptop (that am using to write this to you) so I could 'catch up on some study'.

1:10 pm – Libs, with girlie mags, Pringles (pizza) and mysterious 'gift' from friend of hers (some sort of letter, will explain below). Damage to head has caused loss of appetite, so Libs ate most of Pringles, then chocs, then grapes.

2 pm – Duncs, just popping in to check I was still OK, with more flowers (in case the other bunch had died, one assumes).

2:27 pm – Abby waddled in, with 'slight twinges' (she's due any day now).

3:40 pm – Reuben (at last – hurrah!), with card. His visit cut short by...

4 pm – Duncs, just checking... with more chocs and grapes (in case Libs should visit again, one assumes).

6:48 pm – Lydia and Jon (her fiance!), with card.

All in all, have not had chance to be bored... other kids on ward have looked on in awe, wondering why they (with legs broken in several places, or in need of heart transplants or whatever) have only had ONE visit all day... from their lousy parents... ha ha titty ha ha!

Oh, am on children's ward, due to lack of available beds – when they saw I was just 18 they thought I'd fit right in... huh, how embarrassing. Leave home to become an adult, only to end up on a ward with a wall to wall *Bob the Builder* theme...

No, no it can't be... please no... yeah, it is, it's him... am going to have to go now as can see next visitor approaching, with yet MORE flowers... will pretend to be asleep...

9:23 pm Yuk yukkie yuk yuk... faked sleep for a good 20 mins. Assumed he'd LEAVE... but no. At one point he kissed my hand. IS THAT ALLOWED?! Yuk. Eventually he called over the hot nurse, saying I needed immediate attention as had slipped into a coma. Hoped that if anyone was going to give me kiss of life it would be hot nurse and NOT the champion hosp visitor. Before he comes again ought to try to get moved to another ward/hosp/planet.

V thoughtful of Oren to lend me laptop – saved me from complete bore-dom, tho don't think am well enough to study yet.

Right, must do something stimulating now all alone and visitor-free.

Ah, now Libs brought me something from her HorrorMovie pal (the one doing law) apparently all I have to do is to sign it, pop it in envelope and send…

Dear Sir/Madam (Editor of heat)

On Monday 17th November of this year I was reading a copy of your magazine. My enjoyment of it, however, was impaired due to the following: when placed on a slightly damp surface it turned into a near-fatal weapon. I am currently in hospital being treated for a broken toe and possible serious damage to my brain.

The Consumer Protection Act of 1897 states that manufacturers are strictly liable if the products they make are defective and cause personal injury.

In addition to this, the Misrepresentation Act of 1967 states that if a consumer enters an agreement on the basis of a statement purporting to be a fact but which turns out to be untrue, they have the right to cancel the deal and get their money back, or get compensation.

Finally, the Trade Descriptions Act of 1968 states it is a criminal offence for traders to make false statements about the goods they sell.

On the front cover of the magazine in question it said 'Chill out with heat'. Due to this misrepresentation/false statement, and to my injuries, I expect to receive your cheque for £5,000 (the price of the magazine, plus some compensation) within 14 working days. If you fail to reimburse/compensate me I shall have no alternative but to issue a summons against you in the county court for recovery of the money without further reference to you.

Yours sincerely…

Never quite sure whether to take that gal (or those who associate with her) seriously or not.

'Serious damage to my brain'? Do they know something I don't? Prob not… saw Libs chatting with hot nurse when she visited… thought it was sweet that she should enquire re my health. When she came back to me, asked her just how long I had to live.

'At least long enough to find out what happens when I meet that hot nurse of yours at Fusion tonight… but after that… anybody's guess, my sweet…'

Huh – the tart!

OK, so let's have a look at these cards then – haven't had a chance to open them yet. Ah – that's Reuben's writing…

NOOooooo!! It reads 'love Reuben and Saskia'.

Huh – guess they're a couple then. Great. Timing couldn't be better. That scheming little madam – GIVE HIM BACK! He's mine, all mine!! Well, he will be one day, you'll see…

Ah, and he's included card from Nazarene which has been signed by all the band members – cute.

Right, next one from… 'Get well soon, from Oren and Maisie'. Ahhhh… that's nice. Even old Ms GroanForEngland has spared me a thought in my hour of need.

Next one, 'love Jon and Lydia. PS Look up these verses: John 8:32 and Psalm 51'. Hmmmmm.

Last one – puke-city… involves lots of little hearts drawn (badly) with arrows through them… someone tell him we left primary school a long long time ago…

Pretty late Have tried sleeping but to no avail (ace word). Doors to ward keep banging and continual stream of nurses' banter coming from some-where. Aren't they expecting any of us kiddies to sleep in here? Huh?

Just got up to shut doors, but within minutes they were flung open again. Perhaps sleep deprivation is all part of NHS policy – who am I to complain?

Is all dark and unfamiliar in here. Don't know a soul. Am lonely.

Still don't know whether am virgin or not. Still feeling guilty re whole Tate thing. Still not sure re whole God/truth thing. Bit fed up with this 'search' for the answers. Other people have only served to misunderstand, confuse and annoy me. Gggrrrrrrrrrrrrrrrr.

Wonder if there's a book you can buy called The Truth – something you can read and then know it all.

Ahhhhh, guess some would say that's the Bible. Huh. Haven't read the thing in ages…

Good job there's no Bible here as having to squash little niggling desire to get my hands on one.

Just as I typed that last bit, 2 things occurred to me at the exact same time: Lydia's card, and the Gideons…

Yeah, sure enough those ancient suited blokes have struck again – a Gideon Bible is now in my hand, after being extracted from bedside table. Right, now to those verses (can't believe am doing this)…

'Jesus said… you will know the truth, and the truth will set you free,' and Psalm 51 – a ton of stuff from old Dave re sin and forgiveness.

Hmmmmmmm. OK, spooky coincidence or something of a more divine nature? I WILL know the truth… when? How? Would sure like to be 'set free' from whatever it is that is messing my head up. Guess, if there is a God, he can forgive me for excessive drinking and poss sex. Dave thinks God can, anyhow. Boy – HE must have done something REALLY bad. Sort of said 'sorry' to God and kinda asked him to show me the truth – my 1st 'almost prayer' since JimDream. Don't feel any different. Perhaps he doesn't visit hospitals… perhaps he's getting some kip, like I should be right now.

Thur 18 Nov

1:46 pm

If Mum rings one more time to check am 'taking it easy', will top myself… THEN she'll be sorry…

Oh, came out of hosp yesterday… twas finally decided that damage to my head had made no difference to mental state (have always been this way)… toe has been told to heal itself – the NHS doesn't 'do' broken toes, don't ya know. Also, they needed my bed for little lad having wisdom teeth out – ouch city!

V much hoping toe is fully better for wedding – will look a bit of a minger if am still hobbling pitifully around, as am now.

MUST start planning wedding gear/hair… will get Libs to help. Not eaten anything today so far in attempt to lose extra weight put on in hosp (not sure why people complain about hosp food – thought it was cool – was allowed triple helpings!).

Hacked off as can't find all cards and stuff that got given whilst in hosp – must have left a pile in bedside table… never mind, at least have L&J's card, with the verses in… have stuck to noticeboard – keep thinking about God/forgiveness/ truth/freedom etc, each time it catches my eye. Wonder if L&J really believe in it all? Guess so. Bit unfair tho – prob easy-peasy to have faith in God when you're all hunky-dory in lurve and about to tie the knot. Not quite the same when you're single, bored stiff with being alone, and desperate for a bloke. Huh.

3:12 pm Oooooooooh, quite peckish now… ought to eat something soon, after all, am a recent concussion sufferer with slow-healing broken toe… need to keep up what little strength I have left…

5 pm Not sure meal from refectory (roast chicken+yoghurt for pud), followed by 3 bowls of Coco Pops back here in room, was such a good idea. Thing is, fab offer on C Pops box… only need to get through another 6 boxes and will qualify for cool monkey-shaped keyring!! Have often fantasised about having cool keyring to keep car keys on when I pass.

Not that am likely to pass in near future.

Not that am likely to get a car if do pass, but hey… a girl can dream! Got to go…

That interruption was due to Mum on my mobile… almost launched into my 'Hi, this is Jude. Please leave a msg' routine, to avoid having to talk to her, but she beat me to it with – 'ABIGAIL HAS HAD THE BABY!!!'

Wow – it's a girl, called Eve… would tell you her weight… if hadn't forgotten it already.

Why is everyone always so interested in a baby's weight? Mum told me weight before she said it was a girl, or what her name was. Good job people fast lose interest in children's weight as they get older. Would be a nightmare if, when Mum told a new friend that she had a daughter at uni, the friend said:

'Oh how lovely… and how much does she weigh?'

People are strange. Bob, when I (we) have children, let's ban them from being weighed at birth and successfully annoy the world by depriving them of such information.

Anyway, Abby and Eve are fine, and coming home tomorrow. Mum wants me to go to Abby's after my last lecture tomorrow and 'help', whatever that means. Her and Dad are travelling up in a couple of days, to stay a week at Abby's.

(If I'd had a baby the last thing on earth I'd want would be to live with Mum and Dad for a week.)

Being an auntie all over again calls for a celebration… now, to the C Pops…

Fri 19 Nov

Estimate that if eat, on average, 5 bowls of C Pops per day, for next 2 weeks… should be able to send off for keyring.

Just booked app with fashion/image consultant – Liberty Young… tomorrow before BURP. Can't wait! Wedding just over 2 wks away…

Arrggghhhh!

Slight prob has arisen… was just making card for Abby and Amos re new baby (in attempt to save couple of quid, so can put toward wedding outfit) when recalled had told Mum would go there today, after last lecture, but already said would go to Libs for eve of telly n chat – would be rude to break a promise. Will give Abby a ring – can't make too much difference if I go tomorrow instead.

Right, off to Tesco to stock up C Pops…

Sat 20 Nov

9:13 am

Made a grand start to the day – 3 bowls C Pops! Ya know how it is when you eat lots and lots of something, however scrummy it is, and it begins to get on your nerves a tad…

No… mustn't grumble – keyring will be worth it.

Right, off to Abby's now… tried to get Libs to come with me again – she claimed she was spending the day matching up all her odd socks. Surely most people would give that a miss to see brand spanking new baby, wouldn't they?

How many odd socks can one lass have, anyway?

1:46 pm Huh… that didn't go too well. Baby Eve is v v cute… twas great to give her a cuddle and feel all auntie-ish. Nat doesn't like her much – has transformed himself from little angel to little gremlin (poured whole bottle of Ribena over Abby's freshly polished flute, pulled Eve's hair and pulled all the ribbon out of one of his many *VeggieTales* videos, all in the space of the hour I was there!).

Gremlin aside, the main prob was that Abby had been expecting me to go there yesterday, and I didn't. Told her had left msg on their answerphone explaining that I'd come today instead, but they didn't get it. Amos was working til late (he seems to do this quite often I've noticed – hmmmmm). Abby said that she'd really needed someone here on the day she came out of hosp and that my help would have been much appreciated. Got the feeling that she was a bit crosser than she was letting on.

As penance I offered to do some ironing/watch Nat, whilst Abby took baby Eve for a walk in the pram (to get her off to sleep – someone should explain the whole 'sleep' thing to that child – she hasn't got the hang of it yet!). Was ironing away while Amos was making a call from the lounge – he'd asked if I could keep Nat in the kitchen with me for a bit, so did. After a bit, he said he was popping to shops for more Ribena, so let Nat back in the lounge. Before I knew it he'd grabbed the phone and started pressing keys (pesky kid). Snatched it off him, but not before he'd managed to hit the redial key. Didn't want to just hang up as whoever Amos just rung might think it odd, so hung on to talk to them, and to apologise for GremlinNephew's behaviour. It was a woman:

'Ah, Amos – glad you rang again – I forgot to say you left your stuff here last night and…

Amos, is that you? Ah…'
and she hung up. Working late? Huh.

Didn't tell Abby – she looked a bit distant after her walk, which was weird as Eve fast asleep… AND I'd done a ton of ironing (5 of Amos's smart work-shirts, 3 pairs of his trousers and a billion hankies/tea towels/etc – when we are married Bob, I shan't waste what valuable time we have together ironing things that, quite frankly, really don't NEED flattening and would still function OK if a tad creased).

Odd… really wouldn't have thought Amos would mess around. He's a super-Cn after all… isn't he? Perhaps is no such thing, and we all mess up now and then. Still, an affair is a pretty big mess-up, as mess-ups go. If he leaves Abby, my sis will officially be a single mum – not Abby's style. Not sure is poss to be a flautist and a single mum – just doesn't fit.

6:45 pm Just got in from session with Libs re sorting me out for wedding. Started by informing her that want to look like cross between Jen Anniston, Posh and Ally McB. She said this wouldn't be a prob and started scribbling frantically on a pad. She then showed me what she'd written:

Jude needs: Boob job, liposuction (several areas), wig, major plastic surgery – most of face and other parts of body including…

and so on. Huh.

Won't tell you where else she was suggesting I had plastic surgery... didn't even know it was possible to have THAT done! She told me that only snag would be I'd have to live in poverty until the day I died, due to paying back hefalump-sized loan will have to get to afford it all.

Glancing at Libs' list caused me to pinch myself all over, quite hard, much to her bewilderment. Explained that was just checking I was in the real world and not trapped in an episode of *Sex in the City*.

'Ah, OK sugar,' said Libs.

That's the thing about being friends with someone who's nuttier than an overgrown Snickers bar... whatever small nuttiness I produce seems totally normal to her. She did add tho that she wondered if I was practising some new anti-cellulite technique involving pinching, and was looking forward to learning it...

does she think I have cellulite?

Do I have cellulite?
Isn't that when you get old,
like 30 plus?
On a more realistic note, she commented that my eyebrows needed 'doing'.

Asked what was wrong with my eyebrows.
'EyeBROW, Jude love... you only have one and it runs from one side of your face to the other.'

10:32 pm Darn it – just remembered need to eat 2 bowls C Pops before the day is out... when keyring is finally mine will NEVER eat them again! Not sure will ever lose weight for this wedding – wish could move fat from hips/stomach/bum up to boobs...

Sun 21 Nov

SICK OF C POPS... offloaded remaining 2 boxes on Mr NextDoor, who seemed only too pleased to relieve me of breakfast rejects. Left me with nothing suitable for breakie tho, so resorted to Pot Noodle from goodie bag that got given in Freshers' Week (along with condom, mini can of coke, leaflets on safe sex etc).

Glad to see condom still in bag – if Tate didn't use it then perhaps we did-n't do it after all. Tho if we did, and he didn't use one… then that's even worse. Huh.

After church, Oren asked me and Lydia if we'd be free to see Maisie again sometime, as she so much enjoyed our last visit. Huh – glad someone did! Lydia was all up for it, but at the same time v busy with 'wedding plans'. This made my jealousy of Lydia two fold:

1] Coz she has good reason to get out of visiting moody Maisie.
2] Coz she has wedding plans – I WANT WEDDING PLANS!!!

But Lydia's alright – can't let my jealousy get in the way of our friendship and all that, blah blah blah…

Said would consider it (seeing Maisie). Oren said that would be a start. He really does seem to care for her – weird – don't think of lads as caring crea-tures – perhaps he's gay.

Mon 22 Nov

D lesson – no StiltonBreath! Whoo-hoo!

He has flu – may I just take this opportunity to sincerely thank whoever sneezed in his presence and gave him the virus – THANK YOU!!

In his place was a rather hot young thing… kept wanting to grab his knee instead of the gearstick, but managed to control myself, just. Now with this guy (Darren) I would be happy to remain a hopeless driver til the world ends, just so I can sit in his presence for 2 hours every week.

Occurred to me that IF I ever pass, I'll have to live/work/socialise etc in Bymouth and Bymouth alone… it's the only place have ever driven in. Can't see myself attempting to venture elsewhere, this will be my home for life. Let's hope you live in Bymouth, Bob, or are planning to visit real soon.

Post-plucking Have just been plucked to death by Libs. My once sin-gleton eyebrow is now 2 separate ones… which are neatly shaped like lit-tle West-Country bridges… Posh would be proud of me. It really hurt mind, but my torturer kept reminding me that weddings demand neat eye-brows… and if I was wanting to pull I'd better sit still and shut my BEEEP gob.

Thur 25 Nov

No, Oren's not gay – he's got himself a girlfriend, apparently. Well, HE says she's just a good friend, but Reuben said that 'Caroline's' as keen as keen can be. All sounds a bit immature to me – if he's going out with her he should just get on and say so. Why would we mind anyway? He's a free man – we don't own him – he can marry the lovely 'Caroline' for all we care – seems the 'in' thing to do at the mo.

Boring lecture on the central nervous system, along with details of the parasympathetic system and such and such… might have even spelt that right, but don't check up, just in case. Forget para… wotsit, it's ALL plain pathetic if you ask me… like, what's this supposed to be – psychology or flippin' human biology?

Am now watching old Jamie (Oliver)…

Oh Jamie, as much as I fancy you with your cute lisp and squiffy hair, deep within I have the urge to burst in on your kitchen 'set' during filming, drag you away from all those fresh ingredients and whisk you away to Tesco, where the fab Pot-Noodle-and-tiramisu-combo can be found, along with a side order of Pringles… but keep trying mate – you're a joy to watch!

Fri 26 Nov

Arrrgghhhhhhh!! Just looked at my eyebrows… the hairs that were so brutally plucked have started coming back with a vengeance… is all stubbly… I HAVE EYEBROW STUBBLE!!

Will txt Libs – this can't be normal, can it?

She just rang me straight back (prob coz I said emergency ring jude now)! Slightly narked as she was busy with 'Graham'.

Dr Young said 'regrowth' was to be expected, and that I should get plucking.

Why didn't Libs tell me this beforehand? Huh. Right, to the tweezers then…

Sat 27 Nov

Tweezers a tad blunt – some of the little blighters got away with it. Think I need to let them get a bit longer so are easier to pluck. In light of this, will stick shades on (is a bit sunny – honest!). Only need to do bit of shopping in town – not likely to meet anyone and, even if I do, will just keep shades on and hope for best. Hair also a tad greasy, so will add baseball cap to my accessories for the day…

Later Hmmm… well that was one of the worst decisions I ever made. Was just coming out of TopShop (had been looking for wedding outfit – no luck tho) when who should I bump into but Reuben and Saskia. OK, so they may be going out, but still keen to impress him – he is the hottest thing around after all. 'They' invited me to join them for lunch in McDs. Then Oren and Fax appeared, and said they'd come too (no sign of this 'Caroline' person – perhaps it's all ended in tears).

Yeah, had to take off my cap and shades. Tried not to, but after 10 mins or so of sitting in McDs, the pressure from the guys was too much. Think I made it worse by keeping them on so long as they all were v keen to see just what I'd been hiding… they failed to see what my problem was tho – must have been struck with momentary blindness, poor things. Fax just stared for a bit, then went back to his nuggets.

I am developing a theory that many female Hollywood stars must have eyebrow stubble and greasy hair on a regular basis, as they're nearly always wearing shades and baseball caps when they're not tarting around in front of the camera. This means I have something in common with the stars… this means I might BE one some day… watch out Jude Law – Jude Singleton's not far from superstar status.

Skipped BURP as busy plucking/washing hair – it's a tough life being a woman.

Am I a woman yet, or still a girl?

You decide, Bob, you decide.

Mon 29 Nov

5:43 pm

Why oh why am I taking Psychology? Is hard – harder than the A level, but guess it's supposed to be, being a degree and all. All 4 assignments are due in NEXT WEEK. Has kinda crept up on me… well, have been so busy, what with preparing for the wedding, becoming an auntie again, making people laugh with my *heat*/broken toe story (which is a lot better now, thanks for asking).

None of assignments finished... 2 of them aren't exactly started either... must get down to it asap. Thing is, really not that interested in 'The psychodynamic approach' or 'Systematic desensitization', whatever they are... thought this subject was supposed to be vital and alive... huh, more life in my hair.

9:32 pm Libs just called by – unable to BELIEVE I'd worked on assignments for a good 3½ hrs (tho didn't tell her that this time span also involved several trips to Mr NextDoor to ask him to turn M Manson down, and one slightly longer trip to Tesco to stock up on Pot Noodles).

So appalled was she also to hear I didn't go out Sat eve due to beautifying myself, she said we'd both hit the town tonight.

No more yapping to you – need to get ready now... she's coming back in few mins – need to pluck some more, as haven't done it since lunchtime!

2:16 am Yeah, note the time – v late! Have really made it as a student! An interesting night out... Libs took me and two blokes she knew from somewhere (both pretty hot!) to club on other side of town. Hadn't heard of it before. Bit nervous that would be expected to pair up with one of the blokes, but they seemed pretty happy chatting to each other, and knew Libs would look after me this time... she knew about the whole Tate thing after all.

Got some drinks (I had my usual ½ pt Dry B) and had a bit of a boogie... fine. Seemed like entire uni girl's rugby team was there – fine, as much as I detest ANY sport that involves effort, must not be prejudiced. Then gradually it dawned on me – something was different. No, not the music... Kylie can be heard in any self-respecting club. No, not the Dry B – tasted fab as always... what then?

Glanced over at our 'dates'. They were both snogging...
each other!!!
It was a gay club.

I was outta there...

Found Libs and told her it wasn't my scene – she only just managed to miss blowing huge amount of smoke in my face, laughed and said she'd catch me later.

Is SHE gay?

Don't feel like going to bed yet – still a little disturbed by all this. If God's there, would he be cross that I went to gay club? Hmmmmmm.

At what point am I gonna suss it all out? Life, I mean. Life and what it all means. Should I talk to Abby? She has kids – she must know stuff… or will she just force-feed me Christianese til I can bear it no longer?

OK, so what can I read to cheer me up…

Psychology for today? Nope.
One of Oscar's sex books? Nope (must return those).
Lydia's card? Ah, now what was that verse about the truth… 'You will know the truth and the truth will set you free…'
It almost brings tears to my eyes – dunno why.

PMS/blended frog

Tues 30 Nov

Watching Delia Smith on 2...

Not sure 'English gooseberry cobbler' is quite where am at right now... perhaps next year when in house, as opposed to halls.

Anyhow, she's failing to distract me from PMS.

No, Bob, nothing to do with periods... Pre-Marital-Stress. MUST look hot. No, not just hot... v v hot. WHEN am I gonna lose weight? Only 4 days to go now...

Would look so much improved if could shed a stone...

so, 14 lbs divided by 4 = 3.5

so, if could lose 3.5 lbs each day until wedding on Sat... wonder if could book liposuction app before Sat?

Bit narked that invite is for 'Jude and partner'. What does that mean? Boyfriend? Best pal? Does 'partner' have to be of the opposite sex to qualify? Hmmmm. Have been hinting quite a bit recently that am in need of escort to wedding, in front of certain hot males, like Reuben... and, well, just him really. Thought it might be his chance to dump the blonde and discover his true destiny (rumour has it that Nazarene are playing at the evening 'do' – he could dedicate a song to moi!).

Oren lit up when asked if he was going with anyone... but then pulled a v 'oh-I-just-remembered-something' face and said he was taking his 'friend' Caroline.

Tried Fax next, but was already fixed up with a lass to go with (does she know what she's let herself in for?!). Never mind, if worst comes to worst... can always go with Duncs – will just have to remember to ban anyone from taking photos of me and him together – yuk!

Dec tomorrow – means will have to start thinking about Xmas and all (Xmas? Christmas? If not sure about God, does it matter?). Slight snag – have hardly any cash to speak of... will start begging on streets of Bymouth in due course... or perhaps could busk with lass who sings in 'harmony' at

BURP – if she does her stuff to 'Away in a manger', will happily hum along!

Wed 1 Dec

5:12pm

Spent most of today's lecture composing the following:

Dear Mr and Mrs Ford,

Thank you for your kind invitation to the forthcoming wedding of Lydia to Jonathan Blake. Unfortunately, I am such a minger that not a single bloke in the entire universe is interested in accompanying me to said wedding. Therefore, it is with deep regret that I inform you that I cannot possibly attend said wedding, as to go alone would be the saddest thing a person in my position could possibly do.

With my fondest regards,

Miss Jude (forever-a-)Singleton

Really need a partner asap! Should I advertise on noticeboard outside union bar?!

Don't they WANT me to come alone – is it a CRIME to be single? Why do people always want everyone paired up? Many singletons are fulfilled, interesting, confident people, who don't NEED a trophy partner hanging off their arms (me excluded – I DO need!).

Eating v little – jeans still as tight as ever – not got outfit yet – only 3 days to go!!

9:46 pm Odd – Saskia just rang me, asking if I knew where Reuben was... how careless of her to lose her boyfriend... if I were going out with someone, would never lose them as would set up GPS to track their every move, esp if that someone were Reuben! Why would I know where he is?

Has he told her that he really loves me instead?

Huh – dream on Jude...

Thur 2 Dec

9:35 pm

Had severe lack of non-homeostatic motivation today... spent most of it at Oren's watching TV (house, not halls – can't wait to be 2nd yr like him!). Translated into non-psychology lingo... this means I was dead lazy! Thing is, his house gets SKY.

We had SKY at home (only for GOD channel, so parents claimed... rather think Dad would spontaneously combust without daily fix of SKY Sports – 1, 2 AND 3!). We didn't even have a telly when was v young – was fine with me – just spent loads of time round at pal Hannah's, whose parents, although Cns, were not quite so hung up on us being 'polluted with the evil secular world'.

Was just about coming to terms with loss of SKY (as obviously can't get it here in halls) when made discovery about Oren's house. Make a point of calling in now and then (only down road from here) to ask Oren when next BURP mtg is or enquire about Maisie... then say, 'Oooohhh... is that Friends just starting?' and make myself comfy. He doesn't seem to mind – prob too busy with the illusive Caroline to notice. It means get to have weekly fix of all things trashy.

Did I say 'trashy'? I meant 'wholesome'!

Anyhow, somehow ended up staying there for most of the day, glued to several such progs, and other daytime TV stuff. Oren and housemates all out for most of the time. Didn't eat til 2 pm... then raided their kitchen for yummies (½ pack jaffa cakes + 2 bowls Shreddies – Oren had said to help myself!). Know should've been searching for wedding outfit/finishing off assignments that are due in TOMORROW/planning next move in search for 'truth'... but couldn't be bothered. Figure this is what student life is ultimately about after all – doing what you want when you want, with no parents to hassle you about it...

(This said, when one house-occupier returned – female – I got ear-bashing for not washing up bowls etc... but shall overlook.)

Only 2 days to go!

Fri 3 Dec

5:34 am

No, am not up early... have been up ALL NIGHT doing stupid assignments! Are all finished now, if a tad rushed. Bet Abby never left things to the v last min when she was a student. Think Libs did all 4 of hers this week... but then she has multiple brain-cells and finds them easy-peasy. Huh.

10:16 am Just back from town to hunt for outfit (no luck)... sick of Xmas already – stuff's been in shops since Sept but big day still ages away yet... should be a law that doesn't allow shops to display anything Xmassy until a wk before. Who wants to celebrate anything when you're single anyhow, let alone the biggest day of entire year?

Is it really Jesus' b'day? If so, was he really that special that, 2,000 odd yrs later, much of the world devotes an entire day to naff pressies, calorie-laden grub, boozy parties, Queen's speech (Zzzzzzzzz) tedious games of charades with rellies... etc etc, because of HIM, when most of them are at ease ignoring his existence for the other 364 days? Hmmmmm.

Have one mission and one mission only – to find partner for tomorrow. Perhaps will have to go with female after all... will call on Libs, and beg...

10:27 am Nope – Libs busy with 'Jack' tomorrow, surprise surprise.
M Manson blasting through wall again – will tell him to turn down...
Back again. Mr NextDoor said he'd stick some headphones on (why didn't he think of this back in Sept?). Asked him if he was free tomorrow (yeah, am getting desperate now) but he said his parents were visiting for the day (bringing him more food supplies, no doubt).

So, still stuck for an 'other ½' and outfit. Why did Abby inherit the 'organising' gene, while it bypassed me altogether? Huh. Right, only one thing for it.

Will have to ask yukky geeky freaky Duncs... will ring him now (why why why?!?!).

Post-call Nope – Duncs is already taking 'Lauren' to wedding. Amazing! Huh! She's a BURPer, and a complete geek, which I guess is why they are attracted to each other. 2 geeks all lovey-dovey on geek cloud 9, giving geek kisses and... yuk.

Now feel super-ugly – can't even pull Duncs, my ex-biggest fan. Am fat and ugly – shouldn't even bother going to wedding... sight of me might cause people to choke on their vollervonts (correct spelling?). Oooohhh... just LOVE vollervonts – esp prawn ones... Will have to go tomorrow – even if go as singleton-of-the-year.

Enuf of such misery – will pop back into town to get stunning outfit – how hard can that be?

Post-town Had been walking past McDs when spotted Saskia in window, alone, uneaten burger/fries in front of her, staring into space, face all red and blotchy as if been crying muchly. Ha! Was pleased – must have meant something had gone wrong with her and my hubbie-to-be! It spurred me on to look even harder for outfit...

TopShop, New Look, River Island... everything made me look too fat, too geekie or too slutty... walked back past McDs – Saskia still there, crying real tears now – almost felt sorry for her, but had to get on...

Debenhams, Dorothy P, Primark (just in case they had cool wedding gear for under a fiver!)... but nowt. Had spent good few hours now on task – fed up and still without outfit – considered making a statement and going nude...

but, again, people might choke on vollervonts.

Sauntered past McDs again – crying lady still there. Was no good. Must have been the Cn hidden deep within... had to go and comfort her. She may have been a tart, and stolen my true love, but if it had been me...

so went in...

Ate her (cold) meal as she poured it all out – Reuben had dumped her. She said he'd been so keen when they 1st went out – often talked about their future together, making her feel really special etc (got jealous at this point, tried to focus on my luck at getting free meal instead). Turns out she'd hardly had any boyfriends before – not quite as tarty as had thought. Through the sniffs she said how he'd not turned up at cinema on Wed eve (where they'd arranged to meet) and that's why she'd rung me, and most of BURP, just in case he'd forgotten or whatever. Then he ended it all yesterday, saying:

'I need to give my time and energy to Nazarene right now.'

Apparently they think they're on course to be playing on main stage at Greenbelt next summer – he's so dedicated to that band – I for one respect his decision to end his relationship with Sas and focus on greater things. Sas however is not so chuffed.

Thought a change of subject might help, so mentioned my wedding outfit (severe lack of). She brightened up, grabbed me by the arm and marched me back down the High St (shame as 9 fries still to go) visiting all of the shops had been in previously, until she'd got me sorted... she really knows clothes!

The skirt/top she finally chose for me actually makes me look good, and not like a bloated elephant about to hit the town... whoo-hoo!

Just as we were parting ways she suddenly gasped, having just realised she now didn't have anyone to go to wedding with... we decided to go together,

me and Saskia,
Sas and I.
How bizarre is that, eh?!

7:43 pm Am off to bed now – all-night study session finally caught up with me... mustn't be full of yawns tomorrow!

Sat 4 Dec

7:14 am

Is the big day! Wonder how Lydia and Jon feel right now (had to get up early as soooooooo excited!). Is odd – hate seeing couples together all settled and cosy as makes me feel extra-extra single and depressed. For some reason tho – love weddings! Is the bigness (if that's a word) of whole thing – the drama, excitement, glamour... free posh grub! Am going to call on Libs for some pre-wedding-glamour advice – spots have chosen the wrong day to come out to play...

Ahhhhh, had forgotten quite how early it is (esp in student halls). Libs not too chuffed with my visit/zits enquiry... flung book at me from her bed, mumbling: 'see page 3.8.3.'

Was one of those Adrian Mole books... the page in question contained detailed info re curing zits using blended frog (too detailed).

Yeah – you heard me right – FROG... as in the 'ribbet ribbet' variety.

Blended.

Applied to face...

Huh. Libs. That gal – fat lot of use.

Wondered if a facial sauna would perk up my skin, then remembered don't own such a contraption. Went in kitchen for early am snack, spotted saucepans and – hey presto – boiled water on hob, shoved face into steam at regular intervals – my pores are truly opened – spots not looking quite as bad as before.

Shaved everything (inc armpits) applied 2 coats clear nail varnish to nails to prevent them snapping off. Had shower – washed extra thoroughly.

Finally arranged hair into trendy style (after 3 trillion attempts) with lots of grips, mousse and spray. Will just put new outfit on (chosen for me by my newly appointed personal shopper) and will be ready for the off…

Yep – it's official, am drop dead gorgeous. Look out world (wedding party) here comes meeeeeeeee…!!

Post-wedding Well, Jon and Lydia made a fab-er-oonie couple, as did Sas and I! Where to start? Hmmmm… ahh – Caroline!

We finally met Oren's 'friend' Caroline (why not Caz, Cazzer or Carrie – why the whole 3 syllables of Car-o-line… how pretentious is that?). She seemed to be under the impression that they were an item, but he looked less sure. In actual fact, he couldn't take his eyes of Sas – the geezer. I was with Sas for the whole time and, trust me, he kept looking over at her, looking all wishful. So, Caroline's not enuf for him – he has one gal but lusts after another – I dunno, the state of Cn lads today – really gone downhill…

While we were sitting in the church, waiting for Lydia to arrive, got to thinking how L&J are kind of an odd match. To put it bluntly – he's hot and she's not. Not that am one to brag, but sure 'most would agree that, when compared with Lydia, I am hotter. Wondered if ought to nip up to front row and confront Jon, 'There's been a mistake mate – I'm hotter than she is – marry me instead…' but thought it futile.

Wondered what he saw in her… then remembered seeing him watch her intently as she led a BURP Bible study last month – she's so full of God it's unreal.

If I were full of God, would Jon like me?
Would anyone?
Is there a God to be full of?
Hmmmmmm.
Was slightly worried about actual vows – a certain part always makes me weepy, regardless of who's wedding it is:

'Till death do us part.'

It's so sad – thinking about dying and all. At the same time – is so sweet, to picture the couple still together when all old n wrinkly… is just what I want out of life (to have someone who stays with me till the end – not to be old n wrinkly, tho guess it comes to us all one day).

Kind of coped with it:

'To love and to cherish,' (I *take deep breath*.)

'for richer for poorer,' (*Not long now.*)

'in sickness and in health,' (*Still holding breath -mustn't cry.*)

'til death do us part.' (*Phew – did it – eyes dry – can release breath.*)

As they jigged merrily back down the aisle (to jazzed up version of 'Over all the earth'), began to think how wonderful whole thing was – how much I wanted what they had, and how lovely it was they'd be together til they were applying for zimmer frames and claiming cheap bus tickets. Could feel the water pressing hard behind my eyes, waiting for release. Quickly announced to Sas what was coming... then let it go – she gave me a quick hug – bless.

The tucker was superb-er-oonie... yeah – prawn vollervonts city! Stuffed my face just a tad. Sas and I chatted together most of the time, but got lumbered at one point with Prince Oren and Princess Caroline... what a bore! She ended a long speech about globalisation (huh?) and other such stuff, with:

'So by the year 2010 I hope to be something big in politics over in the States.'

As she turned away to grab a toasting champers I murmured:

'Yeah, well start walking now and you should just about make it.'

Sas laughed so much she began choking on her vollervont (tuna, not prawn). Oren smiled – prob an attempt to impress Sas with his appreciation of humour (come on, it was funny, esp for me!). Cazzer deserved it tho – she was so snobby – talked 'at' us like we were underprivileged 7-yr-olds.

She was constantly on at Oren re what he ate, and how, and when... what a nag. Her and his gran Maisie would get on just fine – they could nag in stereo.

At the eve 'do', Sas & I hung out by the bar, pretending we weren't watching Nazarene do their thing on stage. Both witnessed something gruesome – during a break from playing, Reuben got v touchy-feely with Sarah (a hot/skeletal lass from BURP). Not good – for me or Sas (not that she knows I like him). The lead singer and his new gal looked v cosy together – a bit too cosy, rather like they'd been that way many times before...

Fax joined us at the bar, so we asked him if he knew much about Skeletal Sarah. He said he'd never spoken with her... then added that he'd seen her only the other day in McDs with Reuben. Sas demanded to know what day.

He said Weds eve...

She began to cry again – handed her a 'Jon & Lydia' serviette, before she blew her nose on my new top.

All I can think is that sketetal woman has led him astray – he's clearly being manipulated by her and can't be held responsible for his actions.

Fax tried to comfort Sas by declaring that at least Reuben wasn't a chimpanzee, as they are 5 times hornier than the average human male. It didn't do much for Sas tho – sent her to the loos to sort out her face (smeared mascara). Spotted Oren looking in our direction again, and I'm like, 'Hello, Oren – she's not here mate – be patient – she won't be long' (but not out loud).

Sas sorted herself out (as much as is poss when you've just been dumped for no good reason, then find out your boyfriend was seeing someone else behind your back and is now all over them, boa-constrictor-style). We had a good time after that – boogying, munching on pricey finger food and knocking back Bacardi Breezers like they were water (amount of food consumed meant alc wouldn't be a prob).

Got back around 2 am… flaked out for a bit, then wrote this letter to you (now that's REAL commitment, Bob!).

Mon 6 Dec

D lesson – StiltonBreath fully recovered (why oh why?). Asked if Darren was OK and would be likely to be taking any more of my lessons.

Tap… tap… tap (his pencil on clipboard). Then he answered in the negative (perhaps is jealous… deep down is in love with me and is threatened by Darren's charm and hotness).

Couldn't concentrate on reverse parking due to tiredness, due to sleepless night followed by v late night – don't think he noticed tho – is not like have ever been able to do it properly.

Wed 8 Dec

11:34 pm

A tad depressed as just learnt (from Sas, who txted me with the bad news) that Reuben n Skeleton are def going out. She, in my opinion, is 2nd hottest gal at BURP, after Sas. By my reckoning then, if he goes out with each BURP gal, in order of hotness, finishes with each after 3 wks (allowing for some overlap, as in recent case) then it should be my turn in… hang on (using computer calc)… roughly 3 yrs time… when we've all left uni!

Well, that's fine with me – that'll be a grand time for the 2 of us to settle down and be wed. Deep down he needs me, he just doesn't know it yet. Still, not sure am happy about him seeing other gals so much – if only there weren't so many Cn tarts around to distract him.

3:12 am Unable to sleep due to major feelings of inadequacy. Perhaps rated myself too low in the female BURP hotness chart – but it's just how see myself right now – highly unattractive to the opp sex. Even Duncs has 'dumped' me and is all over Lauren, the love of his life. Huh. Will I ever find such love? Should I give up now and sign up at Bymouth convent (if there is one)?

What do geeks DO on their dates… play chess whilst wearing anoraks and grooving on down to Classic FM?

Thur 9 Dec

3:54 pm Just back from Abby's – thought seeing new niece might cheer me up (and my nephew, but he's not quite so cute right now). Eve is all fine and healthy – still not sleeping much tho, according to Abby, who looked tired. Nat was still playing up – he has it in for Eve… keeps nicking her rattles/dummy/blankets then hiding them in his room. He did show one out-of-character act of cuteness – when I first came in the house he legged it to his room, then back down again, clutching a screwed up piece of paper in his little hand:

'Me maketh thith yoooou.'

It was a little picture of a cross he'd done at Sunday School. His leader had written on a verse: 'You will know the truth and the truth will set you free.'

Stared at it for a few secs, unable to speak. Another freaky coincidence, or something more profound? Snapped back to the real world as Nat was pressing it into my hand – thanked him for it, kissed him on the head, which made him giggle.

Abby later commented that he usually gives things he makes to his daddy, but insisted that THIS picture was for me. Also that he usually forgets things he's made after 5 mins, so twas amazing that he'd remembered this… he'd made it 2 whole days ago!

Left shortly after Amos came home from work. There seemed to be friction between him and Abby of some sort – didn't want to hang around and get involved. Will have to tell her about his affair soon – perhaps she already knows.

Didn't go away empty handed tho – they let me (the poor undernourished student) have some surplus food – 8 tins of sardines + 5 tins of rasberries – Abby had serious cravings during pregnancy which involved these 2 foods… combined!!

When I am pregnant, will invent 'cravings' for the following: Pringles (all flavs except S&V), Pot Noodles, tiramisu, Soleros and will force hubbie (that's you Bob) to get out of bed at 3 am and fix me snack involving the above… yum yum in my tum!!

Fri 10 Dec

A miracle has occurred!

Today's lecture was actually… wait for it… interesting!! Someone alert the press – quick!

Old Prof Carr was talking about gender stereotypes – like how males are independent, aggressive, assertive, dominant and good at maths, science and mechanical stuff… and females are more emotional (nah – ya don't say!), caring, creative, but get hurt easily and need approval.

Some think it's a load of pants, but makes sense to me. Ideally tho, Bob, you'll be one of these all-rounders – nice and masculine, with a sensitive feminine side that you're not afraid to show once in a while!

Anyhow, Carr said that if we all made lists re what we want out of life, comparing the male list to the female list would demonstrate a lot of the above. Totally lost him after this… got down to making my list instead, to discover what it is I REALLY want out of life. Came up with the following:

1] *I want a bloke.*
2] *I want to know the truth about God n stuff.*
3] *I want to lose weight.*
4] *I want to get this degree.*
5] *I want to do something useful with my life, that isn't boring.*

Hmmmm. Is that it? All seems fairly simple, yet highly unattainable at the same time. Would be great to have some of my 'wants' granted real soon, so could tick them off, shorten list and feel more satisfied with life. Well, last 2 'wants' are more in the future... 1st 3 COULD happen any time, couldn't they?

Prof Carr really was on top form today – could I be a professor? Think you need a PhD or whatever. What does PhD stand for anyway? Phrumpy, Haggard & Dull? (OK – slight poetic licence with spelling there). Could be known as Prof Singleton... Dr Singleton has a kinda ring to it too.

Huh – am more into having the title of 'Mrs', to be honest.

Sat 11 Dec

11:35am

Surprised myself last night – almost asked Libs if she wanted to come to BURP with me today. She was saying some stuff about her lonely child-hood, being an only child (omitting mention of her parents, as always). For just a minute she looked all vulnerable and in need of something more in her life... but it soon passed and we moved straight onto spotting the hottest behind on *Friends* (me – Ross, her – tie bet Joey n Monica – does this make her bisexual?!).

Not sure why I assume that taking her to meet other Cns will help her in any way... don't even know what it's all about myself – couldn't BEGIN to answer any awkward questions re suffering/science/sex and wot-not... it's ME who's doing all the asking right now... not in a position to help convert someone... esp when that someone is Libs.

Legs 11

Sun 12 Dec

Need help. (Or is radiator on too high?)

Woken up early by weird moaning noise coming from outside.

Went outside to investigate. It was there I found him… Santa.

The Xmas dude himself, in full gear, perched on a deckchair, moaning, looking glum, like he'd lost his way en route to kiddies' grotto at Debenhams, or some such.

'Hey – this is uni – anything can happen,' thought I, as I approached him, asking if he was alright (hoping he wasn't totally wasted/stoned/a psycho etc etc).

'No no no,' he began.

'No no no no no,' he continued (reminding one a bit of that old guy on *Vicar of Dibley* who says 'no' a lot).

'No no no no no… I'm not alright. It's my back you see – it's been hurting so much this year… I'm not sure I'll be up to delivering all those presents at Christmas. I'd hate to disappoint all those lovely little children.'

(Had quick image of GremlinNephew… was about to say that they're not all lovely, but bit tongue.)

Then, Lydia appeared from round the corner, with a man I didn't recognise.

'Hi, Jude, this is Simon, the man I was telling you about yesterday.' I shook the man's hand (coz he offered me his to shake). Then it clicked – he was the bloke who was taking BURP next week – the healer!

Was about to introduce these 2 to my Santa-pal, but Lydia started offering round sticks of Blackpool rock. Then Simon looked at Santa, Santa looked at Simon, and THEN Simon said:

'Santa – you've got a bad back,'

and Santa said that he had, but how did Simon know?

Simon then gave a brief lecture on the power of the Holy Spirit and the ability he had to heal Santa's back, by calling on such power, if Santa wanted to be healed.

Santa did not hesitate – he wanted his back healed asap... well, as he'd said... all those lovely kiddies were relying on him.

Santa got up from his deckchair and Simon laid his hands on the big guy's back.

Lydia and I knew just what to do... we opened the tins of sardines and rasberries (that were in my pockets) mixed them together and ate them, whilst watching Simon do his thing.

Simon (who now looked v much like Jake from the Tweenies) finished praying and Santa ran off around the campus, yelling:

'It's a miracle – my back's been healed – praise the Lord!!'
I was impressed – had seen healings before at home church, but to heal Santa (the genuine article) – that had to be a 1st. Might even make the headlines: God heals Santa – Xmas back on!
Jake, Lydia (errrrr... who now looked more like Oren's Caroline) and I then went to McDs to see if those 9 cold fries of Saskia's were still there. I bought Jake a Big Mac, but Libs appeared and stole it from him, saying he would make the cow come back to life and spoil the whole experience... Caroline said she didn't want anything to eat (not that had actually offered HER anything – didn't see HER just save the day using supernatural powers).

Jake then said he had to go as Tweenies was starting in a minute.

Caroline said she had to walk to America, and waltzed off (hurrah!).

Libs agreed to share her Big Mac with me... but then started banging on the table shouting, 'Jude – come on... Juuuuude, get it together babe – Jude, are you there?!...' (and am thinking, 'Yes Libs, am right here in front of you, duurrrrrr...').

Then I woke up, to Libs verging on banging door down, yelling the above, but using additional words like BEEEP now and then.

What is it with me and dreams?

Saw Simon at church (the real one – bearing no resemblance to Jake whatsoever). Lydia HAD told us about him yesterday... he IS a healer and IS taking the mtg next Sat.

Not sure am syked (unsure of spelling) about going – these healers are into spotting stuff other than bruised ribs/in-growing toenails etc... some of them are 'discerning machines', aiming their powers in some unsuspecting victim's direction and revealing hidden sins, not just petty ones but whoppers like lusting after married men, spending money earmarked for 'giving' in TopShop sale, skipping a church mtg in case something actually happens in the *Big Brother* house, and so on.

Keen to avoid being exposed as fake Cn... avoided eye contact with Simon today in case he started the show early.

PS Please note that have never been party to above list of sins (ooooohh – now need to add 'being big fat liar' to list!).

Mon 13 Dec

Xmas card from parents today – kind of forgotten about them recently... the tenner that fell out of card made me remember them that little bit better.

D lesson – told StiltonBreath I break up at end of week and going home for Xmas, but will be back beg of Jan for more lessons.

He said he didn't work over Xmas anyway.
I said, 'Fine.'
He said, 'Fine.'
Think we understand each other.

Tue 14 Dec

6:24 pm

Money-free Xmas card from Hannah – my bud from back home, who's still... back home (works in bank). Inside littered with little smiley faces and she'd broken the mould by actually including a personal msg, instead of the obligatory, 'Dear ..., Happy Christmas, love Hannah'.

Unfortunately, her msg was along the following lines:

Hi flower!
How's you and your Pringles?! Everything's just peachy here – God is good!
I've just started going out with Paul (from church – always sat with his parents – you remember?!). We are totally sure that God is calling us to get married, so we've got engaged!!!! God is so good!!!!

I find he confirms it on a regular basis – nearly every time I open my Bible I come across the name 'Paul'. Don't you just love it when God speaks to you this specifically?!! We'll inform you of wedding date soon!!!!!!

Love in Jesus,

Hannah

Why is it that some people think that something isn't written properly unless it contains a few billion exclamation marks? Why do all those smiley faces make me want to puke? WHY is she being so dense?

Shouldn't be too surprised – remember how, few yrs ago, she thought she was being 'called' to marry our pastor, Vic.

Had gently pointed out that he was 15 yrs older than her… and was happily married with 4 kids. She said I was tool of Satan… how did I know wife/kids weren't about to be party to a tragic accident, leaving Vic all alone and in need.

Before I could defend myself (not keen on being accused of being Satan's tool at the best of times – hey, just realised – 'Satan' and 'Santa' look v sim – could there be a connection – was my dream influenced by dark unseen forces?) she added that every Sunday, Vic was preaching on what she herself had studied in the week, and that they were therefore spiritually 'in tune'.

Pointed out (less gently this time) that this might be coz she was using housegroup study notes in her personal study, and that THESE notes were linked with the sermons for that term. Durrrrrrrrrrrrrrrrrr!!!!!!!!!!!!!!!!!!!

(Just experimenting with e marks – is less satisfying than you'd think.)

Ahhh… Hannah – bless her little Cn socks. May she and her God-given Paul live long and prosper (is that biblical, or something off Star Wars?).

11:47pm Phew. Just written 20 Xmas cards – tried to keep it to just people back at home, and pals scattered across other unis (tad annoying that some are ½ way across world doing exciting year out stuff – means will have to go to PO to get them weighed huh… huh and 'bah humbug').

Wed 15 Dec

10:52 am

Cards from:

Abby and co

The catalogue people (that still haven't sent me the actual catalogue…)

Des (apparently, my home church's 'student coordinator'. One of those Cn cards with Xmas verses aplenty. Shame he didn't think to get in touch with me before now, or help me sort out my faith etc.)

9:31 pm Had just been sitting here in room feeling all single (stupid Xmas Ball coming up tomorrow eve and no one to go with – Dey-Jar-Voo city) when had 2 quick visits from 2 people, resulting in 2 invitations! Firstly, Libs called in again and TOLD me I was going back home with her on Sunday, as she couldn't face it alone. Not sure if should feel privileged, or just used – not sure what her problem is about going home anyway. Will go back to hers on Sun, then on to my parents on Weds or something.

Then, Oren popped in. After a bit of small talk ('teeny weeny' talk) he got to the point and asked what I was doing tomorrow eve.

'The ball,' thought I, 'he's asking me to the ball! What – me AND Caroline? Or me, Caroline and Sas?'

Before I could answer he explained that it was Maisie's birthday, and she wanted us all to go to hers for a meal.

Tried v hard to invent v good excuse in under 10 secs, but brain not up to it. Figured it would be a legit reason for not going to ball, so wouldn't look like such a 1st class minger… agreed to go.

Thur 16 Dec

Had 1 card this am:

Dear Jude
Many thanks for your letter regarding your unfortunate accident, that involved a copy of our magazine.
Whilst we have no intention of taking responsibility for your accident, or compensating you with £5,000, we loved your letter so much that it is going in next week's edition! As a little 'thank you' for giving us in the office (and next month – all our readers) such a good cackle, we are giving you a £30 Virgin Megastore voucher along with this week's copy of heat, *absolutely free of charge!*
We sincerely hope that your broken toe and 'possible serious damage to brain' make a speedy recovery,
Have a cool yule!
(signed by editor and several of office staff).

Had to think back to last month and retrace steps (or lack of them, due to broken toe!). Can only think that:

1] *Left* heat *letter in hosp, along with some cards, in bedside table,*
2] *little wisdom teeth lad (who took over my bed) found it… signed it on my behalf (getting my name from cards?!),*
3] *w teeth lad gave it to nurse for posting.*

Kids these days!

At least getting free mag and voucher out of it tho – Libs will be v jealous (as she is only one I know who gets anything for FREE!). Will give voucher to Abby for Christmas – it will save me having to think of something to get her.

5:45 pm Am in bit of a sulk right now. Kind of hoping some gorgeous bloke will knock on door any minute with 2 tickets and ask me to go to ball. Don't care who he is, what he's into or even if he never wanted to see me after this eve… just want to go, with a hot bloke, and feel special. Am Cinderella, but more depressed as not expecting fairy godmother to burst through window, with, 'You SHALL go to the ball.' Huh. The only 'Fairy' will see tonight will be when washing dishes at Maisie's. Must stop munching on these Pringles (SC&O)… tho if Maisie's food matches her convo, won't need to bother about ruining my appetite!

Post-Maisie's Was all a bit odd. Oren picked me up, but no Caz in car. Turns out she goes to a uni up north somewhere, and not here. He didn't seem to want to talk about her anyway, which was more than fine by me. We were the 1st to arrive at Maisie's… or so I thought. When I asked her if the others had rung to say they'd be late, could have sworn (in a Cn way) that she started to say, 'Wot uv-ers…' when Oren abruptly asked her to go get all her b'day cards to show us. When she was out the room he told me that the gang were all busy and couldn't make it… it was just me, him… and HER!

Sad to see that the old girl only had 2 cards – and one of them was from Oren. Guess she really doesn't have any friends. Gave her a card from me, along with box of Maltesers:

'Ha – shows just ha much ya young uns knows abat Dia-be-ees… eat 'em ya-self!' and she thrust them back in my hand.

She should've considered herself lucky I didn't go for the sardines/rasberries double act! While she was serving up in the kitchen, Oren explained that she hates it that her doctor forbids her to have sweet stuff due to her health – said it was just a sensitive area of hers and I wasn't to take it personally... huh!

Maisie's b'day meal consisted of:

Starter – *prawn cocktail (but prawns were swimming in mayo and BROWN sauce, as she'd run out of red = tasted like it looked – brown and ugly).*

Main course – *spag bol (turns out this was the 1st time she'd ever cooked 'real' spag, as opposed to the tinned stuff – would never have guessed – she freely admitted she had a bath while spag was cooking).*

Pud – *unidentifiable sugar-free pud (sponge?) with sugar-free custard... it's her theory that if she has to suffer by not eating sugar, the rest of the world ought to suffer also.*

(Come back sardines/rasberries... all is forgiven.)

Convo was stilted – she went on and on about Tony Blair, her new Asian neighbours, and the price of Radox these days (don't think the 3 were linked, but wasn't listening that closely... she seems to have an obsession with Radox baths tho). Any comment I made she made fun of, pointing out how young I was, how 'experienced' she was... blah blah blah. Couldn't wait to leave.

When she went to loo (where she stayed for good ½ hr) Oren and I shared the Malteser-rejects (at last – real food!). He apologised for her a billion times, and thanked me for coming. Had a good chat – he's not so bad without Caz hanging around.

Started to say something about getting back for the Bond film on telly this eve... but she had other plans, like us all watching it together at hers. Hmmmmm – not my idea of bliss, but still, company is company... us singletons must learn not to knock it!

So, the 3 of us cosy-ed on down on sofa for an evening of action, violence and sex (in film). She'd dropped off by the time the 1st ads were on – Oren lovingly covered her legs with a blanket, making her look as tho she had a one way ticket to old folks' home.

In car on way home (roughly midnight) told Oren it was cool that he did so much for his gran.

Not sure it was good plan to eat quite so much this near to Xmas, when stomach will be treated to annual stretching.

Fri 17 Dec

8:24am

Just got up, got dressed... then wondered where strong whiff of lavender puke was coming from... realised it was my clothes (the ones wore last night). Had to change... huh – OAPs and their lethal air-fresheners – should be a law against them.

9:30pm Last lecture today – whoo-hoo! Found it hard to concentrate, what with Xmas only 8 days away and all.

While Carr droned on about research methods in psychology (something we're gonna have to learn a lot about next semester apparently – what joy) began thinking about the new BURP committee. At last BURP mtg Lydia said a new committee would be sorted in soon.

Changing subject... Lydia and Jon seem so cool re their newly found married status. Am jealous, of course, but they are soooooooooo sweet! Turns out his parents had given them a stack of dosh for a 'decent' honeymoon (abroad). L&J however had felt they didn't want to waste money when so many in the world were in need etc etc... so they donated much of it to Tear Fund, and spent the rest on a short break in Blackpool! It'd rained buckets all wk, but they sure look as though they enjoyed themselves (prob all that sex!).

Bob, when we are getting wed... if your parents give us honeymoon dosh, I promise I won't risk offending them by giving one penny of it away to charity – shall do the decent thing and use ALL of it to book classy hol in Mauritius or sim (wow – sex AND chance of finally getting all-over tan!).

Anyhow, back to the new committee... rumour has it that Fax is up for president! Ha – Fax! Can't see him leading Bible studies, which tend to involve saying whole sentences (that relate to study, and not to how many times the letter 'z' appears in the Bible, or whatever). Still, he's a stable Cn with a lifestyle to prove it... let's see:

Sex: check – don't think he's had it – doesn't tart around, has gal-pals without need to snog them.

Language: check – he is one of those Cns whose creativity in the area of non-offensive remarks of exclamation is unbeatable: 'Oh my life' 'Oh my word' 'Man alive' 'Oh my goodness' 'Goodness me' 'Drat' 'Darn-it' etc etc.

Booze/smoking/drugs: check – doesn't get past tipsy stage, avoids latter 2.

He might do an OK job. Hmmmm... wonder if Reuben will be on new com

– he'd get my vote any day! But he's prob too busy with Nazarene and

1:42 am Sorry didn't finish that – suddenly remembered was supposed to be at F&Ferret. We (select BURP pals and moi) went on to Fusion for a final Xmas boogie – had a good laf. Asked others why they hadn't made it to Maisie's yesterday, but they didn't seem to know anything about it… odd.

Must ask Oren about it.

Must return those books to Oscar.

Must not eat between now and Xmas so that can have a guilt-free 25th Dec, for a change.

Must talk myself out of skiving BURP tomorrow (healing mtg). Am scared/sceptical. Perhaps will go to laundrette tomorrow and break other toe… which is fine if it helps me miss mtg, but not fine if he calls in at hosp wanting to heal me, or even worse… sends someone with a prayed-over hankie!

Sat 18 Dec

If God exists, and can really make someone's leg longer, curing their back-ache… what's stopping me from requesting he make BOTH my legs longer… thus making me taller/slimmer (due to fat being stretched in upwards direction)?

Could he do that? WOULD he do that? The NHS does cosmetic surgery to help people feel better about themselves, don't they?

If I told him I'd believe in him and follow him for always if he made me taller, would that help? God – are you out there? Can you hear me – Jude – the short one?!

If faked having one leg shorter than other (would sit with legs outstretched, but one not quite so stretched as the other) would Simon suss me? Would God? If God's there, then he'd know, would dob me in to Simon and would-n't lengthen legs. If he's NOT there, he's not gonna heal me anyway… huh – stalemate.

Post-mtg Just back. Simon really did his stuff to the max, and the crowd (of 40ish) lapped it up! OK, so they were all as nervous as moi at 1st, but the guy knew how to explain it all really simply – said it was down to the fact that God loved us so much and wants us to be free from whatever it is that is holding us back in life, whether it be a physical pain, a deep-rooted hurt from the past, or whatever. After the usual singing (sorry, 'worship time') and a little preachy bit, he launched into his act.

It wasn't how had remembered it back at my home church... instead of him saying, 'I think there's someone here with a bad neck/swollen ankle!' etc, and then letting them come forward... he was pointing at certain people and urging them to come to the front, which they did. 'Rather them than me,' thought I.

With each victim he'd ask if they were suffering in this area, or that area (sometimes physical, sometimes emotional... sometimes downright juicy, and willed them to move nearer to mike!).

Soon sussed that he was a man with a plan... he was systematic with his selection process... had started with those in front row, then moved to the next, was now dealing with the next... I WAS IN THE NEXT!

Hmmmmmm... no way! No way was I gonna hang around to have him say:

'Ah – Jude – you're an impostor here, aren't you? God's told me that you don't believe in him any more, and now I'm going to pray for you – for your faith to return... blah blah blah.'

Couldn't face thought of everyone knowing... esp the likes of Lydia, who actually seems to think I'm OK...

Decided I wasn't gonna be bullied into this – got up to leave.

Was no escape from Simon's eagle eyes (that were closed in prayer at the time, but he prob had supernatural x-ray vision – it's not just for Superman!).

He called out to me, 'Why don't you come up here before you go?'

So, up I go... thinking that if I got in there 1st, saying my once broken toe was still playing up on occasion, then perhaps we'd avoid any other messy reference to my current state. No chance – remember... he's a pro. We stood there, face to face, in silence. I was dumbstruck... which doesn't happen often. I could just feel... something. If I were a poet I'd be able to express myself better (perhaps should have done BA in English instead) but you'll just have to believe me... there was something about Simon and the look in his eyes that freaked me out... but at the same time made me excited, scared, secure, exposed, safe, trapped... free (?).

It all came at once... ½ of me was ready to make a run for it while the other ½ wanted to throw my arms around him (God?) and never let go. Mainly, I wanted to cry, but couldn't.

Then he said it:

'Jude – I don't normally do this, but God's just told me to give you this verse, so I will... "You will know the truth and the truth will set you free." You can be free Jude... you really can.'

Tears. Rivers of them. From me. He hugged me. It was good. Have been crying on and off ever since, and typing this now is getting me started again...

As soon as ordeal was over, got out, fast. Nope – it wasn't an ordeal, just emotional, with a touch of humiliation thrown in... did I really sob like that in front of everyone? Arrggghhhhhhh! Quick, find a hole in the ground and ask it to swallow me up for all eternity.

Ooooh... phone...

Twas Lydia. Cringed at 1st as thought she was gonna say something re healing mtg. She didn't – her purpose in ringing was to inform me that we had each other's phones! We'd been comparing phones (like ya do) just before Simon arrived, and must have pocketed each other's by mistake. We agreed to meet tomorrow to swap them back, before I leave with Libs.

Looking at her phone now – it's waaaaay cooler than mine. Will just have a little play on it to see what this baby is capable of...

Ahhh, perhaps not such a good idea – am stuck in some weird mode that can't seem to get out of (story of my life)... ah, that's better, now it's saying... nope, that's messed it up again – why don't mobiles come with mini-manuals hanging from them, for thickies like me who can't suss out how to... yeah – that's done it... if I now press this then it'll... ahhh – no it won't... now it wants to know if I want to read msgs...

If I want to read msgs!!

Nope – mustn't – THEY'RE NOT MY MSGS... but then again, what if they're important and Lydia needs to know, like that Jon now wants socks for Xmas instead of hankies (my yawnyawn Dad always asks for these yawnyawn items at Xmas). Hmmmmm... it wouldn't be intrusive, just thoughtful – helpful – concerned. Will tell her what have done, so won't even be lying or anything (why am I so keen on doing what's right?). Here goes then...

no them NOT *ok for social sec bye oren*

Who?

Who's not 'OK' for role of social secretary? Hmmmmm. How v annoying.

Guess she and Oren have been discussing new com and now he's eliminating some poor loser who HE considers isn't suitable. Huh! If you're not up for organising a few BBQs and bowling trips then you really have failed in life!

Thinking now that won't tell Lydia about viewing msg.

Wish Simon hadn't come up with THAT verse.

It's prob all a big fat coincidental load of nothing... but at the same time, can't help feeling all weepy when think of not just what Simon said, but the way he said it.

He knew...

man did he know.

Sun 19 Dec

Libs was v quiet in car as she drove us to her place, which took a good couple of hrs. Clearly she was anxious about going back home... wasn't much I could say to take her mind off things. Flicked through a brochure of hers that offered 'Experiences' to give as Xmas pressies... like hang-gliding or driving a steam train (ooohh – big thrills!) and also a flirting course for £200. Joked to Libs that such a course would be of no use to her – she could RUN the thing!

No lafs from her tho.

Tried chatting about baby Eve's progress (she can say 'ga ga' now) but Libs tends to switch off at mention of anything smaller than a 15-yr-old.

Eventually we pulled up in a lay-by, she looked me in the eyes and said,

'OK – we're nearly there... please don't be too shocked – it's not like I'd let anyone else meet my parents, or see our... house.'

And off we went. Prepared myself for manky flat on rough council estate, or sim... prepared for the worst...

You should've seen the SIZE of the place! Did I say 'place', I meant 'palace'!

A mansion – not quite Beckingham Palace but not far off! Yeah – totally unreal! The drive through the 'grounds' alone was enough to make you say, 'Boy – they must be LOADED!'

As we pulled up on the gravel outside the house (next to someone's brand new Mercedes, which looked oddly jeep-like) she made her 1st comment re it all, 'Jude – I know it looks impressive, but I hate it. My parents won the lottery last year. Didn't get on with them before – hate them now... money's turned them into BEEEPs.'

Panicked as we went in... felt underdressed and under-posh to be anywhere near this place – let alone stay here for 3 days... is it breakfast, dinner and tea... or breakfast, lunch and tea/dinner? Serviette or napkin? Handshake, peck on cheek/both cheeks... or should I just be done with it and curtsy?

Needn't have worried – without being too snobbish about it – they were as common as I am! Weird – all dressed in designer stuff, but in no way designed for it, if you catch my drift. Clear from the start that there was serious friction between them all – her mum and her dad, Libs and her mum, and esp Libs and her dad. Just kept smiling and accepting the offers of designer food, designer cocktails (at midday!) and a dip in the jacuzzi!

Am typing this in the study (errr... one of several studies on this floor) and will email it to myself. Libs has had an early night (it's just gone 9pm!) due to stress of parents. Her and Ern (her dad) had a bust-up during tea (which was tons of Chinese takeaway, that they had delivered). From what I can gather, she gets her bad language, temper and free spirit from him... perhaps 2 people so alike are bound to clash.

He was saying she should accept the money they send her (what money? How much? Can I have some?!) and not keep sending the cheques back to them, ripped into tiny pieces... at this point Marge (her mum) started to cry quietly.

Her and Ern have separate rooms, in separate wings. Libs' theory (as she told me in the jacuzzi) was that the money had ruined what little relationship her parents had and it wouldn't be long before they'd separate. Libs can't stand that they try to buy her affection with money and is totally determined to fend for herself... and not use a penny of theirs.

Right, off to my fancy room with 4-poster bed, silk sheets and telly in the wall!

I, for one, could get used to all this...

Wed 22 Dec

Arrived home this am. That's MY home... the 3-bed semi, with 10-yr-old Ford parked outside!

Felt bad about leaving Libs on her own, but she said she'd see her old pals – stay away from her parents as much as poss.

Had forgotten how slow/old fashioned/dull my mum is... or is it just that being surrounded by students for a whole semester has changed me? She says stuff like, 'Judith, are you wanting baked beans with your Cornish pasty?' when a fellow-student might say, 'Jude, d'ya want beans with ya pasty?'

Also forgotten how boring my home town is – all so slow and grey. At least Bymouth has a little colour, magic, life... must stop before burst into song!

Evening You won't belieeeeve the convo that's just taken place between me and my parents! Mum came in my room with v grim look on her face, saying we all needed to talk, and Dad followed on behind. Then she started (whilst focussing on my Delirious? poster, not looking me in the eyes once)...

'I just can't believe this Judith – after all we've done for you.' She starts crying uncontrollably and leaves the room with, 'Your... (sniff) fa-(sniff)-ther... (sniff) will (sniff) tell you (sniff sniiiiiiiiiff).'

Turn to Dad for explanation... he takes his time – is clearly embarrassed...

'Your mother and I... well, your mother... feels very strongly about this... issue and is distraught... we were up till the early hours this morning discussing... it. She thinks it's the end of the world, and is already talking about AIDS and...'

'AIDS?!' (Seemed like a suitable point for me to interrupt.) 'Who's got AIDS?'

'...and your future and how all this will effect it, but...'

'You think I've got AIDS?!'

Usually a quiet bloke, now Dad was on a roll he wasn't able to stop. '...but Jude, I love you. If this is what you want for your life, however much it pains me, however much I can't understand it... I'll let you be, pray for you and offer you any help I can. Your mother is even talking about special clinics she could book you into, in America... they've had really great results apparently. She has plans to ring the Pastor today to arrange your counselling sessions. But Jude love, hear what I'm saying here…'

'Dad, I have no IDEA what you're saying…'

'I'll support you in this – try to protect you from, well… your mother, and the gossip… she says it all makes sense now, why you've never had a boyfriend and…'

'Dad – I haven't got AIDS and have no immediate plans to visit America… WHAT IS GOING ON?!'

He starts a guppy impersonation (opens mouth, closes mouth, opens mouth, closes mouth… you get the picture). Then he takes my hand and leads me into the lounge, presses a few buttons on keyboard and points me in direction of computer screen. I then read an email that had been retrieved from my inbox…

> Dear Friend,
>
> Your details have been passed on to us recently, which means you have visited one of our clubs or local groups. We welcome you aboard!
>
> We will be sending you further emails with details of our forthcoming events/rallies etc.
>
> All the best,
>
> Damian Barratt-Smyth
>
> On behalf of GaysRus

Burst out laughing – recall my freaky night in gay club with Libs, and how we filled in some forms the barmaid gave us, just for something to do…

But then turn to Dad and see his face – he isn't laughing.

So I take his hand, lead him to the sofa, sit him down and explain the whole thing. He is very relieved.

He is very relieved.

(Yeah – have put that in twice to stress just how relieved he really was.)

He went to find Mum to explain.

All this has just happened, and am now sitting at computer emailing this to me (you)… needed to sit as legs came over a tad jelly-like. OK, so it's funny, but Mum's obviously been to hell and back over it. She couldn't even LOOK at me. Wonder how many people she's already called to 'discuss' my newly found sinful state of 'homosexuality'?

Kind of impressed with Dad – standing up to Mum is no easy option – think have got more respect for him now. Wonder how many times he's gone along with Mum's plans before, when his heart's not been in it.

Xmas day

Huh. Xmas.

Funny how one misunderstood email can cause soooo much trouble. OK, so now Mum knows am not gay... but notice she still has trouble looking me in the eye. Still in shock I guess.

We're all off to church now (inc Abby and co, who arrived here yesterday). Wonder if my old pals will be there or not... wonder if God will be there or not...

Post-church Found it hard to concentrate. Kept thinking – would Mum have been just as upset if she knew I was questioning the existence of God? More upset? More upset than when she thought I was gay? Doubt it, which makes me think there's either something wrong with her, or with me. Dad had said he still loved me... does that mean Mum DIDN'T love me when she thought I was batting for the other team?

Someone read out Xmas greetings from absent church members... one of which was from Jim (ex-youth leader/star of the dream that's to blame for my messed up head). Jim's msg included a plea for people to write to him... esp members of his old youth group! Hmmmmmmmm.

Sounds like he's doing fabo stuff in Uganda – tho breeding the required number of goats has challenged the team no end (will write and suggest they rig up soft lighting and romantic music in goat pens...).

High stress, but low carb

Sun 9 Jan

Just paused *Brookside* as remembered you are well-due a letter! Yeah – I did say 'paused'… parents got me video player for Xmas – woo-hoo! Now don't miss all my fave progs due to heavy social calendar… only got to finish *Brookside* (omnibus), *Friends*, ER, *EastEnders* (omnibus) and *Casualty*… and am all done!

Came back here (Bymouth) yesterday. Was nice to be home for Xmas, see old pals, old room, old parents etc… but been getting a bit itchy for uni these last couple of days. Things between me and Mum still… odd, with all that stuff re stupid *GaysRus* email – let's hope she sees the funny side one day…

Right, off to church now… need to locate WWJD band (that now only sees the light of day at BURP and church, poor thing!).

1:12 pm Saw Fax scribbling away at church – was v nearly impressed with his dedication to the sermon… until after, when he showed me what he'd written:

50 *sermons per yr* (*ish*)
exposure to sermons from age 16 *to age* 80 (*ish*)
= 3200 *sermons per lifetime* (*ish*)

Wow – 3200 opportunities to count the no of old biddies in hats/old blokes in ties/young 'wannabe' lasses that look like Britney (ish!).

At coffee, got involved with a convo re 'the future'.

Duncs has just read book re how Cns need to consider the future… and 'act now', blah blah blah. Tried not to look interested (Lauren looked interested enuf for all of us put together) but now he's got me pondering…

All that messing around with genes and stuff – yuk!
Will couples be able to choose the sex/looks/intelligence/sporting abilities/hair colour/etc of their unborn child?
Will gay couples be allowed to marry?
Will planet earth run out of oil?

Will Beckham ever get bored of football?

Hmmmmm. Who knows…

Not me.

God?

If God DOES know – why doesn't he come and tell me, or even Duncs (he's the one reading the book after all)? Why can't we know the future in advance… or would that mess everything up, like in film Back to the Future?

What about MY future? Didn't make any new year resolutions this year – didn't feel I was in a good 'place' to do so.

As a sign of respect for the new year, shall now attempt to picture MY future…

Finish degree (hopefully!) – 2½ yrs time – will be 21.
Track down potential boyfriend – 1 more yr? – will be 22.
Go out with him (you) – 1 yr (need lots of time to get to know each other) – will be 23.
Get engaged, then married – takes 1 yr (takes a long time to plan a wedding these days) – will be 24.
Have 1st kid… Hmmmm… now that's just taking it too far – not ready to think about that yet.

24?! That's SIX years away from now!

Is that OK – to get married at 24? Sounds a bit old to me – would do it tomorrow if could find you, Bob. Guess Mum would rather I waited until I was well-old, like 30 or something. Guess Libs would rather I never got married, but went from lad to lad to lad, as she does, like they were invented for the purpose.

Huh – stuff the future… it stinks.

Mon 10 Jan

9:54 am

Bit stressed now due to future of planet/mankind/me… wish Duncs had been reading Good Food mag instead – there's nowt wrong with having good food on the brain.

Food – huh… am massive right now. No, really, am HUGE-MUNGUS, in every sense of the word. Xmas was a real killer. Predict my future will involve Slimfast shakes if don't get act together asap.

11:19 pm Bizarre! Got chatting with BURP lasses at F&Ferret about diets. Seems that am not the only one with Xmas blubber to shed. Lydia, Sas and Lauren all feel as fat as I do. I say 'feel' as in my opinion:

1] *Lydia's married, so really doesn't need to think about such things any more, does she?*
2] *Sas is almost as skinny as skeletal Sarah – who knows what holds such gals together…*
3] And Lauren's… *a geek… like, who cares if they're fat?*

But hey, that aside… it was cool to feel some kind of unity in the arena of 'fatness'. We got so carried away, that by the time we left we'd all agreed to diet for next 2 wks.

We're gonna have weigh-ins!
We're gonna get SKINNY LIKE POSH!

All agreed to try out different diets on the market – so we could see which one was most effective. We've agreed NOT to cheat! Called in at Smith's on the way back to campus and picked up the following:

Eat Right For Your Type
Dr Atkins' New Diet Revolution
Fit For Life

and one on counting calories that can't recall name of.

I selected the Dr Atkins one – haven't read it yet tho.

Feel more positive about future of body shape!

Forgot to query Lydia about new BURP committee… dig about a bit and find out who (whom?) Oren was referring to in that txt msg.

Must stop eating out – money running v low. Don't understand it – felt soooooo rich in Sept when loan appeared in bank account – now bordering on poverty line. Huh.

Tue 11 Jan

3:32 pm

Grim yuk arghhh!! Just been to Lydia's for 1st 'weigh-in'… won't tell you my result, but is not good… not good at all. Others all lighter than me – great boost for self-esteem. They were all discussing 'their' diets… had to admit hadn't read up on mine yet. Must do it now…

4:12 pm Arrrgggghhhhhhhh – what have I let myself in for?! You won't BELIEVE what am going to have to eat over next 2 wks (starting tomorrow)… well, let's just say that CAN'T eat any of following:

bread
potatoes
pasta
rice
pizza
Pringles
Pot Noodles
tiramisu (in fact, no puds at all!).

Yet, oddly enuf, CAN eat:

meat
cheese
cream
eggs
veg and fruit (but not all types, coz that would be, like, waaay too simple!).

HOW DOES ONE MAKE SARNIES WITHOUT BREAD? Huh – trust me to pick the worst diet book out there… do people actually DO this diet? Are they M.A.D.?!

Right, off to Tesco to stock up on… meat and stuff. Crazy as it sounds, am gonna do this and lose weight, coz really want to. Would also like to totally thrash the others and lose more than they do – hah hah titty hah haaaaah!

6:03 pm Back again… got 3 whole chickens, variety of cheese (v expensive – must be a lot of rich cows out there), 2 doz eggs, 2 pints double cream and a swede. Hmmmmmmmm.

Had a job to squeeze into tiny fridge in communal kitchen – hope the others don't mind. Prob not a good idea to boycott refectory meals for 2 wks, as they are free and this stuff I've had to pay for… but if that's the price you pay for a decent body shape… then so be it!

Wonder if could get a job to get more cash? Most of pals here have jobs… don't really fancy one tho – got enuf on (tiny) mind as it is.

Just glanced up at noticeboard here in room – have got reminders of all 3 'truth' verses up there – Lydia's card, Nat's piccie and a flyer re Simon the healer.

What would God think about me trying to lose weight?

Is it OK, or wrong, coz of all the people in the world that are starving etc?

Considering writing to Jim re mysterious disappearance of God since that dream.

Naaaa… he'll be too busy with those goats…

Must ring Abby – haven't seen her since Xmas. Still not sure when to inform her re Amos's suspicious behaviour… if to tell her at all.

Wed 12 Jan

4:32 pm

Strange noises distracted me all through d lesson. Soon located source of noises to stomach (mine)… twas rumbling/yelling:

'Give me food – stuff the diet – give me food – stuff the diet…'

StiltonBreath took me by surprise by asking if I thought I was ready for my test.
He said he thought I nearly was.
We agreed to differ.
'Nearly'? Huh – what a confidence booster… he prob means 'nearly', as in 'this time next yr' I might be ready.

8:28 pm Just rang Abby to complain about StiltonBreath, and life in general (being fat, running out of cash, no boyfriend etc). She didn't say much. Got the feeling she was itching to say something when I told her about my new diet support group… but she didn't. Perhaps she thinks am anorexic.

Huh – now she'll tell Mum and then

Sorry, had to break for phone – twas Oren, asking if I was up to visiting Maisie tomorrow. He said he was doing a prison visit, and that she'd said she'd like ME to visit. Hmmm.

Said, 'Yeah, OK,' before could give it real consideration (which would have resulted in reply being, 'No no no no no no no no no no no no no no no no no no!').

11:57 pm Am v knackered. Just had session with fellow-fatties here in my room… we shared the 'rules' of each of our diets – helped each other think of creative meals to suit each other… is becoming a bit like Alcoholics Anonymous (not that have ever been to an AA mtg).

Today have only eaten cold chicken (almost a whole one), a fried egg and a stick of Pepperami. Sas suggested I cook myself an omelette every morning for breakfast… she really doesn't know me that well – like I could cook an omelette!

Lydia brought a mag containing article re women on TV compared with women in the real world… said that 31% on TV are underweight, compared with 5% in real world… also that 3% were obese on TV, compared with 25% in the real world (figure that TV-world looks cooler than the real one anyday… didn't say this tho).

Libs gatecrashed and was highly amused to learn what we were up to. Cringed when Lauren asked her if she wanted to join in (Libs is just a tad bigger than me). Libs took it well…

'My dear petal – I'd rather eat your HEAD than diet.'

(Can't help but agree – remind me again why am doing this… ah, yes – to be a part of TV-world.)

Libs snuck out later, mumbling, 'If you can keep your fat… when all around you are losing theirs…'

Said about prediction re being 24 by the time I finally get wed. Sas said 24 was far too young to get married.

Then we all remembered Lydia was there, and said stuff like:

'Yeah, but SOME people are like really ready to get married when they're young…'

Lauren said that age didn't matter – if you love someone and God's confirmed that they are the right person for you… you can get married, end of story. Nearly asked her if her and Duncs had made any plans yet, and if I could be bridesmaid (joke) but bit tongue. Can't forgive her for stealing Duncs from me.

OK, so he's a geek.. but he was MY geek, and now he's gone, forever.

'Rumble rumble rumble… why why why?'

Thur 13 Jan

That catalogue came in post today… finally. Libs now getting all excited, wanting me to order something so she can claim her voucher – doesn't she realise I HAVE NO MONEY!

Went to Maisie's. Went OK. For some bizarre reason, she seems to like me, I think. Doesn't stop her from criticising everything I say and do… but hey – she's old. Hideous having to turn down slice of (diabetic, but scrummy-looking) choc cake (could hear stomach begging, 'Please oh please let me have it…').

Maisie thinks 'diets is stoo-pid' and that young men want brains and personality, not stick insects. Huh – she would say that – she must weigh the same as me… several times over!

Am not saying I find her totally likeable, yet… perhaps it will come.

Need to go do some more plucking – have discovered that if stand in front of mirror for ages, plucking them one by one, they cotton on, digging their roots in deeper, making it impossible to remove them (eyebrow hairs) but if I say out loud, 'Oh, I'll do my hair at the bathroom mirror now…' then suddenly produce weapon (tweezers) on reaching the mirror, and 'go for the kill' of pesky-est ones asap… they ain't got no chance.

Post-surprise eyebrow massacre Am so bored that will write to Jim. He might have the answers have been looking so hard for, re God and all. He was so good at teaching us stuff at youth group – kept all his handouts – got them here in front of me, but can't find one entitled: 'What to do if you have weird dream and lose your faith, when just started at uni.' Hmmmm.

How much shall I tell him? About Tate? Nope – he'd be horrified, as per 'Sex and Relationships' handout.
About Reuben?
About these letters to you?
Nope – he'd just refer me on to Cns who have a specialised ministry in dealing with raving loonies…

How come HE gets to go to Uganda anyway? If I'd gone abroad somewhere to do Cn work, instead of to uni… would I still have had JimDream and got all messed up?
Huh – perhaps my calling to Hawaii got lost in the post.

In need of real food. What good's a fried egg if you can't have it on toast? What good's a hunk of cheese if you can't stick it in a sarnie?

Soooooooooo hungry!

Fri 14 Jan

Prof Carr enlightened us about 'stress' today. Great – like JUDE's the stressed one here, mate… forget the theory – study me! (Swipe that – don't want Carr to do any such thing…).

Big chart in textbook, showing how stressful different events/changes in life are… for example:

most stressful = death of spouse, 100 points
least stressful = Christmas, 11 points

Will photocopy chart and bung on noticeboard – then can know in advance exactly how much certain changes are gonna do my head in – can feel justified when crack under pressure…

Carr said that the greater the change/the higher the no of points… the more likely the person was to get ill, or to have psychological probs in the next couple of years… plenty for me to look forward to then.

Instead of taking useful notes from lecture, found myself scribbling:

Stress. I am stressed. I have stress. Stress and me are united.
Stress-ed. Stresssssssssed.
'Stressed' backwards is 'desserts'…

and so on. Would kill for a pud right now.

Got too stressed listening about stress, so used remainder of lecture to perfect my 'Christian categories' idea. Have always viewed Cns as being one of 3 types, but never really had sufficient time (or motivation) to put thoughts re this on paper. That's the beauty of lectures – can get on with completing such tasks!

Here's my finished work, for purpose of judging fellow Cns, related to flaves of Pringles:

Salt and vinegar (S&V) = just too much – too OTT
Don't set foot in pubs.
Read Bible every day, sometimes more than once.
Do tons at church.
No telly, or strictly educational/wildlife documentaries only.
Cn music, mags, books ONLY.
No alcohol, smoking, lottery… don't know how to swear.
V familiar with certain UK Butlins resorts.
Friends all Cns (or have no friends).

Campaign against Harry Potter, Pokemon and suchlike... and as for devilled eggs...
Can tolerate SC&Os (as below) and pray mightily for Paprikas (and avoid them like Satan himself).

V godly... too darn godly.

For example – my mum.

Sour creme and onion (SC&O) = cool

At home in pub or church alike.

Get on with S&Vs and Paprikas... have non-Cn pals.

Regular Bible readers, but don't flip if miss days out here and there.

Involved with church (S School, housegroup leaders).

Also involved with community – school governors, on local darts team/council – or sim.

Pretty godly.

Enjoy glass of wine (or 4).

Tend to have cool kids/cars/houses/lives.

For example – Abby n Amos.

Paprika = too 'out there'

More at home in pub than church.

Swear, drink, smoke, lottery (some or all).

Tart around.

Not v godly.

Fit in with non-Cns a bit TOO well.

For example – Saskia.

Judging... did I say judging fellow Cns? I meant ASSESSING.

Course, there's always room for overlap in such categorisation...

Fairly sure I was a SC&O, but now have tendencies to wander into Paprika territory, due to shattering of faith. V good at faking being SC&O still, or even slightly S&V, should the need arise. Always hard to figure out who's faking one category when they're really another, and who's not.

10:43 pm Jim's letter now sent – hope he replies soon. Hope he can tell me the way out of this hole am in, where the truth is hovering overhead... always out of my reach. If verse is right... knowing what truth is will set me free from hole. IF verse is right, which still not sure about.

Hope he (and you) understand what am waffling on about!

Sat 15 Jan

Got headache. Feel like poo. Don't normally get headaches, so is prob a massive tumour or sim. Ahhhh, will just consult my 'stress' chart on this one… 'personal illness' comes in with a high score of 53 points… fab.

On further examination of chart, can see that have recently gone through a fair old no of these 'life changes' :

New family member = 39 (*Eve*)
Financial state = 38
Living conditions = 25
Residence = 20
Schools = 20 (*uni*)
Church activities = 19
Social activities = 18
Mortgage or loan = 17
Sleeping habits = 16
Eating habits = 15
Christmas = 11

Total = 238

So technically, should be at least twice as stressed as someone who's spouse has just died… this explains headache…

Got BURP this eve – will ask Lydia if we can have a private chat sometime. She's a sound sort of person (def a SC&O) so intend to grill her re life/God etc.

Diet going well, in the sense that am sticking to it… but am getting bored with all this cold chicken and cheese… recipe ideas on a postcard please!

Ahhh, perhaps headache due to lack of carb (diet lingo for 'carbohydrate') in diet. Might sue someone if head gets any worse…

Post-BURP Freaky. Have been asked to be on BURP committee!!!!! Social secretary – me? Hah!

Said no, of course.
Lydia said I ought to think about it, rather than give them an answer now (which had just done – how deaf can they be?).
Fax then added that I'd need to tell them soonish… as TOMORROW EVE they're having a mtg of present com + new com Huh!

Subtly took Fax aside and asked him who else was considered for SocSec (was thinking about Oren's txt – wanted to know who he'd rejected before I was chosen).

'Errrrrrrr… no one,' he replied calmly.
I was less calm… asked him if they'd all been agreed on me being on new com.

'Errrrr… yeah. No. Well, Oren didn't say much when we discussed it – said he'd ring Lydia about it later or something…'
Hmmmmmm. The truth is out. Oren hates me.

Oren, who thinks that spending an entire wedding staring at one lass, when another lass is on his arm, is completely acceptable.

Oren, who FORCES people to visit his grumpy gran, while he spends time perfecting his ability to be the most yawnyawn bloke EVER.

Why? What have I done that's so bad? Is it coz am sometimes late for BURP mtg? Coz am too fat? Coz I said bad things behind Caroline's back at the wedding?

Def not gonna be on com if Oren doesn't think am up to it. Let them suffer. Let them struggle to find a replacement – another person to organise their social life for them… another MUG!! Left BURP a bit early due to growing feelings of inadequacy…

9:32 pm Just had call from Lydia, trying to convince me to sign up. Said, 'Thanks, but no!' like 100 times… then she said something that caught my attention:

'Jude, you do know who else has been nominated for the new committee, don't you?'

I didn't – my wallowing in self-pity (who, me?) had made me forget to ask. So she told me… and then it happened… heard his name… 'Reuben'.

Don't ask what his role on com is to be, as can't remember… but did hear his name, loud and clear… like a refreshing shower after a game of squash (not that I play it, but have good imagination), like a Solero after… another game of imaginary squash… like getting a 1st for your degree, without having to do any work…

R.E.U.B.E.N… funny how one person can make such a difference.

So said would be SocSec… and she asked me to meet them at Tesco IN 10 MINS, to shop for tomorrow eve's mtg… which turns out to be something to do with Romania… huh?!

Haven't even started my 'term' on com yet (start next month) and am already confused! Still, sure can have long chats with Reuben about such com related matters… this is gonna be sooooooo cool!

Must catch up on a bit of plucking before Tesco…

Post-Tesco

While the newly recruited mug (moi) struggled to manoover (correct spelling?) highly dodgy trolley around v annoying old people who kept getting in the way… Fax and Lydia explained to the rest of us (Reuben, Sas and Duncs) about this Romania thing.

Is all to do with Oren (which, for me, is huge turn-off from the start). His home church are organising a group to go to Romania, this March. They are a few people short, and have asked Oren if he and a few friends would be interested. There are 4 spare places.

Just after trolley developed loud dying-herd-of-mice-type sound, suddenly realised that Oren wasn't with us. Asked Fax… he said he didn't know. Huh! He's prob v pee-ed off that am on com after all, and can't bear to see me… fine. He'll prob quit BURP altogether now, which is equally FINE with me!

We split up a bit to grab supplies for tomorrow's mtg… at one point it was only me and Reuben walking down the 'tinned food' aisle…

Oh Reuben… if only you knew of my plans to one day be walking down another aisle with you

decorated with green orchids,
rather than tins of mushy peas,
tuna in brine,

and Postman Pat pasta-shapes in tomato sauce, with those mini processed sausages…

Daydream extinguished by the others appearing and lobbing food into trolley. Reuben then said he wouldn't walk with me any more as dying-herd-of-mice noise too embarrassing.

Glanced down at trolley contents… spotted that Sas had added 2 tubs of cottage cheese, of the 'v low in fat' variety (she's doing low-calorie). Realised I wouldn't be able to eat most of the other stuff (Pringles, choccies etc) so grabbed some cheese for myself (brie).

Duncs rudely pointed out that brie was a bad choice if I was trying to lose weight. Told him to get educated re modern dieting, as opposed to dark-ages dieting. He looked confused, and wandered off into drinks aisle (returning with more booze than is advisable to attempt to carry!).

Remembered that was gonna ask Lydia about having that chat... decided against it – seems like she's one of the few people who thinks I'm OK... don't want to spoil that illusion, not yet anyway. Wouldn't want her to think she'd ignored Oren's advice at her peril... made a big mistake in choosing me...

Head still hurts lots – dying-herd-of-mice noise remains in head... do mice live in herds?

Sun 16 Jan

9:16 am

Just glanced at today's date and remembered it's my nan's b'day.

Well... 'was' my nan's b'day – she died 2 yrs ago. Wish she hadn't – she was cool. Really miss her...

Had to stop for a bit due to tears in eyes... crying sort of helps tho.

Sometimes think that the longer she's been gone, the more I miss her – odd. It was her who always read me *Winnie the Pooh* when I stayed with her (even when I was 15 or so... we both enjoyed them so didn't see the harm!). Now and then, and esp today, just think it would be cool to get to see her for an hour or so, have her read me a *Pooh* story... and then say goodbye again...

Head still bad.

Tins of rasberries and sardines finally coming in useful (never thought would hear myself say that!). Am allowed rasberries with cream, and sardines in a salad. Thanks, Sis – you're a star for having such pregnancy-craving leftovers!

12:48 pm Sermon was on John the Baptist... sounds like he too was accustomed to weird diets... wonder if HE lost any weight?

Chatted with Fax over coffee re the whole 'Simon the healer' thing. Feel can confide in Fax a bit (only a bit, mind) – he's pretty much SC&O. Told him about me hoping Simon could 'do' both my legs to make me taller. He looked mildly amused, then added that American astronauts are required to be under 6 feet, and perhaps God was calling me to such an occupation.

Huh – I sure know how to pick people to confide in.

He must have sensed my lack of enthusiasm, so he then added that Geri Halliwell and Madonna are both only 5ft 1.

This helped.

Am now off to see my personal financial adviser, who goes by the name of Liberty Young…

Back again. She knows so much about money (and other such tricky stuff). She helped me work out a kind of budget thing, the aim of which is to prevent me from spending too much on stupid stuff and helping me to actually save money, for when really need it. Sounds great, in theory…

She also reckons I need job.

Not what I wanted to hear. She now works at Fusion, behind the bar. In fact she organises the rota for bar staff/glass collectors… reckons she can put in a word for me and get me 'in' by next semester. She more told me than asked me.

Fine by me… need the cash. Never worked at a club before tho – mustn't tell Mum!

Hmmmmm… Mum. Ought to ring parents sometime and ask for a little financial assistance, just until start at Fusion.

Here's what I did with remainder of aft:

2:05 pm Went to Tesco – realised we didn't have any Fanta for Oren (the yawnyawn teetotaller).

2:37 pm Back to Tesco – also didn't have any peanuts – they always go down well, and I CAN EAT THEM!

3:02 pm Tesco – popcorn (both salt AND sugar).

3:31 pm Tesco – dips and celery (for me, again!).

3:58 pm Tesco – to collect purse that had left at till…

Tesco's staff beginning to look at me oddly toward the end.

Don't tell Mum I shopped on a Sunday.

If God's there, would he mind me shopping today? It's all for the 'Lord's work' after all…

Lydia had asked me to get anything else I thought we might need (you'd think we were actually GOING to Romania… not just planning the thing!).

Know it's not really a big deal, but sort of my 1st official task as new SocSec-to-be, and want to show am capable.

Now, if my good Sis Abby had been given such a task, things would have been v different...

SHE has this printed weekly shopping list that has 3 separate columns for 3 local supermarkets, and what she needs for the week is in the appropriate column. She studies those leaflets you get through the door with offers from said supermarkets, and will add to her list accordingly. Finally, she'll consult her monthly meal-planner and add the finishing touches. This goes to ensure that she gets exactly what she wants, at a good price... ALWAYS!

There'd be no return journey to Tesco for her... let alone 4!

Sort of wish could be as organised... but then again, where's the FUN in all that?

Also, doing 4 return journeys to Tesco in short space of time = plenty of aerobic exercise and toned legs... whoo-hoo!

Right – BURP com mtg in 9 mins... just enough time to check on map exact location of Romania, just in case...

Found it – looks like a pigs head...

Mon 17 Jan

Last night's mtg... during the pre-'getting-down-to-business' chat... Sas complained about her recent 'one-off' trip to the gym (on other campus, on far side of town). She'd thought it cool that the treadmill actually told her how many calories she was burning off. At the end of her exhausting 30-min 'jog' she noted that she'd rid herself of a whole 140 calories.

On returning to her room, however... she noted that 1 Mars bar contained a whopping 281 calories. She had therefore rid herself of ½ an M Bar – all that effort and for what? So depressed was she that she ate 1 (M bar). Don't think she's gonna be winning our weigh-in next wk!

So, this Rom trip... they're gonna paint some schools and give out some stuff to the poor villagers. The idea of helping those in need kind of appealed to me, not sure why tho. It's not like would have to go to church much (it'd all be in Romania-ese anyway, wouldn't it?). So put my name down to go...

Oh, and... REUBEN's going!!

I really bug myself sometimes. Would be fab, on one occasion, to actually make a decision without 1st considering Reuben, or blokes in general. Why am I so pathetic? Why can't I be my own woman and think of genuine reasons for going on trip, like to broaden my horizons or to clear my head etc?

Huh?

So the 4 places have been filled by me Lydia, Jon, Reuben and me (am I doing the right thing?). Oh, and Oren's coming, obviously... worse luck. No Sarah/Saskia, so have got more of a chance with my true love. No Duncs... him and Lauren are off to Spring Harvest... huh! How romantic!

The carefully selected grub went down well, as did all that booze. Was kinda nice, being a tad tipsy. Hadn't been like that since Tate thing (tho that was more 'off my head' than tipsy). Felt safe with these guys – like it didn't matter what I said or did – they wouldn't do a 'Tate' on me, or judge me (oh, Judge Oren not yet there at this point).

After much discussion re Romania trip... moved onto more serious matters, like playing Mouse Trap, followed by Twister. Am not v good at the latter... must practice more! Was such a laf.

Duncs still on about this 'future' stuff. After he'd gone on for ages, Jon told him that if he heard the words 'future', 'rainforest' or 'responsibility' one more time... he'd personally arrange for Duncs's future to involve a heavy duty chainsaw (but the beer made him say 'sain-chore'). Doesn't seem funny now, but at the time, after a couple (OK, 5) B Breezers and it being late and all – it was v v hilarious – nearly wet my knickers!

Just as we were all falling around the Twister mat, holding our sides due to Jon's newly discovered threatening side, knocking over bowls of Pringles/brie in the process... it happened.

He arrived.
Oren.

Has been raining lots this wk. Not your nice pitter-patter raindrops...
more your nightmare blowing-in-yer-face,
up-yer-nose,
mess-up-yer-hair,
rain.
Rain rain rain – puddles/umbrellas/geeky anoraks... you get the picture.

And here was Oren, all wet and drowned-looking… it may have been raining tons outside, but the real storm was still to come…

He went ape. Knew he didn't drink himself, but hadn't thought he'd have a prob with us drinking. Anyhow, we weren't 'drinking' in the sense that Libs does… we were just slightly more merry than on your average Sun eve.

He went around collecting cans and bottles (some still full) and stuffed them in a bag, all the time saying how we were pathetic losers, blah blah blah. He just didn't stop. Were all a bit stunned, so just let him tell us off (I made desparate attempt to prise lump of brie off Twister mat, so as to avoid eye contact with Ogre Oren).

When he'd gone (with remainder of our booze), Lydia said we ought to call it a day. Wanted to thank them all for being such good mates – tell them that loved them lots etc etc… but the magic was gone. Oren had extinguished the little flame of fun we were so much enjoying – the best time I'd had in ages.

Grrrrrrr. That lad – he's a pain.
More than a pain – he's a git – will get Jon to take his 'sain-chore' to him…

Head hurts more than usual… due to last night's drink? Brain tumour that doubles in size every day? Extended period of low-carb dieting? Stress? Oren?

Did well food-wise last night, but totally forgot about alcohol – shouldn't have had B Breezers (they contain sinful sugar). Think red wine (dry) is my best bet – must remember for next time… not that there'll BE a next time if Oren has his way… yawnyawnyawn…

Right, off to see Dr Young for several hundred paracetamol…

Pink caterpillars

Tue 18 Jan

10:43 am

Ought to be:

1] *Planning how to cut down on 'Tesco snacks' in attempt to follow Lib's budget plan.*
2] *Ringing surgery for app re headaches.*
3] *Going to town to buy dinghy (still raining tons).*
4] *Revising (ha ha – like THAT'S a priority!).*

Libs says am only allowed to buy 2 packets of Pringles, 2 mini-tiramisus and 2 Pot Noodles per wk (when am off diet).

Can only buy multi-pack Soleros and a few B Breezers (to go) when is a close pal's b'day. Had a bit of a row over Soleros – Libs saying they were an unnec food item to be purchasing in Jan... me saying they were LUSH and couldn't live without weekly (daily?) fix...

Thing is, how does one define a 'close' pal these days? Feel 'close' to many of my fellow students... on my floor/in these halls/on this campus... that's a whole lota Soleros/B Breezers!

Am pretty buddy-like with most on this floor now... hang out with them quite a bit. Mr NextDoor sticks out like Marilyn Manson at a Will Young concert... but we cope with him OK, just pretending that the smell coming from his room isn't too illegal, the noise not too deafening and his visiting mates not too pierced/tattooed/satanic-looking...

Libs has always got on with him fine... should I be worried?

Right, will ring surgery now re my HEAD that HURTS a LOT...

Have app for MONDAY! Assumed they'd try to squeeze me in asap when they heard just how bad head is... no, instead have to endure it for another 6 days! Receptionist prob thought me a student with hangover... failing to appreciate poss nature of complaint... ie BRAIN TUMOUR... Hope have only got 5 days to live – that'll show 'em!

Will do assignment... but not now – is raining far too much to concentrate.

What really puts me off about studying is the darn spellchecker! It underlines all my misspelt words (most words) with a wiggly red worm. I add a letter – line still there. Change another letter – line still there. Then wonder if should go back and change initial letter back to what it was, but keep in 2nd letter change… and so on.

Let's just test my theory out a sec… take the word 'rasberries' – every time I type it in your letters it attracts aforementioned wiggly red worm. Don't usually bother to spellcheck these letters (sorry bud, but students are v pushed for time) but this word has continually bugged me, so let's see if can get it right…

rasberries (no, worm has appeared)
rasbberries (worm)
rassberies (worm)
rasberrys (worm)

Is no good – will have to right click on mouse and summon Mr Spellcheck… and low and behold – it's got a 'p' in it! Who'd have thought?!

7:52 pm Diet still going well. Weigh-in day tomorrow! Jeans poss a tad looser, tho might just be wishful thinking, and

Short pause in letter due to quick visit from Libs (to ask if I'd ordered anything from catalogue yet – huh!).

She has taken to chewing gum a lot… find this annoying (yeah – that sounds snobbish – so shoot me).

Tried not to let it get to me, but kept seeing it all the time (the gum) yuk. Only use for gum, in humble opinion, is to rid oneself of bad breath after consumption of garlic bread or sim… and for sticking posters to wall when out of Blu-tack.

Wed 19 Jan

10:15 am

Arghhhhhh! Just woke up… had mad dream about an army of giant worms that ate only raspberries… but then turned on me, coz I couldn't spell raspberries… and tried to eat me instead…

Will eat peanuts to calm me down…

Also having major freak-out over this weigh-in thing…

What if haven't lost any weight, and others all lost loads?

What if they laugh at me?

Will try to refocus by meditating on peaceful things, like the birds singing outside in the tree-tops, the cool refreshing breeze coming from my open window, the

Arrghhhhh!!

Will someone please inform Mr NextDoor that M Manson is NOT my idea of peaceful meditation... has he LOST those headphones, or did he eat them for a midnight snack? Will gladly invest in a new pair for him... stuff the budget (typed that v quietly so Libs didn't hear).

Will again attempt to distract myself from weigh-in by... errrrrrrr... ah – ringing Mum. Could do with a bit of extra cash. Will tell her have got job lined up – she'll be so proud of me (hopefully) that she'll send me big fat cheque...

Sorted!

She asked if I could 'check up' on Abby as she hadn't heard from her recently (by this she prob means a whole 24 hrs). Yeah, like Abby's someone who needs checking on! Was feeling full of gratitude (due to promise of cash) so said would call in tomorrow if not too busy with study (ha ha).

Post-d lesson StiltonBreath reckons am ready for test!

Protested, but he was insistent (prob just wants to get rid of me – the worst driving pupil in automotive history).

Finally gave in and told him to do the biz (book test).

11:32 pm Post-weigh in Yea! Yeah! Yes yes yes yes yes... whoo-hoo!

Am 2 lbs lighter than this time last wk!

Can't believe it... wish Dr Atkins was (were?) here right now so could give him great big bear hug!

Lydia, who's been doing the blood-type one, lost nothing, but says she feels good and will persevere (bless 'er).
Lauren (food combining) – lost 1 lb – grinned geekily at us all eve.
Saskia (calorie counting) – gained 1 lb – due to depression, brought on by hunger, resulting in large consumption of Mars Bars...

Didn't want to gloat or anything, but highly recommended MY diet to the others, who were well-impressed... until later, when mentioned the headaches... then they all said it must be my diet, and tried to talk me off it!

Dear Bob

Huh! Like I'd quit now!

Fri 21 Jan

Couldn't write yesterday – was all a bit much…

It involved big Sis Abby and… well, just her really.
Right, let's take it from the top (Thurs am)…

Was feeling obliged to visit Abby, but not really looking forward to it. Aside from how she (unintentionally) makes me feel (inadequate/boring/useless/immature etc) always dread one of her 'Mumsie-pals' being there for coffee… had heard it said in the past that Mums (of babies) sit around talking about the colour of baby poo all day. Know this to be untrue.

They talk about a whole VARIETY of topics, such as:

1] *the price of nappy sacks,*
2] *baby names,*
3] *sale on at Mothercare,*
4] Teletubbies…

and as for the BIRTH STORIES – yuk yuk yuk!
You catch my drift – it makes me cringe.

Anyhow, knew I had to, keen to see Nat and Eve, so went there, partly by bus, partly by swimming (OK, not really, but still raining loads).

Decided that, as long as Amos was at work, would tell Abby about his affair – she's gotta deal with it soon.

Let myself in as door ajar… no sign of Abby at first.

1st impression was that had walked into a student house by mistake… could hardly see carpet. Figured GremlinNat had been on a wrecking spree without his Mum knowing… and where was she anyway?

Chaos consisted of piles of nappy sacks on floor, wipes and related stuff in more piles, changing mat… lots of wet stuff – buggy, coats, socks, boots etc.

Found Eve crying (she was in pram in lounge). Think she'd been crying from when I got there, but had thought noise was coming from upstairs, where had assumed my sis was lurking. Stuck Eve's dummy in – she shut straight up and dropped straight off! Wondered if would make a good m… but squished that thought before it got out.

'Why isn't Abby seeing to her? How long had she been yelling like that?' I wondered.

Nat was absorbed with Laa-Laa's toast antics (on TV) quite oblivious to the fact that Mummy was nowhere in sight.

So, had she fallen asleep? Popped to the shops? Fallen and knocked herself out? Ventured upstairs to investigate...

And there she was, on her bed, all curled up in foetal position, glazed expression on her face.

'Abby, are you... OK?'

She didn't speak or move (tho she may have been rocking, just slightly).

'Errrr... Abby? Can I...? Are you...? Should I... errr...?'

Then she spoke, 'Take them away.'

'Urrmmm... what, sorry – who?' I said.

Wondered if she'd lost all her marbles at once and was referring to little green men that only she could see...

'Take them away – the kids – please.'

'Ahh, well, you see that might not be possible right now as I'm meeting friends in town soon and...'

She turned to face me. Could see that she'd been having major crying session – had never seen her look so upset, or angry...

'Oh, so you have to meet your friends do you? Well, of course, don't let me keep you from your oh-so-important social life... your boys to impress, your new clothes to buy, your student parties and balls and... don't let me or my problems stand in the way... please!'

'I... I'm sorry. I can stay for a bit and help with the kids if...'

'Oh yeah,' she said, now kneeling up on the bed, kind of towering over me, using her arms to gesticulate. 'Stay for an hour... then leave me to it. Leave ME to deal with the sick, the poo, the crying, the tantrums, the mess and the... the stupid pathetic buggy board that falls off when you're in the middle of a busy road and it's pouring with rain and makes Nat cry... that blasted buggy board... do you know how much that cost?

Fifty pounds.

Fifty bloody pounds... and then it falls off...'

Was temporarily stunned at sister having just sworn. On the issue of swearing she's a complete S&V – never ever does it. Hoped Mum didn't have the place bugged.

Did quick equation in head… Abby swearing = something v wrong.

Wasn't sure what to do. Wished Lydia were there – she'd know. Am no good in a crisis… and trust me, this WAS a crisis.

Searched desperately for some soothing words. Came out with:

'Shall I watch them while you get some rest or… something?'

'Ah yes, give Mummy a quick rest and she'll be as right as rain – ready to take on the world again, and her kids. Do you really think that's how it works? Do you have any idea what it's like to look after them day in, day out, stuck in the house… day in, day out?'

No, I didn't… but was beg to build up a fairly clear picture…

'…and when Amos gets back they're practically in bed already – fat lot of use he is…'

Concluded that this would be bad time to speak of his affair.

'Tell me, do you have stretch marks that look like an army of overgrown pink caterpillars? Do you wee every time you cough or sneeze? Do you have a huge flabby stomach and can't diet because you're breastfeeding? Do you have a baby who just cries and cries and cries all through the night, and never wants to sleep, and that HATES you? DO YOU?'

She slumped down to the bed, resuming 'in-the-womb' position.

Rang Amos at work, telling him to come straight home as there was an emergency.

He was like, 'Errrr… yeah, but isn't Abby there?' So explained that she WAS the emergency, and that he'd better get his butt in gear, fast. (OK, so didn't use those exact words… he's my bro-in-law after all.)

So that was yesterday… and am now about to go to Abby's again, to look after the kids for a bit while A&A 'go out' for a bit. A tad unsure about having GremlinNephew AND tiny baby, together, on my own…

What if Nat finds and plays with matches while am changing Eve's nappy, and sets house on fire?

What if Nat insists we watch *Teletubbies* when I want to watch *Hollyoaks*? (Suppose *Tweenies* would make a suitable compromise.)

What if Eve does that projectile vomiting thing on new River Island top (budget only allows one new item of clothing per month).

Hmmmmmm… am going to ring for reinforcements…

Libs = busy (could hear some guy in the background)
Lydia = busy
Fax = busy (pleaded with him, mentioning the whole 'baby sick' thing…
he said that the best recorded distance for projectile vomiting is 27 feet)
Sas = busy
Oren = busy, but will come anyway (guess he feels he owes me, what with
me visiting Maisie and all).

Ringing Oren really was a last resort, for obvious reasons… now not sure
if have done the right thing, but no time to have regrets as just realised
he's picking me up in 7 mins!

Post-Mary Poppins attempt Please say you don't want kids, Bob –
they're SUCH a nightmare… no wonder Abby's gone nuts…

Nat started off all angelic (a bit in awe of 'Oren the Stranger'). Eve slept for
1st ½ hr – considered quitting degree and pursuing career as nanny (to kids
of the rich and famous… pref Brooklyn and Romeo) as watched her sleep.
She is well-cute.

Then Nat, now fully introduced to Oren, overcame his shyness and threw a
wobbly… something to do with not being allowed to use Daddy's 'worn-
moder' (lawnmower?) to mow the lounge rug. The noise of the angel-
turned-Angelica (*Rugrats*) woke Eve, and things turned nasty.
Both kids were yelling.
Nat looked as tho he was about to do something v violent to the next person who said he couldn't worn-moder the rug.
Eve smelt pooey…
wanted to scream, but thought it not appropriate in front of Oren.

Oren didn't panic – he produced some bubbles from his coat pocket and
blew some for Nat… who thought they were the best thing he'd ever seen
in his tiny life.

When Nat was all calmed down, Oren told me to take Eve upstairs to
change her, then give her a bottle (of 'expressed' milk) from kitchen (ahhh
– had completely forgotten about feeding the thing… I mean, the baby).
Did as was told, and harmony was soon restored.

Congratulated Oren on being so good with kids… he said that when it
comes to kids, bubbles are always 50p well-spent. Our convo got a tad

stilted after that tho. Asked him about Caroline, but he started talking about one of his housemates who never does his washing up, and what a pain it was. Wasn't quite sure how this answered my question… odd. Considered challenging him about why he thought me unsuitable for SocSec, but didn't (cluck cluck… am complete chicken).

He left for lecture when Eve had returned to dream-land (if she sleeps this much in the day no wonder she's up all night – poor Abby).

Abby had said it was fine for me to use their computer if got bored, so decided to surf the web for a bit. Screen was displaying their email page, so had a quick peek at it. Noticed that Mum appeared to email them at least once a day – typical. THEN…

Saw one for Amos, from someone called 'Kate'.

Took all of 2 secs to recall that it was a 'Kate' he'd been speaking to on the phone that time had overheard him.

Opened email and read it – this is my sister's future at steak here – like she hasn't got enuf on her plate without her husband's mistress emailing him AT HOME!

'Kate' was saying she'd meet him at 6:30 pm, at The Rock, tomorrow.

Some Cns should have a sign on their back, like lorries do: 'How is my lifestyle – ring this number?' and Amos is one of them. Then could ring someone and report him for his crime against innocent wife and kiddies. Huh.

To top it all, got back here exhausted, looking forward to a TV/snacks (low-carb) night with Libs. She came here to my room, showed her photos of Eve (as she STILL hasn't come with me to see her). Then she said she'd changed her mind about this eve… wanted an early night instead… and left.

Just like that, with no warning.

Why am I making people cry/leave all of a sudden? 1st my sister and then my best bud? Or is it something in the air? Or is it their TOM?

(TOM = Time Of the Month, in case you didn't know.)

Correction: think that should read 'my sister's future at STAKE' not 'STEAK'… food on the brain, again…

Sat 22 Jan

Is odd, but the fact that Abby is having this… mini-breakdown (?) makes me feel better. That sounds awful. Really hope she gets better soon – but now feel more secure, knowing that she's not 100% perfect.

Same goes for Libs – meeting her parents made me see is not all easy for her – she doesn't have parents she's close to. The fact that she's not all 'sorted' makes ME feel that bit more sorted – my parents are a bit of a pain, but they're not that bad, and get on with them most of the time. As for Libs getting all weird and walking out on me…?

Does this make me a bad person?

Why should I say 'yippeeeee' when people I thought had it all sussed turn out to be worse off than me? Hmmmm.

Have decided to do a 007 and check out Amos and Kate's little rendezvous today. Had considered recruiting a bud to join me, but decided against it. Couldn't ask my upright Cn pals to come and help me… spy on people.

Wondered about Oren, seeing as he proved himself so useful yesterday, but concluded he'd only come so he could see what I was up to, and then report all to Lydia and try to have me de-nominated from committee…

Right, am off on mission – feel as tho need binoculars or bugging equipment etc… never mind – will take treasured copy of *heat* mag to hide behind – perhaps could drop it on floor in front of Amos and hope he slips and breaks HIS toes on a Coke machine.

Or would I feel better if did this to Kate? Can't decide…

6:19 pm Sharon's Cafe Am in Internet cafe directly across road from The Rock (yuppie bar/restaurant). So as not to look suspicious, am at computer, emailing myself, so can copy n paste into your letters later. V tempted by cream cakes at counter, but ordered coffee with cream, which is low-carb and nice and… creamy.

OK, 6:21 now, and no sign of Amos. Rock pretty empty – should be easy to spot them. Just looking at who's sitting at tables… a family, a couple, 2 blokes in suits… ahhhh!… there's a woman sitting on her own, sipping at something brown in a tall glass… keeps looking over her shoulder… quite old – maybe even 35. Sort of attractive, for a woman of her age. Got ya Kate!

6:32 pm Kate still sipping brown stuff (beer?) looking more nervous by the minute – bet she'd jump a mile if crept up behind her shouting 'boo!', which v tempted to do coz... there he is!!

Amos, my bro-in-law, the adulterer.

He's coming toward her... hope they won't snog – my nerves couldn't cope right now... he's nearly there... (get out of the way large waitress-lady...) he's at her table and...

he's walked straight past – perhaps part of their 'being subtle' plan?

He's now trying to squeeze between large waitress-lady and a table (could SHE be Kate?)...

He's now... sitting down at a table... with a bloke!

A bloke? Kate's a bloke? Is he GAY as well as a cheat? A cheating gay bro-in-law – that'd be just my luck (if believed in luck... blah blah blah...).

Nope – no snogging – phew! (2 gs in snogging or 1?)

They're having some kind of in-depth looking convo.

7:32 pm Bored out of tiny mind, still at Sharon's – only me and one other girl left in here now – suspect will be chucked out soon... coffee gone cold – forgot it due to all the excitement earlier. Is v non-exciting now... they've been chatting and eating for ages... perhaps should go to BURP – am late already and Oren might think that

Oh – hang on – they're shaking hands, smiling, now getting up to leave. Amos is putting on coat, looking toward the street outside. Is he checking that there's no one out there he knows?

He's now looking directly at Sharon's – perhaps he thinks this would make a more discreet mtg place...

he's still looking this way and

waving.

He's waving at Sharon's... HE'S WAVING AT MEEEEEEEEEEE!!!

Just gave quick feeble non-committal wave back, trying to convey that:

1] *have acknowledged his presence across st, but*

2] *unfortunately am far too busy to be able to actually talk to him right now...*

It didn't work... he's on his way here now, so better end this letter before he

11:41 pm back in room OK, so will never have a career as private dick. Amos joined me in Sharon's and we chatted for a good hour (does that place EVER close?). Turned out he'd spotted me before he entered The

Rock, and had rather wondered why I'd been staring over at him for over an hour...

Was embarrassed, and then cross, which lead to being V cross... it was him in the wrong here – not me. HE was the one having an affair, tho not quite sure why he'd just met a bloke instead of Kate...

'Amos – I know what you're doing and it's got to stop. Abby doesn't deserve to be treated in this way!' I blurted.

He seemed unphased – asked how I knew about it.
Said had overheard phonecalls, read email from 'Kate' and so on.
He said that now was a good time to tell her, and did I think she'd mind? Huh? MIND? What planet was he ON?
Turned out it was ME who was on planet Ga-Ga.

The explanation: Amos has been unhappy in his current job for a long time (something in computers). He's been planning a new career in the caring profession – something to do with autistic adults (I think). This has involved regular meetings with his mate who runs a 'home' (with his wife – Kate) for such adults, to suss out Amos' suitability and sort out the training he'll need.

Amos didn't want Abby to know anything about it as it's such a big step for him to take... he wanted to surprise her with the news when he had it all sorted.

Wanted to top myself there and then – what a prat! What MUST he think of me to accuse him of... well, you know. Made it back to BURP (Amos gave me a lift back).

Cool to have Sas there again (she hasn't been for a bit). She's a bit of a drifter really – likes coming to BURP/church, but not that committed (in true Paprika-like style) – goes elsewhere if gets better offer. Was there all the time when going out with Reuben, of course.

Get on well with her – after Libs she's one of my fav people here. Totally love most BURPers (with exception of Oren) but sometimes their S&V super-spiritual comments freak me out a bit.

Really need my sleep now – has been an emotionally exhausting last 3 days... may have to miss Monday's lecture – don't want to overdo it...

(Think there might be 3 gs in snogging – sorry for confusion.)

Sun 23 Jan

Church

Found 'worship' slot a bit tough... kind of miss being a part of it. Miss the feeling used to get 'knowing' that God was on the receiving end...

Please don't think I sit there with eyes open and arms folded tho... guess I fake it without thinking – eyes shut, arms raised (one at 1st, then 2 when the chorus starts, or things really get going) singing my little guts out (or should that be heart out?) then... when the song dies off a bit, bringing hands together in 'praying saint' fashion, with fingers resting on lips, slightly rocking from heel to toe... which says to any onlookers:

'I've been on an exciting worshipping high... but am now moving on to a phase of deep meditation.'

Now what's that old film with Meg Ryan in? Doesn't she fake her own death in a restaurant or something?

Am the Cn equivalent of Meg... I fake it.

Did however say little word to God/inner self/thin air re being sorry for neglecting Abby and wrongly accusing Amos. Didn't work tho – still feel like poo.

Would really appreciate priest + confessional box... must be great to confess, then say 10 Hail Marys (whatever they may be) and go out feeling all holy again... perhaps should check out local Catholic Church... hmmmm-mmm.

Head still bad – never looked forward to a Dr's app so much in my life (is tomorrow).

Just looked in mirror – wish looked less like Jude and more like Meg...

Was it her death...?

Mon 24 Jan

10:21 am

Just got post from my box downstairs... got letter from Mum – whoo-hoo! Can only mean one thing!

£20? Huh? 20 quid – is that IT?! Pause for a min to push 'ripping-cheque-up-and-sending-it-back-to-parents, Libs-style' thoughts aside...

Have they any IDEA how much things cost? Let's ponder for a min where £20 might go...

1] *Toward weekly snacks from Tesco (but wouldn't cover it).*
2] *New top from TopShop/a CD or sim.*
3] *Almost cover the cost of eve out – round of drinks, entrance to club... McDs on way home etc.*

Huh! Thought they'd send me some REAL money – like in the region of 3 figures at least... am REALLY gonna have to cut back now...

12:32 pm Sorry to go on about this, but are my loving parents aware that my annual tuition fees are £1000 (at least), rent – £3,500 (ish) and so am likely to leave uni owing £13,000 (or more) in student loan debts? And they send me 20 measly little pounds... why why WHY?!

3:47 pm Just been on phone while (whilst?) walking back after lecture... call from StiltonBreath... test is on 14th Feb – that's 3 wks time!

HELP! Am not ready!

Dear residents of Bymouth,

I am due to take my driving test on Monday 14th February.
I would be most grateful if you could cease from driving in or around Bymouth on this day, from 2–2:30 pm. This will give me a better chance of passing. I am not a good driver at the best of times, and will be well-stressed on day of test – so I am saying this with the well-being and safety of you and your families in mind.
Cheers,

Jude

Post-Dr's app He says I need an eye test! Have to go to opticians and make app.
Sure have got perfect eyesight – Dr (with some weird name) just embarrassed he couldn't cure me – typical.

Considered asking if he could check me to see if still virgin or not.

1] *Not sure if this was poss anyway.*
2] *He got up my nose as failed to take away head pain.*
3] *He wasn't female.*

Tue 25 Jan

11:58 am Not sure what's wrong with me, but have decided to see Maisie today. Perhaps she knows how to get rid of bad headaches (migraines?).

Way past my bedtime Just back from Fusion – had a 'trial go' to see if can cope with glass collecting/hanging up coats/taking money on door etc. All v simple, but quite stressful, what with all the drunks, tarts, snogging couples getting in the way and all.

Fusion is not that different to union Bar... TVs suspended from ceiling, pool, black leather sofas, students working there, students drinking there... students getting chucked out coz they can no longer stand unaided... once you've seen one student hangout you've seen them all (OK, so Libs prob wouldn't agree, but then she gets around far more than I do – in more ways than one!).

It's recommended, by the people who know these things, that students work a maximum of 15 hrs per wk. Think Libs says will get £5.50 per hr, so that's... errrrrrrr... £82.50 per wk – hurrah! Will be rich at last!

That's if can get 15 hrs out of this rota Libs is in charge of... she'll sort it out, won't she?

Oh, nearly forgot about Maisie... did call on her today. On opening the door she told me off for not being in a lecture or in library studying etc etc. Was tempted to obey her and go (tho not to lecture or library) but then she asked me if I was coming in or just trying to drown the both of us (still raining) so went in.

Told her about the Abby/Amos sagas... was good to have someone to tell – at one point really felt she was taking it all in, and not interrupting for a change... then realised she was just snoring more quietly than usual – huh!

Wed 26 Jan

Final weigh in SKINNY AT LAST!!!

OK – not actually skinny in sense of Vic Becks... but a whopping 5 lbs lighter than 2 wks ago – ta-daaaaaaaar!

JUDE-IS-THE-WINN-EEEEER!

The others did OK, but not as well as my good self. Sas has continued to binge on M Bars – she may even get FAT at some point... oh, to see the day...

'So, will Jude continue with the Atkins diet?' you ask. Not sure yet. To go off it might cause missing 5 lbs to come home again... couldn't face that now – feel sooooo great!

D lesson Roads v wet. Can't believe test is 12 days away... hope it doesn't rain for test.

Thur 27 Jan

Eye test

2 surprises awaited me at opticians...

1] *Eye test was FREE (on production of form HC2, which also entitles me to free dental check-ups!). However, this didn't make up for the news...*
2]*Have got BAD eyesight – wait for it...* NEED GLASSES!

So old Dr Whatsisname was right – headaches caused by squinting, caused by my need for geeky goggles to be attached to my face. Am short-sighted, so will need to wear them loads, like for driving, lectures etc etc... this is NOT GOOD NEWS for a hot chick like myself who's recently got slim(mer).

Have got to go back a wk tomorrow to collect the darn things... just in time for test – phew!

8:23 pm Today is now a day to remember. Have just had a visit from VIP – still feeling awe-struck/week at the knees (no, haven't been on the B Breezers). No, not Vic Becks, not Matt Redman, not even Nicky Gumbel...

but the PRESIDENT of the SU (Students' union)... here in MY ROOM!

She was doing the rounds, talking about the forthcoming elections (for SU com), her campaign to end the loan system (hurrah, I think) and all that stuff. Didn't really get all she said, but still, was an honour just to have her here, for almost 7 mins.

Told Libs about weight loss today – she suspects I have a tapeworm... read out to me passage from *Bridget Jones* that says how to rid oneself of tapeworm... it involved holding a bowl of warm milk near my mouth, then winding it's head round a pencil when it surfaced.

She THEN informed me that SHE's lost 4 lbs in past 2 wks.

She said wanted to lose a bit, just to see if she could, and wanted to do it her way... she always did her teeth after last meal of the day, at 6 pm-ish, and made sure she chewed gum continuously after that, for whole eve, so wouldn't be tempted to eat anything else... and it worked!

Bizarre! Not only has she lost weight, but she's got the best smelling breath on campus!

PS Did Atkins diet today... until about 10 am-ish... when popped to Tesco to stock up on my fav snacks that have missed so much (don't tell Libs – might have gone slightly over budget).

Perhaps will market Lib's way of dieting, and get rich rich RICH!

Fri 28 Jan

9:47 am

Abby's just rung to ask me over for lunch. Not keen to go. Embarrassed (re 'Amos affair' thing) and scared (re Abby's manic depressive behaviour). Will go tho – would be rude not to I guess. Will take her flowers (like that'll help...).

Post-Abby's Things a lot better than had expected. Abby almost normal again.

She was well-chuffed with flowers – asked me to put them in a vase while she fed Eve. Did so, but hashed it up a bit – they looked not dissimilar to the bushes that surround our halls. On returning to the lounge after the meal (her yummy lasagne – 3 and ½ helpings), examined my weed arrangement again... thought it didn't look as bad as before – had been too hard on myself. Then realised that Abby had been at it, transforming the bush into something beautiful...

So how do I sign up for the course? Assume there must be a course in existence that everyone goes on when they reach a certain age (18?) that teaches such things as flower arranging, along with cooking, sewing, DIY, car maintenance, finances etc etc. How come people like Abby (and Libs) know all this stuff and I don't? Anyhow – mustn't let jealousy take over again – can now fall back on fact that she's NOT perfect and struggles with life just like the rest of us.

She seemed more relaxed... noticed she'd raided Tesco freezer compartment... pizzas, g bread, puds and more pizzas. She used to do all her cooking from scratch, Delia S-style... guess now she's realised she needs to take things easy for a bit. The house was slightly less tidy than normal... and they've now got SKY! Nat now addicted to kiddie-channels... there's only so much VeggieTales a kid can take...!

Her and Amos seem OK now – she's OK with his job changing idea, esp now she knows what it's like to be stuck doing something you don't enjoy…

She said how Nat had been an easy baby, and she'd coped fine. Eve has been awful, and what with her arrival causing Nat to find the Gremlin within…

Now she's admitted she needs help, she said, she's on the road to recovery. Her Dr is keeping an eye on her… so will Mum, to be sure! Mum even suggested travelling to Abby's one day a wk to help out… but Abby declined, saying that Amos would be around more when he quits his job. Phew – not sure how comfortable would feel knowing that Mum was a few miles away on weekly basis!

1 wk til G-day (goggles)!

Skived lecture today as enjoying being with Abby and co.

1st ever lecture skive… will try not to let it become a habit… must get down to serious revision soon – exams only 2 wks away!

Sat 29 Jan

Not sure now that ought to go to Romania… don't really have enough cash spare (we all have to contribute £200 for travelling costs etc). Will speak to Oren after BURP.

Enjoying eating all foods sky-high in carb again – will try to keep AMOUNT of food intake down to prevent those 5 lbs from sneeking back. If that fails, will go for the chewing gum/teeth-cleaning idea.

10:46 pm Reuben and Sarah are finito!!

Is it my turn now Reuben my sweet? Is it – huh?

He finished it… said he needed to devote more time to his course… wow – to be that committed to doing a degree – is a lesson for us all. Made this comment to Fax, who creased up and said, 'Nice one Jude!' as if had told him a joke or something… huh?

Great – I pull hot blokes as often as *heat* mag ring me and ask me to be on next week's cover… and yet a living breathing skeleton gets the pleasure of 8 wks + 1 day (errrrrr… not that was crossing days off my calendar or anything) with my Reuben.

My (now single) true love/soulmate has taken to wearing this amaaaaaaaaazing aftershave… it kinda smells like burning wood… but in a good way (log fire? camp fire?).

Sat extra close to him, inhaling deeply… was going fine til Lydia said she didn't know I got asthma too, and did I want to borrow her inhaler…

Toward the end of mtg, Lydia said we'd have a few mins of chat… with someone we didn't normally talk to (don't ya just hate it when that happens?). Before could cunningly approach someone I knew, with 'Oh, hello – my name's Jude – what's yours?', this tall girl (who had never really noticed at BURP before) came up to ME, placed a tatty pink envelope in my hand, saying…

'God told me to give you this… oh, and my name's Beth – what's yours?'

Wandered off to loos as soon as mtg over.
Opened tatty pink envelope with haste…
a one-way ticket to Jamaica?
The address of my future hubbie?
The 'truth' at last?
Nope.
A cheque.
A cheque, payable to me… for £200!

OK, so had a few fleeting thoughts re several items of clothing have been eying up in TopShop lately… then PING! Penny dropped – Romania!

Can go!

Do I really WANT to go?

Hmmmmm. Don't have much choice now. Either Beth (my new best mate in whole wide world) KNEW I needed that money for trip, or…

or it was… God?

So, say it was all Beth and not God, coz he doesn't exist… WHY would she give me her money? Can hardly be compared to lending a mate a tenner. £200 is no laughing matter… she's never even met me before…

Tue 1 Feb

Today so far…

1] *Eaten lots.*

2] *Thought about d test lots – will Jude be a qualified driver in 2 wks time?*
3] *Thought about wearing goggles a lot – will this be Jude's one-way ticket to geekland?*
4] *Thought about that £200 lots and*

Woooahh… arghhhhh!!!!! What on earth?…?!

You're not gonna believe this… all the lights have just gone out! Can see across to block of halls opposite – their lights are out too. Hmmmm. Still have power to PC, but all around me is black. Not an ideal thing when you're in a room on your own and are the type of person to dislike the dark…

or things associated with it, like…
murder,
monsters,
ghosts,
spiders (huge hairy man-eating ones)…
Will stop list – not doing myself any favours…

This screen in front of me is all lit up – the only light in the whole room.

A tiny light – not enough to be able to see the rest of the room, making it all scary and unknown.

Rather like my life really – keep getting little 'rays of sunshine' that give me hope… but it's never enough – there's still too much darkness, too much unknown… the truth is still out of reach.

OK, so now succeeded in scaring pants off myself AND depressing myself to point of breakdown… will get outta here – will visit Libs…

Post-Libs Odd. Had to bang on her door for ages before she'd let me in. Could hear a bloke in there… wondered if they were putting their clothes back on – would be typical of Libs to take advantage of a blackout…!

When she eventually let me in… the room was blokeless. Checked the loo/shower… asked where he'd gone.

'Huh babe? Naa – no talent tonight – just old Libs on 'er tod… enjoying the… errrr… dark…'

Am back in my room now.

Without a doubt, she had a bloke in that room that she didn't want me to know about. Either he is a superhero and can make himself invisible (or morph himself into a can of Dry B), or he escaped, Bond-style, out the window.

Finding a different lad in Libs' room every time I visit is just part of my uni experience so far… and she knows that… so why didn't she want me to see this one?

Has he got 2 heads?
Is he over 30? 50? (not even thinkable, forget that).
A geek?
Prof Carr?!

11:43 pm Just to report that light has now been restored to the campus residents… will go to bed, now that I know I CAN switch light on, if needs be…

Sorry – the above should read as 'person-eating spider' (must keep up with inclusive language trend).

Twelve pancakes and a funeral

Fri 4 Feb

8:32pm Collected glasses today... no, not at Fusion, at SpecSavers. Feel sooooooo old. Is my b'day Wednesday... perhaps will turn 59, not 19... what comes after glasses... a zimmer frame? Hearing aid?

Popped into Boots (to view 'the new me' in their teeny mirror in sunglasses section). Had quick whiff of men's aftershaves to see if could suss out what Reuben wears... want to get some so can pour on pillow, sprinkle on textbooks, and perhaps even use in Maisie's lounge to exorcise the lavender puke. Found one that was close (tho not an exact match – more fresh wood than burnt wood)... cost £35... gave it a miss.

Exams in 11 DAYS! Argghhhh!
Right, will do daily action plan for this coming 'revision' wk:

8 am – *get up, shower, de-hair appropriate body parts etc.*
10 am – *enjoy 'sensible' breakie before heading to library, to REVISE until:*
5 pm – *eat.*

6–9 pm – *REVISION in library.*

Hmmmmm. Haven't included lunch... no probs – will help keep those 5 lbs off.
Is library open that late? Have no idea.
Plan allows for 10 hrs of revision per day... that should do it.

9:33 pm Queen of Budgetland has just been here (Libs) with yet more ideas, one of which is to use sticky tape instead of buying waxing strips to rid oneself of unsightly tache. She went on to demonstrate this idea... ON ME...

OUCH OUCH OUCH!!!
She managed to wax a teeny bit of my LIP in the process = LOTS of blood.
NOT for the squeemish (which I am).
Told her she'd make a pathetic beautician...
'Torturer' yes, but 'administrator-of-delicate-beauty-treatments' no.

Just after this, had txt from Lydia, asking if I wanted to go over as she was all lonely (Jon leading Alpha at church). Can't understand married persons saying they're lonely... at least they're MARRIED for crying out loud! Anyhow, it was Libs who read txt to me (while was tending to blood-flow from lip)... asked her to txt Lydia back with, 'Thanks, but busy.'

Why did I assume the sticky-tape torturer would obey orders? She later informed me that she'd txted her back, saying I was busy... with my new boyfriend, Bob! (SO regret ever telling Libs about these letters...)

She seemed to think it no big deal.

'Help put a bomb up your lazy arse, get out there and FIND this Bob... yeah, groovy baby yeeaaaahhhh!'

Sometimes she forgets she isn't Mrs Austin Powers.
Sometimes I forget she isn't helpful/truthful/of this planet.

Sat 5 Feb

6:41 pm

Whoops! Just remembered my carefully thought out revision action plan... hmmmm – will start it tomorrow...

Post-BURP Got all excited when my love asked me to go and stand next to him. Heart went crazy... tried desperately not to sweat more than is lady-like. Turned out he needed someone to hold his upper left arm so he could get optimum reception for his mini-radio thing. At least he chose ME to assist him... must think my body's well-tuned.

Upper left arm was gorgeously muscular and manly... must be all that surfing.

Lydia took me aside and asked if I was still interested in the Romania trip... would the fact I now have 'Bob' make a difference? Neither of us had seen Reuben lurking behind us... before I had chance to put Lydia straight, Reuben blurts out, for all to hear...

'Yo – our Jude's found herself a boyfriend!'

Gals then all over me in style of ugly rash... questions – height? Age? Course? Saved? (last one asked by Lauren, who then scurried over to a concerned looking Duncs, to report back... her news put a smile back amongst his acne).

I DID say he was a Cn.

Had tried to explain about the mix-up (honest) but then caught a brief glimpse of Reuben, looking at me as he'd never done before… just like he used to look at Saskia/Sarah. Wondered if he might be interested in ME now he thinks am spoken for. Might have denied charge of having boyfriend if my love didn't stand so close to me, exciting my olfactory organs with 'essence of burnt wood'…

Escaped from clutches of newly-formed 'Fans-Of-Jude-Now-She's-Not-a-Sad-Singleton' and took Beth aside (if Lyd can 'take people aside for a quiet word' then am darn sure I can too… officially start as SocSec from today anyway!). Asked her why she gave me that £200.

(After all, as Cns we HEAR about this kinda out-of-blue-donation-giving all the time… but never thought would be on the receiving end… all v well for those S&Vs who 'live by faith'… didn't really think would apply to those who aren't really sure if they HAVE a faith to live by…)

She said, 'God just told me you needed the money… that's all there is to it really.' Slapped her round the face, EastEnders-style.

OK, so didn't really, but acted it out in head, causing me delay of a good 10 secs before could reply, with voice more raised than would normally be expected by someone who has taken another someone aside for 'quiet word'…

'But what do you MEAN he "told you"? Did he write it on stone tablets? Yell down to you from the clouds? Order a computer-literate angel to email you? Huh? Eh?'

Beth looked at me like I were a couple of Noodles short of a Pot… thought she was gonna burst into tears, Tweenie-style. She took a deep breath and asked if I wanted to chat about it sometime, over a Big Mac or sim. Didn't know what to say – hadn't wanted to upset her – just to get some decent answers for a change…

Found myself saying that 'Bob and I…' had a busy week planned, but maybe sometime after… when our exams are out the way, blah blah, lie lie, blah, lie… etc.

Beth is far more worthy than me to serve on the BURP com – why wasn't she nominated? God SPEAKS to HER… bet SHE never lies!

Fax led the study-bit – seems there's more to him than random useless (tho interesting) facts… he started with:

'Right. Scenario. A church feels God is telling them to plant a new sister church on a large needy council estate in their town. They spend 2 years raising money, and receiving gifts of money, until they finally have enough to start building. The project starts off well, and those from the estate show an interest – some are even employed by the church to help with the building, decorating etc.

The church is then told they need a further twenty grand (due to something being overlooked in the original plans). They are also told that this isn't a problem – they have been offered a lottery grant.

They don't feel they can raise the money themselves, and no one has come forward to donate it. They need the money straight away. If they don't get it, the project will have to be abandoned.

Should they take the lottery grant, or not?

Please split into 2s and discuss…'

Went with Sas (v much hoping she didn't come to BURP just coz she knew Reuben was single again)… in true Paprika style she thought the church should take the lottery money and not let everyone down, blah blah. In true 'no-idea-where-am-coming-from' style… I agreed.

When we all regrouped for 'feedback', was only me and Sas who were pro-grant – all the rest were against it. Huh. Can't get anything right.

Still, Fax's bit was v interesting. Overheard Duncs complaining to Lauren that it didn't include any Bible verses. From my POV, know that I actually used brain for once, and we were all still mulling over 'scenario' in F&Ferret afterward, until closing time… is THAT a bad thing Duncs, eh?

Another thing discussed at F&Ferret was 'Fairtrade'. Well, Reuben discussed it and we all listened… he could sit and discuss the life cycle of the toad for all I care – he's just so good to hear, and watch, and smell, and…

Anyhow, was all v interesting – seems that in some countries there are companies that exploit their workers – naff pay, crap working conditions, child labour etc. Then the produce is shipped around the world… even to England, AND WE BUY IT, unaware of what's been involved.

'It's an outrage!' said Reuben. Some BRITISH companies use/abuse workers abroad, and we are none the wiser. Seems to mainly involve stuff like rugs, clothes, coffee… he MAY have said chocolate, but will discount for now, not prepared to alter choccie buying habits until have all the facts… could take YEARS.

O-K-Doe-K… will start this revision tomorrow, without a doubt.

Ah, hang on… is Sunday tomorrow… day of rest and all that…

Sun 6 Feb

Reuben kept us all amused during yawnyawn sermon by writing jokes on Lauren's pad (she always takes notes – the swot)…

What chorus do you sing if you are wanting to work behind a bar?
'I want to serve…'

What chorus do you sing if you've got a friend who is thinking of dating a girl called Joy, and you think he should go for it?
'You shall go out with joy…'

Not sure others got jokes, didn't even snigger (inc Sas, which = phew, she's not after him again). Personally found them rib-ticklingly-ace… added lots of 'ha ha has' over several pages of notebook… Reuben looked my way and WINKED when he saw them… Lauren gave me the look of death.

Went to Lydia and Jon's for lunch, with some others… Reuben spent most of the meal telling us about Nazarene and how they're now 'ready' for gigs. How cool. He even asked ME if I'd be his groupy… said no, but only coz don't know what a groupy is… must ask Libs…

Lydia then added that Bob probably wouldn't be keen on me being Reuben's groupy… which triggered off a load more questions re Bob and me and us etc.

ALMOST told them the truth, but thought again about the attention Reuben's been paying me recently… and lied for England.

Mon 7 Feb

4:31 pm

Started revision plan with professional precision – up at 8 am, de-haired/showered, breakie by 10 am… then got txt from Abby, asking if I wanted to come over.

OK, so revision is important… but family comes 1st, eh?

Nat's speech really coming on… said I was 'wuv-wee' – cute-er-oonie! Pointed at Eve and asked what she was… 'thh-tinky'. Hmmmmm.

Grabbed a book of baby names from bookshelf while Abby doing Eve's nappy – did you know that 'Oren' means 'Gift of God'? Huh – typical... he sure thinks he's God's gift to women... his parents must have prophetic gift of sorts...

Abby seemed good. Seeing her so tired and busy always makes me feel guilty now – I can do what I want, when I want... is not like she'll ever be able to lie in til 1:30 pm... not for next 18 yrs anyway (errr... not that have ever done this myself or anything, well, not this wk so far...).

She looks more relaxed tho, on the whole. Feel like can talk to her now – she seems less distant – on the same planet as me for a change – is nice.

Brought Nat back here (my room) for a bit... he's here right now, playing with my hair straightener... assume 2 yr olds don't know how to plug things into the wall – those things get well-hot.

Ah, now he's found a ½ eaten packet of Hula Hoops in my underwear drawer – wondered where they'd gone...

Now he's eating the H Hoops... seeing how many he can get in his mouth before he has to chew... time to intervene...

a\ng@~[q03ui q[e3tojut p;w9j;s#;
 KF[0FOJ@lsdgIHILGGNBOsidD

Ahhhh, sorry bout that – Nat got to computer whilst was checking room for anything else that might be hazardous in Gremlin-hands... why can't kids just sit still and read or something? Huh? Think his keyboard attack was my punishment for confiscating the H Hoops.

D'ya think his typing is code for something? Hmmmmmmm.

5:45 pm Abby just been here to collect Nat... am exhausted... only had him here for an hour (whilst Abby took Eve for a check-up in town). Sure this doesn't mean won't make excellent parent – just that will be a v tired one – perhaps will find faith in God again, and as a reward he'll give me several extra hours in the day when am parent so can sleeeeeeeeeeeeeeeeeeep!

Really ought to start some revision now... will just lie down on bed for a few mins to recover...

8:45 pm Whoops! Just woken up! M Manson is coming through wall again... will go help find those headphones, then go to bed properly... was obviously more tired than thought – don't tell anyone – don't think students are allowed to go to bed before midnight!

Tue 8 Feb

8:32 am

Ouch – toes in much pain! Just woke up thinking, 'Oh no, got to get up for lecture.' Put one leg out of bed. Then remembered there are none this wk, and put leg back again. Then remembered that this is coz it's revision wk... my exams start in a wk and have done NO revision yet... jumped energetically out of bed, straight onto straightener, plus a whole load of other stuff that Nat left on the floor.

9:34 am All going to plan, am just gonna eat Pot Noodle (beef and tomato) for breakie, then will head for library...

10:02 am AM IN LIBRARY! Have finally made it – someone call the uni paper and get it on the front page! Thought would begin by emailing you (errr... me) to share this good news.

Am a student who studies... in the library.

Am a keen student who is aware her exams aren't far off and am revising... in the library.

Am person who can manage her time so that

10:57 am Sorry, had spotted Sas in nearby booth - went for chinwag.

11:06 am Hard to revise when toes hurt so much... perhaps toe that was broken has broken again. Will give them quick massage...

11:29 am Right, so looking briefly at my notes on 'memory', looks like am needing 'maintenance rehearsal'... meaning a shallow kind of memory, involving no more than simple repetition. Don't aim to understand it, just to spew it back out on exam papers, making it LOOK like understand it. Will this work? Huh. When I chose psychology, had a sneaky suspicion it was a bad idea to study something I found so hard to spell...

12:15 pm Have just been over with Sas asking her opinion on likelihood of broken toes getting broken again... she suggested we get some food, so am off to McDs...will be back asap...

4:46 pm Just got back (to room). We had long chat over burgers (Sas paid by way of a b'day pressie for me – is tomorrow!). Then got sidetracked in TopShop, etc... never made it back to library... still, is always tomorrow.

Am off to F&Ferret now to meet the others... cheers, Bob.

11:43 pm Bizarre evening. Waited at F&Ferret for ONE HOUR for the others, when got a txt to say they were at Fusion and where was I? Did they give me the wrong info on purpose? Has Oren poisoned their minds against me so they all secretly hate me, and this is their way of telling me? Had no desire to go and find out, so continued to chat with various people I recognised from my course. Then that group left... Jude-no-friends was left propping up the bar, alone.

Then met cool guy, who was oldish (nearly 30?) but cool. We got chatting... turned out he was a Cn... spent 30 seconds wondering if he were you, when he explained that he was the new uni chaplain!

Turns out the old one (Ms Anna-the-feminist) left unexpectedly, with 'issues', as he so tactfully put it. 'Mike' has now taken over. Is married with kiddie.

Chatted til last orders... he said that my joy at finding out that others aren't perfect (Abby, Libs etc) was all part of life and was normal/not evil.

Hurrah!

Mike invited me to his place for Sun lunch this wk... said yes – a good person to be around, methinks.

Wed 9 Feb

Appy birthday to me
appy birthday to me
appy birthday to mmm-eeee-eeeeee
appy birthday to me!

Am 19 today!
In fact, am 228 months old,
= 988 wks,
= 6,940 days,
= 166,560 hours,
= 9,993,600 mins.

Would go on, but just been interrupted by txt from Fax:

Every1 shares a bday with at least nine million other ppl in the world

That's great Fax, but WHERE'S MY PRESSIE – huh?! Still pee-ed off re being deserted by so-called pals last night... do they even CARE it's my b'day?

Pressies opened so far:

Money: £30 (*Abby and Amos, bless 'em*)
Book: Delia Smiths Complete Illustrated Cookery Course (*from parents – don't they know I get fed here? Why not Jamie Oliver's book? He's so much prettier...*)
Book: Victoria Beckham – Learning to Fly (*Libs. Hmmm... OK, so Vic's my hero but not sure is nec to READ about her... maybe when exams are over...*)

Phone's ringing – perhaps is Reuben to ask me out on my b'day...

No, was Maisie, who started with:

Her: Ello – is tha young Jude?
Me: Yeah.
Her: Ha – call ya-self stoodents an ya still dunno ha ta talk proper... the word you is searchin for is 'YES'... gottit?
Me: Yeah, I mean... yes... errr... is that Maisie?
Her: Corse it is ya dimwit... d'ya wanna come an ave coffee wiv a luvely old lady?
Me: (*Slight hesitation as considered saying, 'Sure – what's her name?' but bit tongue.*) Ummm... actually, it's my birthday today and... and...
Her: And wot love? Naa! Ya stoo-pid dimwit... gerr-off.. off the phone GERR- OFF THE PHONE!!
Me: Huh? I didn't mean to—
Her: Wot? Oh, nat yoo stoo-pid... Radox – she's all over the... Ger-off... off off off!

Turns out her cat is called Radox. Figures.

Ended up agreeing to go, as haven't got anything big planned for today, apart from scary d lesson (last one B4 test)... just sort of thought that something MIGHT happen, being my b'day and all.

Ooohhhhh, now have made myself all homesick-y. Weird not having parents around on b'day. Will stick on Radio 2 for a bit...

Post-'lovely old lady' Went OK. Had good chat, v long... only interrupted twice – once so she could listen to Shipping Forecast on Radio 4 (the point of this being...?) and then so we (I) could separate Radox from the dead unidentified small beast he'd caught in the garden (not the kind of b'day treat I'd had in mind).

Had bought Maisie some Radox (lavender flave – to match her lounge) on way over there – she was v pleased with it – said no one 'bovered to giv me nof-in no more'. Left her to have a bath in peace, and also coz she was complaining of 'gut-rot' (her words) – probably been poisoned by her own cooking!

Post-fab eve! Was about to have 2nd v early night in a row (9ish) deciding that no one cared about my turning 19 today, when Lyd, Jon and whole gang came a-knocking on my door! Showered me with cards etc. All went to Fusion – had cool time – lots of boogying – no one got too drunk – felt v loved! Danced with Oren, but only to make myself more appealing to Reuben, who was still looking at me in that special way. They'd all assumed I'd be with Bob today... wanted to know exactly when they'll be meeting him.

Great.

What to do?

Lyd said Sarah is leaving uni! She does some kind of science course apparently, which is v demanding. She's had to work to get by, but hasn't had time to study AND work. Is a blessing... Bymouth uni will be free of one of it's hardest working 'perfect bloke snatchers'.

Duncs overheard this convo and mentioned that a guy on his course is quitting, just coz he doesn't like it here.
Huh? Does he need glasses?
How come everyone's leaving all of a sudden?
Will it be my turn next – will those on my floor group together and vote 'Jude Singleton' to be the next one to be evicted... will Davina come and lead me away?

V cool day on whole... even seeing Maisie was cool – she seems to need me, which makes me feel like am actually of some use to someone... must get down to revision tomorrow (couldn't revise on my b'day now, could I?).

Must return those sex books to Oscar soon, before they biodegrade...

Thur 10 Feb

Vic Becks is human being! As a kid she had giant gap in her teeth, was picked on by kids at school (AND some teachers) had to endure adults saying her younger sister was pretty, but not her (oh, how I relate...).

6:32 pm Done bit of revision today, at last... prob not enuf to get me through exams tho.

Just off to Tesco. Got mtg re Romania trip this eve, in my room. Occurred to me that could get in a bunch of 'Fairtrade' foodstuffs to impress Reuben.

7:16 pm Back again. Sorted. Got bananas, wine, choc, hot choc, coffee and tea... all FT! (Had to go to several supermarkets in the end – why can't they all stock all this stuff?)

11:43 pm NOT a good eve. Reuben not at mtg. Oren began to ask how come I'd bought bananas for them to eat... then picked them up, reading the label and said huffily, 'Ahhhh. Fairly. Traded. Bananas... Say. No. More'.

Huh?

Libs joined us in the kitchen for a bit... took 2 coffees back to her room. Hope that BURP lot think am super S&V Cn as have such a 'close' non-Cn pal.

Tad depressed after mtg... all that FT food was NOT part of budget for this wk. Wasted. Headed to Libs room.

Stopped outside door – could hear voices. About to knock when nose became alert... distinct smell of burnt wood in the air... pressed ear to door... was him, my love, in her room...

Ran back to my room, v v MAAADDDDDD!

Can't believe she'd do this to me, her bestest pal.

What DOES she think she's doing?

She doesn't even KNOW him?

Was just chilling out a bit, telling myself it might all be in imagination, when Libs came over.

Asked if she'd been with a guy called Reuben.

She had.

Pointed out that she KNEW I liked a guy called Reuben.

She said she didn't know this was the one I liked.

Asked how many blokes called Reuben she would expect to be at this uni?

She gave up being sorry and turned defensive, said he didn't kiss like a Christian.

Said he was, 'good at tongues... that isn't something you happy clappers are into, is it?'

Pushed her out the door with great force.

No, really, I did... and slammed it with even greater force.

How DARE she?

Fri 11 Feb

Did fair amount of revision today – exams make up 50% of final mark… scary thought.

Not talking to Libs.

Picked Lauren as my Libs-substitute for the day (only motive being hope that her brains would rub off on me). Spent ages pouring out my heart re stress due to exams and fight with Libs etc… ended with asking her what she thought I should do… she looked up from her books and said, 'How many cs in necessary?' Honestly… thought geeks were supposed to KNOW how to spell. At least Libs is a good listener… huh.

Moved on to Lydia, who pointed out that exams are only 50% of THIS yrs mark, not overall mark when we leave… sort of helped, but still well-stressed.

Letter back from Jim – says I ought to keep going to BURP… give it time… don't rush into quitting God just coz of a dream… keep in touch… blah blah…

Huh – easier said than done mate. Don't WANT to give it time – need to sort it out NOW so can get on with my life, knowing which direction to take etc.

As a teenager Vic Becks had spots and no boobs. I am her, reincarnated! No, that can't be right – she's alive.

Whoops – sorry Vic!

9:34 pm Oren just rang – Maisie's died.

Keep thinking, 'No, she can't have – was with her just 2 days ago – must be some mistake…' but there's no mistake. That 'gut-rot' turned out to be more serious than… well, it was serious. Oren said she wouldn't have suffered much – that she looked 'at peace' when they found her…

Always figured there was some kind of pattern to follow when it came to oldies and death… they fall ill, eventually go to hosp/old folks home coz can no longer cope… deteriorate slowly… then die with loved ones at bedside.

How can Maisie just DIE, just like that?
Why?
Huh?

Oren offered to come over… told him would rather be alone.

Don't want to be alone.

Can't even try to make things up with Libs as will look like only doing it coz I need her.

Sat 12 Feb

So is Maisie in heaven now? Is there a heaven? Know it's been asked before, but... what happens when we die? Eh?

Perhaps Jim was right – a decision about God/faith is an important one, not to be taken lightly. On other hand... if we're all fragile humans who could pop clogs at any given time...

What if still in pondering mode, then die?

Maisie didn't think much of Oren being a Cn.

Did God give her a 2nd chance at the last minute?

That wouldn't really be fair tho, would it, coz...

Right, am not gonna think about this any more today... not ready to deal with all this yet. Really want to talk to Libs... haven't even SEEN her since our fight.

Will go to BURP – try to pretend this isn't happening to me...

Post-BURP Asked Jon why he thought we've lost so many BURPers since Sept, when we had about 100 (only got about 40 now). Wasn't really that interested – just trying to make convo, but turns out Jon has thought muchly re this, he thinks it's coz BURP can be:

1] *out of touch with student culture,*
2] *judgemental of Cns who vary from the 'standard Evangelical norm',*
3] *like yet another lecture,*
4] *a 'holy huddle',*
5] *a few people doing everything... the rest being spare parts.*

Asked Reuben why he didn't always come... he said,

'Coz it's boring.'

Mike the new chaplain was there and was immediate hit with all.

He led short bit where we split into small groups and discussed our fave book in the Bible. Managed to get into Reuben's group (or did HE manage to get into mine?). When it was his turn he just looked my way and said,

'I'm beginning to find Jude quite interesting...'

Have been hearing him say this (in head) all evening – like music to my ears. No… my soul. No… my heart.

Perhaps my new look (glasses) is having an effect on him.

Yeah, know he just snogged Libs – trying to blot this out.

No chance am telling him there's no Bob now, not while it's having this effect.

Oren brought me back down to earth as we were leaving when he mentioned that Maisie's funeral was next Fri, and would I like to come.

Said would think about it.

He said he'd like me to, and kind of patted my shoulder. Thought he was gonna hug me, but Reuben appeared from nowhere, and the convo went something like:

R: Oh yeah, what's all this unusually physical behaviour in aid of then Oren?

O: Errrr… I was just trying to get into Jude's…

R: (*Interrupting.*) …knickers?

O: …shoes.

Oren, ignoring Reuben's remark went on to explain about Maisie and how he knew I'd got close to her and how he suspected I might be upset.

Was Reuben jealous that Oren touched my arm?

Hope so.

Shall I go to funeral? Will it help or make it worse?
D test on Mon… will current state of mind cause me to fail?

Sun 13 Feb

Sermon on 'the heart of Christ'. Was sitting within 2 metre radius of Fax, so learnt that earthworms have 5 hearts… poor them.

At Mike's for scrumptious Sunday roast.

We (err… I) talked til end of *EastEnders* omnibus when Jane, his wife, joined us in the kitchen to update us on events in the Square.

She's nice too. Normal. SC&O. Cool.

1st time since JimDream that felt genuinely understood. He'd had a similar thing happen back along, due to some kinda TV documentary re Jesus and how his resurrection was all invented crap. Had same effect on him… lost his faith. Couldn't wait to hear how he'd pulled through… but he said it was a long slow process – that there're no magic wands etc.

He ended by saying that his aim wasn't to convince me that God was real… it was something I had to discover for myself. Also that God was waiting for me with open arms, like in story of Prodigal Son…

I cried, a lot.

7:34 pm Really evil smell in room – no idea where source lies. Me? Will have shower…

Just out of shower and found card pushed under door – is from Libs (hand-made). Is 'Good Luck' card, for tomorrow's test.

Mum would shred or burn it if it fell into her holy hands… is full monty – black cat, horseshoes, 4-leaf clover etc.

Ought to forgive Libs now – lot of effort went into card – she loves me still…

Have to admit – for few secs really thought that card might be early V Day card… from my love. No such luck (said v quietly so Mum can't hear).

V late Thought: if Jesus is real… hope he comes again during the night, so don't have to do D test tomorrow…

Valentine's Day

5:21 am

Daft time to be awake – thoughts of crashing into cars/pedestrians/much-loved family pets etc racing around head.

Keep forgetting Maisie's dead… is hard not to cry each time I remember, so usually do.

7:46 am Soooo want to pass. So want my own novelty keyring (such as that cool monkey one from Coco Pops offer) to fiddle with at pub… want to be able to use 'car problems' as an excuse for being late to something… want to be able to give that little courteous wave to fellow drivers when they let me pass etc.

WANT TO DRIVE A CAR!!! Is this too much to ask?

Post-test Failed. Examiner (female) had to use her brakes to prevent what she THOUGHT would be a collision on mini-roundabout, about 1 min into test.

Equation: No V Day cards + failing D test in humiliating fashion = major depression.

Just watched 4 solid hrs of 'nothing' telly.
Last batch of adverts were killers – one for animal insurance, featuring piccies of abandoned puppies, made me cry.
Sob.
Wail.
Could life GET any sadder?

Post-F&Ferret Pals tried to cheer me up… didn't work. Passing 1st time is the trend with these guys… ought to chuck them and only make friends with people who can't drive, and who never will drive, EVER. Would feel secure then.

To detract from driving/V day card talk, told them about how you can get £300 toward advertising your pet, if you insure it and it gets lost. Reuben mentioned it might be worth us getting free cat from RSPCA, insuring it, then accidentally losing it on purpose… assume he was joking. Mind you…

Shame is no such thing as 'uni-partner' insurance:

Just pay a small affordable sum each month, and we'll ensure that if, by the time you reach your final semester, you still haven't found your dream man, we'll give you £300 to help with the process – posters for the SU *noticeboard, flyers to stick under all rooms in halls, even an advert in your uni paper – perhaps to include a tasteful photo of yourself (policy covers full makeover)…*

Pity there're no adverts on TV selling hubbies – *This offer is* EXCLUSIVE *to* ChannelWed *– you* CAN'T *buy these in the stores… Order your very own husband from us today and we'll throw in* 100 *Highly Embarrassing and Inappropriate Wedding Speeches ABSOLUTELY FREE! Just dial this number with your credit card details and…*

You know how sleezy blokes order brides from abroad somewhere (Thailand?) well, shame Cns haven't caught on to this – have glossy catalogue full of fit Cn guys from all over the world…

Sexy Sas got 3 V Day cards, pricey-looking bunch of roses and box of chocs.

Why does V Day exist? Surely it causes more misery than pleasure?

Will visit Libs now – try to 'make friends' again – thank her for (evil) good luck card…

Back again… still no V Day card.

OK, so if I DO get an anonymous one, who might be the sender?…

Fax: Nope — *he's said before at BURP that he doesn't want a relationship at uni. Hmmmm.*
Duncs: Nope — *gave Lauren biggest geekiest card in history of geekie cards (also took her out for meal, bought her necklace, blah blah pukie blah).*
Oren: Nope — *he thinks am unsuitable to serve on BURP committee, so clearly hates my guts.*
Prof Carr: Poss — *he's pretty desperate.*
StiltonBreath: Poss — *is perhaps feeling guilty of being crap instructor, causing me to fail…*
Warden (of our halls — don't know actual name): Unlikely — *unless being woken up at 3 am-ish on more than one occasion by me and Libs getting back from Fusion and having to let us in is something that really turns him on (which would be strange as what he shouted at us were no 'sweet nothings' by any stretch of imagination).*

Hmmmmmm.

Things OK with Libs now. Finally agreed to order from stupid catalogue (Wonderbra) so she can get her deal or whatever, by way of an apology (for shouting/pushing/going ape). Likewise, she has GIVEN (not sold) me some of her joss sticks to help rid room of FOUL smell.

Had initially wondered if Reuben had been the mystery bloke in her room the night of the blackout… but she said just now that she'd only met Reuben on the day he came back to her room… hmmmmm.

Just paused from writing to you to cry… thoughts of Maisie, d test failure and abandoned puppies invaded mind yet again.

1st exam tomorrow… hope piddly revision effort pays off…

Tue 15 Feb

Came on this am (meaning it's that special TOM again). Relieved — is OK to cry about life's tragedies, but weeping brought on by TV adverts is not generally accepted behaviour, even for soppy lasses like moi. TOM lets me off hook — was all hormonal.

Post-exam: Not good. Didn't understand many of the questions, let alone know the answers.

Pancake tally:

Breakie, courtesy of ex-enemy Miss Young – 3 *(avec lots choc and banana).*
Lunch, courtesy of uni cooks/government?/myself (as will pay for in distant future) – 2
(avec lemon and sugar).
Tea (or 'dinner' if you're posh), courtesy of Jane (Mrs Chaplain) – 7 *(4 savoury, 2 sweet, then '1 for the road' on leaving…).*

Blame such pig-like gluttony on nerves re funeral on Fri/exams. Told Oren would go with him to funeral (he was at Mike and Jane's – they'd invited us all round for pancake-fest… turns out Mike is 'doing' funeral in Bymouth C of E – Oren asked him to).

Most of 'Romania team' were there, so got a bit more planning done – Mike has been there himself – told us cool stories about the country and stuff (out of the 5 of us going it's only Oren who's been there before).

All came back to my room for continued socialisation (couldn't stay at M&J's too late as their kid Jack had to get to bed – 8 students full of pancakes and wine are not sleep-inducing for a 4-yr-old, apparently).

Libs called by and stayed for a bit. Reuben had gone to Nazarene session, which was relief as wouldn't have wanted him to bump into Libs again.

During a lull in convo, Oren said to Libs,

'So, tell us all about Jude's new boyfriend… she doesn't seem all that keen to tell us about her Bob…'

Libs looked at me with a 'huh?' kind of expression on face.

Looked back at Libs with an 'if-you-love-me-you'll-go-along-with-this' expression on face.

She went along with it alright… told them Bob was heading for a 1st in biophysics, could speak 5 languages with ease, had done modelling in his year out, and was a gold-belt bungee jumper in his spare time.

Lauren queried this, saying that I'd said Bob was doing sport science. Libs then lowered her voice and explained that Bob is, in fact, doing 2 degrees simultaneously… but it's not something he likes to shout about, so if we could all just keep it between ourselves…

You know when you dig a little hole, intending to cover it up again… but then you don't, and find yourself digging deeper
and deeper,
and deeper…?!

Post-bedtime read Aged 15, Vic Becks was 'porky'… her dance teacher said she'd have to put her on a CRANE and FLY her onto stage, as she was so FAT!

Perhaps is hope for me yet then.

Fri 18 Feb

10:46 am

Have actually done oodles of revision over past 2 days, thus no letters for you.

Couldn't face another exam like that 1st one, so put head down and crammed, big-style. Has helped a bit, but yesterday's exam still a bit iffy.

No exam today, but funeral this aft.

Was having a go at Libs on Weds re all that stuff she said about 'Bob', and asked exactly how I was supposed to get myself out of this enormous hole. She pointed out that it was ME who was the big fat liar… she was just helping. Huh.

Thurs am found note from Libs stuck to my door (she left at 5 am for camping trip with some mates… only she would think of camping in Feb):

Jude doll
Here are your options re Bob:
1] Tell them he's died in tragic bungee-jumping accident.
2] Tell them he's dumped you coz you're a bad snogger.
3] Tell them the truth – that you made him up coz you're such a loser and can't get a real boyfriend.
Big snogs,
Libs

Huh. Will deal with her later… re above note, and the fact that her joss sticks aren't clearing room of this pong…

Post-funeral Didn't cry. Not coz wasn't sad beyond words over her death, but coz all cried out already – no tears left.

Service bit was good.

OK, so Mike didn't know her, but then not many people did. He said some comforting stuff re God and love. Only a handful of people there anyway – Oren, his mum, couple of other rellies who looked like they didn't really want to be there but felt obliged...

Turns out that Oren's had to sort out funeral and stuff related to her will etc, as his dad's not around (son of Maisie) and his mum's... well... not really up to it. Quite a frail lady – looked v sad – wondered if it was coz of Maisie, or if she always looked that way. Well, with Maisie as a mother-in-law...

Guess that's why Oren's always felt so responsible for his gran.

Had to speak with Oren at the wake (in church hall) as Mike busy being chaplain, and didn't know anyone else.

He totally freaked me out by saying he knew all about the 'Tate' thing. Turns out he used to hang out with him a bit when they were 1st yrs as they're on the same course. Tate took HIM to Ethan's... then Oren tried to take him to BURP/church, but no joy.

They (O&T) had been chatting at end of a lecture the day after I'd been with Tate. Tate mentioned his 'no-go' date... Oren soon realised he was talking about me. Tate said that just as things were getting interesting in my room, he had a txt telling him to go back to house immediately due to an emergency. Reluctantly, he'd left me and gone back... only to find all his housemates still out, except for one, who was fast asleep in bed and, on being woken up, knew nothing of the txt, or any emergency.

Oren said he'd gathered I was 'a bit under the influence' that night (the phrase 'well-bladdered' would be more fitting), and thought I ought to know what had happened. He ALSO said that his convo with Tate HAD influenced him when he'd been helping choose new BURP com at Xmas, but that maybe he misjudged me...

Looking back, think this was where I was supposed to say that he HAD misjudged me, and prove myself to be worthy of the title of SocSec...

but didn't.

Was too overjoyed at still being virgin.

At same time quite pee-ed off at Oren – he must think I'm an easily manipulated slut. Great. That explains a lot. But why should he care who I go out with? Just checking up on his BURP-flock I guess.

He gave me a lift back, and as was getting out of the car, said:

'Errrr... I think Maisie would have wanted you to have this.'

He reached over to back seat. Had quick visions of some kind of jewellery, that would turn out to be worth loads, and would sort me out financially for life…

He handed me the Radox (lavender) I'd given her the other day as a pressie.

Got big lump in throat – missed her all over again… the crazy bubble-bath-obsessed old woman.

Oren didn't know what to say. Nor did I.

Then asked if he could drop me at Abby's instead… he did.

Burst into Abby's, just about managed to hold tears back. Asked if was OK for me to have bath (there are baths in halls, but are bit grim). Went straight up, ran taps… and my waterworks went into action also. Wasn't all cried out after all. Kept hearing Maisie have a go at Radox for jumping on the phone, or having a go at us students… she must have been so lonely. Did I really do all I could for her? Did anyone?

Poured Radox in liberally and got in. V hot – just how I like it.

Think was crying for my nan too – still miss her lots. Wish she was alive.

She lived in Harrow, in Honeypot Lane. Some hand driers in public loos are made in a factory in this lane, and have Honeypot Lane printed on them. Those hand driers always reminded me of Nan when I was little. If we called at motorway services for loos, me and Abby would always get excited if we checked out the hand driers and found our nan's lane on them. She was famous, in our teeny eyes. Always thought that this was why she told so many W the Pooh stories – he liked honey, after all.

S'pose Radox will always remind me of Maisie. It's good to remember, isn't it?

So is Maisie free now? Is dying freedom? Does she know the truth NOW, or did she miss the truth when it was offered to her during her life?

You will know the truth and the truth will make you free. It SOUNDS good, but is still out of my reach. Am still lost.

I hate death.

Mind you, life stinks too, at times.

Me? Locquacious?

Sat 19 Feb

Early

Got bad cold. Nose runs all the time… need to buy more tissues – soft ones (have delicate nose).

Don't feel like going to BURP this eve, but am supposed to be officially introducing myself as SocSec, and asking for ideas for trips etc for next semester.

Only trip can focus on right now is another trip to uni Dr to cure me of evil stinking cold.

Late BURP involved Lydia giving a talk on 'gifts' – how it's good to know what your gifts are so you can use them to the fullest etc. We went into small groups (like it would be possible to do anything different) and had to say what we thought each other's gifts were…

Lydia was easy – leading, teaching, encouraging… need I go on?
Sim things came up for rest of group.

Then it came to me, and there was a lengthy silence.
No one could think of anything.
I am gift-less.
I couldn't think of anything.
Then Oren said I was good at making people laugh.
He loves to mock me – makes him feel superior I guess.

At prayer time we had work to do – some kind of serious prob at Oren's home church re Romania trip – if not solved, trip might be cancelled.

After prayer, overheard Duncs and Reuben have slightly heated discussion – Duncs said the trip must be in God's will, that's why the devil's attacking it – so it WILL go ahead now we've prayed about it.

Reuben said that if the trip was part of God's overall plan, he would bless it, and such problems with the church might indicate he's NOT blessing it… blah blah Cn-jargon blah doctrine blah like I care blah.

Duncs was fairly irritating all eve – just back from some rally with American evangelists – all name-it-and-claim-it/health-and-wealth stuff.

Had just hinted I wasn't joining those who were going on to F&Ferret, due to cold, when Duncs announced, for all to hear,

'NO Jude, you DON'T have a cold – you are in perfect health – now let's hear you CONFESS it…'

Replied with, 'No Duncs, look – see the snot pouring from my nose, my pockets stuffed with icky tissues, my red swollen eyes… hear my husky voice… smell the minging breath of an ill person… I HAVE A BAD COLD, AM V ILL AND FEEL CRAP… that's just the way it is!'

Ha! He left me well alone after that.

Had almost escaped when Sas queried why Bob didn't come to BURP. I said he was well-involved with a church… a bit outside of Bymouth – they probably wouldn't have heard of it, blah lie blah.

Think she fell for it – is a well-known fact that there ARE other Cns at uni who've never been to BURP coz they're well 'in' with a church. Perhaps you are at Bymouth Uni somewhere Bob, just not at BURP – must do a tour of all local churches sometime…

11:45 pm Too ill to revise – will read in bed instead.

Early (1:12 am) When Vic 1st shared a house with the other soon-to-become-Spice-gals… she was the only one who'd lock the bathroom door. By the end of their time there, she too felt able to pee in front of her fellow housemates.

Arghhhh!
Will it be like that when am in student house in Sept?
Yuk!

Sun 20 Feb

Post-church

Just when you think it's all over… sermon was also on our 'gifts' – bah!
Minister and Lydia must plot these things together, just to humiliate me…
Still in dark about my gifting… can think of areas in which am NOT gifted:

1] *Eyebrow plucking*
2] *Dieting*
3] *Pulling (a future hubbie)*

4] *'Discerning' probs/needs of others (like my Sis)*
5] *Sussing out truth about life*
6] *Blowing nose in non-grim fashion in front of my love*

Still infected with cold of the decade.

Mike says I can babysit Jack sometime for some extra cash – whoo-hoo! Saying that, let's hope 4-yr-olds are easier than 2-yr-olds, eh?

Post-cookies Was just getting into bed when Mr NextDoor called round to see how I was (have been complaining to him re cold non-stop last few days, poor bloke). Asked if I wanted to come to his room as had a few mates over about to watch some film (can't recall name – prob quite a loud/rude/violent one).

So pulled on clothes again (which had done BEFORE answering door, just in case you thought otherwise) and dragged myself and my cold next door.

His mates were OK, if a bit goth-like (actually thought one of them WAS M Manson). One bloke had even brought over some biccies... that he'd MADE! Was so impressed with such a 'Waltons-style' effort that tucked in with gusto (also, scoffing my face makes cold seem more distant – honest!).

By the time the film started, was feeling well-mellow. All feelings of hatred toward all germs responsible for cold melted away... were replaced with thought that these were the best bunch of people on planet... this was the best evening of my life so far etc.

Next thing I knew, was being ushered out of room by OREN... hadn't even realised he was there! Wasn't too bothered tho – so tired... so happy...

So STONED, according to Oren!

He took me outside for fresh air. After a bit things felt more normal... cold had mysteriously returned to plague me again. He explained that some biscuits that are 'student-made' are full of hash...

Hash cookies!

Not sure how long it's gonna take me to come to terms with oddness of this eve.

On walking back to my room, he asked if things were serious between me and Bob. Found myself saying they were, before even realised lips were moving. Perhaps still under effects of cookies, perhaps just wanted him to report back to Reuben, or wanted him off my case – to butt out of my personal life for a change – being interested is one thing, but he's just nosy.

Mon 21 Feb

9:43 am

Still can't believe last night...

Am a student that takes drugs, a junkie, a pot-head...

Does it count if you just eat biccies laden with the stuff, and don't actually smoke anything? Hmmmmm. Sorry Bob – won't let it happen again. OK, so not sure what life's all about yet, but sure it's not about escaping reality for the evening... still, was nice to forget cold for a bit...

4:25 pm Just back from exam – not 2 bad, but suddenly inspired to do non-stop revision for last one on Weds. Will pop into town now, then make start on it when get back...

6:19pm Managed to get 2 FREE mags to read, from Somerfield and Superdrug! Has been great to have complimentary *heat* mag... but have read it enough times now... am only left wanting more... budget doesn't allow. Like to browse S'field one to choose which snacks to buy next, and to learn the vitamin content of smoked haddock etc.

S'drug is all make-up and stuff – it kills time.

Someone at door...

Was Libs. Wanted to know if Wonderbra had arrived (yes. Any good? Nope... turned out had ordered cheap imitation of Wonderbra by mistake – 'Superboobs' or sim). This now means we can split her 'introducing a friend' voucher of £20 – both choose something for a tenner (just in case you didn't do GCSE Maths or anything, Bob).

Have both spent time pouring over catalogue but not sure what to get. Took me long enough to choose the 1st time. Huh. Her and her cunning money-saving ideas...

Bed now covered in mags/catalogue... no room for textbooks/revision – what a shame.

Post-read

Dear Vic (hope it's OK to be on such familiar terms, but feel I know you v well now I've reached chapter 8 of your book),

You had little boobs as a teenager (which I still am, just). Did you ever try a Wonderbra or cheap imitation thereof? Did it work for you?

You've got great boobs now – are they real? Is there any chance I'll develop such boobs in the near future, or is this it?

You know when girls complain that blokes, when talking to them, stare only at their boobs? I've never had that problem. Bet you have tho, eh?!

With me they don't even try... I must have a face that yells, 'I've got no boobs.'

I'm a 36A and stuck with it.

Any advice?

Big hugs... lovin' ya book,

Jude

Tue 22 Feb

10:18 am

Just woken up. Had lie in as no exam today. Think will just

Oh, fire alarm. It goes off now and then, esp when some plonk fries sausages or sim at 4 am... then fire brigade turn up and evacuate us all until they've given us the all clear. Is a pain, but some of those Bymouth firemen... Phwoarrrrrrr!

Can just about read the notice taped to back of door from here (due to super-specs!)... includes all we have to do in the event of a fire... like THAT's ever going to happen!

Hang on, someone at door...

Was Libs, coughing like crazy – assumed she'd caught my cold (mine nearly all gone now). Before could open door she yelled at me not to... in between coughs she said there was a fire. Peeked through the spy hole – she was bent over double coughing/choking/in pain? Said I didn't believe her, and was coming out. Again she begged me not to,

'Not unless, cough, you want to suffer, cough, from smoke inhalation, cough cough, like me, cough, babe... you'll have to jump out the window, cough...'

Then she ran off... huh?

Alarm still going... am still in my room, but can't see or feel any smoke or heat... we had a fire drill in Freshers' Wk – don't remember anything about jumping out the window tho... where's she gone anyway?

Hang on – smoke... under the door... yes, it's

Lots later You won't BELIEVE what happened earlier! Yeah – saw smoke coming under the door – lots of it. When it began to fill the room it occurred to me that this fire was real, and jumping out of the window was no longer a stupid idea. Could just about hear some people outside door running past, shouting and screaming, 'It's huge!' 'Run!' 'Let's get outa here!' etc.

Was enuf to convince me. Opened window. Twas a long way down. Looked down, only to see Libs on the ground under my window, beside a mattress, urging me to jump.

Life flashed before me (didn't take long – wasn't v exciting) and aimed for safety of mattress, after a quick glance back at my soon-to-be-frazzled room that was almost full of smoke by now.

Landed safely on target – managed not to break glasses (they fell off tho). Leapt up to hug Libs, thanking her for saving my life etc.

While doing so, was accosted from behind – a large pair of arms lifted me up, whilst another pair of arms chucked a bag over my head, putting me in total darkness. Screamed a bit, but sensed this was no mugging in the real sense as Libs wasn't exactly attempting to help… or had they got her too, I wondered.

Was bundled into nearby car, which then took off at great speed. Managed to prise bag off head with ease, only to find Jon at the wheel, with Lydia and Reuben also in the car!

Guess what… they took me to the Driving Centre, where I discovered I was booked in for another test.

Guess what… I PASSED!!!!!

Turns out wacky old Libs had been ringing for a cancellation ever since I failed… feeling certain I'd pass it next time. She'd burnt paper in the toaster to set off the alarm, then her and Oren had pumped smoke under my door – using a smoke cannister owned by Nazarene!

Must've just missed firemen – just as well… would've been far too much excitement in one day.

This has truly been one of the best days of my life!

1stly, I didn't die in flames, which at one point I really thought was poss. 2ndly, I CAN DRIVE A CAR AT LAST!

Also… oh, someone at door…

Hmmmm. No one there on opening door, just a v small badly wrapped package, containing the most fab funky monkey keyring ever! Rather like the one featured in the C Pops offer (still haven't eaten any of them since) but larger and cooler... this tops it all! OK, so don't have a car, but who cares... one day...

Guess is from Libs – she's such a doll.

Wed 23 Feb

Have been on a high all am. Am a person who is qualified to drive an automobile... no more StiltonBreath! Also chuffed that my pals cared so much for me that they went to all that trouble to get me to the test centre... aaahhhhhh.

Good mood allowed me to revise all morning so far, as exam this aft (last one – yip yip skippie doo dar!).

Post-exam Not too bad. Assume have passed these exams, but not confident of fab marks... ho hum... no worries – at least I can DRIVE!!

Good mood also inspired me to diet. Think have put on most (all?) of what lost due to low-carbing.

Will start by getting fit – will do one of my sad exercise videos...

No good. As soon as she started talking about stomach crunches, started dreaming of that strawberry-crunch-type cereal, which is my fave, which haven't had in ages. Will pop out and get some now... then start the shrinking process tomorrow.

Back again... saw Fax in cereal aisle of Tesco (he's more of a porridge man, I observed) who said that Oren and Caroline are ENGAGED!
Am not best pleased... seems v sudden... what's the rush?
Will phone Sas... she's gonna LOVE this...

Didn't answer (left msg on voicemail tho).

Why would Oren pick HER of all people? Is bad enuf spending a whole 10 mins in her company... but a lifetime – grim. Ah, phone... will be Sas...

Hmmmmm. Was Oren. Said I was too 'loquacious' for my own good, then hung up. Huh? What planet?
How DARE he call me 'loquacious'.
What's it mean, anyhow, and why am I it?
Oh, phone again...

Was Sas – no, she hadn't got my voicemail msg – she was ringing to congratulate me on passing d test.

Have spent 6½ mins exactly pondering on the above madness... and have now sussed it out – always get BURPers phone nos from my scribbled list on noticeboard. Has been known for me to read the wrong line and dial the person below the person I intended to ring, by mistake. Still with me?

Basically, rang Oren instead of Sas... leaving something resembling the following on HIS voicemail:

'Hi Sas it's me, Jude.
You'll NEVER guess who's just got engaged – Oren! Yeah – I know!
Like – durrrrrrrr – she's a boring, pretentious snob!
He's SO off his head...'
etc.

Whoops. Bad move.

Ideas for torturing people who use words they know full-well I don't know the meaning of:

1] *Make eat whole dictionary – one of the big ones, with no seasoning whatsoever.*
2] *Make quote, from memory, all the NON-famous bits from Shakespeare's plays...
each error = 10 mins enforced Cliff Richard via walkman.*
3] *Make them try to pray without using the word 'just', failure resulting in eating dictionary and listening to Cliff AT SAME TIME!!*

Thur 24 Feb

9:42 am

Lydia just rang – she's also keen to shift weight (hers). She read a bit out to me from a mag, re weighing yourself... it said how you need to rid yourself of all poss excess weight beforehand... such as:

clothes
water (from shower/bath)
jewellery (inc that from body piercings)
pee/poo (go to loo 1st)
earwax
snot
belly button fluff
air (exhale a lot)

Wow – and I thought weighing myself 1st thing in the am was clever!

Am looking forward to chillin' out today... no exams, no d lessons, no hassle...

hold it, door...

1:17 pm Arrggghhhhhhhh! NIGHTMARE city!
Was my parents – yeah, really!
Turned out Mum had mentioned it on the phone the other day... when wasn't giving her 100% attention (more like 14%). Huh!
Dad's been fairly quiet, as always. He's asked questions now and then. He went to uni long ago – think he knows what goes on, like what REALLY goes on. Mum went to Bible College and hasn't the foggiest.

Unsurprisingly her verbal diarorea
diahorea
dhioreah
squits... has covered her opinion on the well-kept campus gardens through to her opinion on my badly kept room.

Grrrrr... my room! On entering it, happened to be burning Libs' joss sticks – one final attempt to ditch the stench that is 'my room'. Mum went straight for them, grabbed them with both hands (ouch!) and chucked out window (that, fortunately, was open), with,

'Drugs... not something we approve of Jude – it's obviously "right" that we came today.'

Before I'd had chance to offer them a cuppa (felt like something a bit stronger personally), she was off again – this time it was Oscar's books (which have been here so long they're part of furniture and don't really notice them)... say no more.

After some explaining (from me) she calmed down a bit.

They're now having lunch in town – said would meet them, so best go now...

Post-tour They've just left – whoo-hoo!
Am so knackered – parents are tiring creatures.
After the yawnyawn tour of the town, Dad said he'd meet us later, while Mum said it'd be 'fun' if me and her went shopping.

Muuummmmmmm... sssssssssssshhhhhooooopppiing.

Nope – however hard I tried, was impossible to bring those 2 words together.

Have avoided shopping with her since was about 10, and for v good reasons.

Didn't want a scene tho, so agreed.

Started in fogey-type department store, of Mum's choice. She selected a handful of clothes she deemed 'suitable' FOR ME and forced ME to try them on.

Yuk.

Told her it wasn't really my type of thing (no idea whose type of thing they are)... she finally agreed to come with ME to clothes shops more... 'suitable' for students.

Grabbed a handful of cool stuff in TopShop and headed for changing rooms (she was paying after all). Left her looking awkward, wedged in tight between a rack of un-Mum-like underwear, and a gaggle of Kylie wannabes... loudly discussing what style of hipster thongs would best suit their tiny rears...

Panicked when came back... to find her gone!
Assumed that she'd:

1| *Got bored and gone to find Dad.*
2| *Gone to complain to the manager about the effect their underwear was having on young impressionable girls.*
3| *Been abducted by aliens (wishful thinking).*

Then, she burst out of changing rooms... dressed in boot-cut jeans and a gypsy top... with an unquestionable 'ta-daaar!'

Never seen her so excited!

She bought ALL the clothes I'd tried on, AND what she tried on! We spent the rest of our expedition in TopMan (where she got 2 tops and some trendy jeans for Dad), River Island (skirt for Abby) and D Perkins (belt for herself).

We ended up at Abby's for tea. Abby and I shared a knowing glance when Mum read Nat his bedtime *Teletubby* book and said that Laa-Laa and 'Poo' loved each other very much...

Parents then went home. Despite bad start, was comforting to see them. Mum seemed to lighten up, which was refreshing.

Do miss them – they've made me who I am (the good and the bad)... I love 'em for it.

Stayed at Abby's for the eve – chick-flick, Pringles (Texacan) and dip – sorted.

At one point she said how much Nat adored me, and how I made such a good auntie. Was touched. Wanted to say how she was a good sister, but just gave her big hug instead... a hug that was long overdue.

Wonder if being a good auntie could be described as my 'gifting'.

Maisie wouldn't have approved of Oren's choice of life-partner.
Wonder how much Caz'll spend on her wedding dress.

Wonder if Mum will be as generous as she was today when we shop for MY w dress.

Oh poo – had meant to ask Abby what 'loquacious' meant...

Fri 25 Feb

Just glanced up at 'stress levels' chart – can't see 'surprise visit from one's parents whilst residing at university' on it... will add it in, giving it 3 billion points... from hereon in I vow to listen to every word Mum says on the phone (hard as this may be) to eliminate possibility of this EVER happening again.

Have traced source of foul smell in room – ½ eaten cheese and Marmite roll stuffed between bed and desk, merrily decomposing... assumedly deposited by GremlinNephew the other wk.

5:46 pm Just been to Abby's with Libs. Surprised Libs agreed to come as she's tended to put off going there with me. Prob coz I told her about Abby's famous lasagne (that we had 3rds of). How anyone can make spinach taste heavenly is one of life's mysteries...

Libs got on with Abby OK. Being an arty-farty lass she was impressed with Abby's plates.

Errr... might not have told you this yet. My talented sis is a painter of plates – she buys plain white plates, paints her own designs onto them, then cooks them in the oven, or whatever, and hey presto...

Try not to be jealous over her talents, but can't help think how fab t'would be to be creative in this way.

As it stands, my tombstone will read: 'Here lies Jude Singleton... she didn't do plates.'

Tried to get Libs to give Eve a cuddle several times, but she declined, saying that babies aren't her thing. At one point, Abby had popped to shops (Nat wanted more *Bob the Builder* yoghurts) and I was helping Nat with his lunch in the kitchen. Eve woke up and started to yell, in a kinda 'pick-me-up-NOW' fashion.

Was about to go when the noised ceased to be. Peeked into the lounge, only to see Libs holding Eve, gently rocking her, whispering into her ear. Then she started to cry quietly (Libs, not Eve). Wanted to say something, but couldn't. Was as if they'd both been transported to... somewhere else, for just a minute or 2. Frozen in time.

Then they came back, as Libs turned to me and handed Eve over, adding in a bad Scottish accent:

'Will ya look at Mamma Liberty here, getting all broody over the Baba...'

She then darted off to the loo.

On her return neither of us made any mention of the incident, mainly coz we were distracted by Nat, who appeared to be threatening to eat Eve's left ear unless his BtheB yoghurt arrived pronto.

Kids.

Remembered to thank her for that monkey keyring (at last)... turned out she knew nothing about it tho... odd. From Reuben then? His 1st move? Also remembered to ask her what 'loquacious' meant. She smiled a wicked smile, then looked all serious and said it was hard to define, and would be best if I looked it up in the dictionary (why didn't I think of this before? Am a student who doesn't use a dictionary... is that allowed?!).

Day ended with a Romania planning mtg. Went OK.

Oren's church all sorted money-wise. Think he's avoiding me. He invited the team to his for a pre-trip meal, this Fri eve. Without looking me in the eye he mumbled something about Bob being invited too, if he 'wasn't too busy being perfect'.

Huh?

Sat 26 Feb

Located dictionary...
Loquacious: talkative.

Huh.

Armed with the full knowledge of the insult he had thrown at me, found myself unable to look HIM in the eye at BURP. DIDN'T agree to keep an eye out for the pricey silver adidas watch he'd lost, that he kept on about (he should check Cazzer's head – you could lose an armoured tank in there…).

Lydia had flu, so Mike stood in and led BURP… told us some more stuff about Romania and its history… all a bit scary really – must I go?

Told us about his work as chaplain, how he particularly sees his mission as helping students who are struggling as Cns – who've lost the plot a bit and need help and support etc.

Said he got his buzz from seeing them recover/grow.

Wondered if I'd ever give him that buzz, or just be one of the few 'strugglers' he'd eventually give up on, writing off as a failure.

He ended up by saying a bit about how we are all prone to judge others, especially our fellow Cns. Glanced over at Oren – hoped he'd listen intently and feel guilty for his childish/judgemental name-calling antics. Mike said he's known Cns to categorise other Cns into groups – like Cns who are super-spiritual and can do no wrong, Cns who are quite worldly and not so committed etc.

Said we're all perfect Cns in the making – none of us are fully cooked yet. People aren't always what they appear to be. To write another Cn off as being a 'backslider' or a 'holy of holies' isn't always the fairest and kindest way to treat them. Just as we hope that others will allow us to change and grow as Cns, sometimes getting it right, sometimes messing up… we must treat our Cn buds (and non-buds) accordingly.

Hmmmm.

Does this mean my Pringle flaves chart goes out the window?
Huh – a lot of hard work went into that.

Borrowed a book off Mike on Romania – am looking at it now (errr… looking at the piccies that is – am a student who's had enuf of words by 11:42pm).

Some fab scenery – can just see Reuben and I, hand-in-hand, standing on the beach at Constanta, at sunset… and as the last rays of sun trickle slowly into the water, he says:

'Jude, my love… will you marry me?'

Or perhaps high up in the beautiful Carpathian Mountains would be better – we could escape our duties for an afternoon, take a picnic there and enjoy our 1st kiss... and THEN he'd propose.

Or... ahhh, just spotted where we'll be based – is nowhere near the above 2 potential marriage proposal sites... ho hum. Is, however, in the region of Transylvania... where Dracula comes from – great.

Will pop down to Libs... haven't seen her since yesterday at Abby's – really want to know why she cried yesterday, and if I can help...

Back again No joy with the above plan – she asked me not to bring it up again. Hmmmm.

Whilst rummaging in her wardrobe in search of a top to borrow for Oren's dinner-party-wot-not, came across a pricey-looking silver men's adidas watch.

Oren's.
The one he said he'd lost.
So, Oren's been in Lib's wardrobe.

So, must have been Oren in her room that night when she hid her bloke from me... he was in her wardrobe.

Why? Why would Oren cheat on Caz, then get engaged to her?
Isn't he supposed to be the classic S&V flave Cn who never sets a foot wrong?

OK, so Reuben's snogged her too – but he's... he does that type of thing. But OREN?

With LIBS?

Didn't say anything to Libs – left it in wardrobe, to rot for all eternity.

As if things weren't bad enuf... just got a txt from Lydia – Reuben's quitting the trip – for Nazarene-related reasons.

Baahhhhh! Argghhhhhhh! Nooooooo!!

Ode to Reuben:

OK *my love, so you're in a band,*
big thrills.
What about us?
Romania could have been our promise land.
You could have promised to be mine,
at last.

We'd get married fast,
have loads of mini-mes and -yous.
What a blast.

Sun 27 Feb

9:41 am

Depressed re Reuben's backing out of trip (and whole Oren/Libs thing). Just read on p148 of textbook that the very ACT of smiling can cause you to feel happy... tried it, but just felt v geeky.

Am crying now... but this is OK as Vic Becks cries on more than one page of her book.

Strange how depression lays a kind of foundation for further depression/stress to rest upon... now find myself stressing about how will explain Bob's absence at Oren's big do on Friday... any ideas?

Don't feel like church... will go anyway – perhaps twill take my blues away.

Post-church Huh. Foundation now built upon to extent that has evolved into small house. Visiting speaker started by asking us to spend a few minutes chatting with someone we don't know – introducing ourselves and saying where we are in our 'walk with God'. HATE it when they do that. Why? What are they trying to achieve? Stress city? If so, they win. Is a bit like when someone leading BURP puts me on the spot and asks me to lead the prayer time... like WHY couldn't they do it themselves? Aren't they qualified? Did I ASK to lead prayer? Do I LOOK like someone who's itching to lead prayer? Huh? Do I?

Stress chart for Cns (all Cns who lead stuff, please note):

Being forced to introduce oneself to total stranger.
500 points
Being asked to 'lead the prayer time'.
400 points
Having to give one's yawnyawn testimony (unless one has an exciting one re drugs, prostitution etc).
300 points
Having to read out Bible passage with long unpronounceable names in it.
200 points
Taking over as OHP operator at the last minute, when you've never done it before and

are therefore prone to getting each acetate upside-down/back-to-front etc.
100 points (but escalates up to region of 500, depending on how badly you do it and how many people chuckle and point)

Whilst babysitting No, not Nat... Jack (Mike's son). Is harder than had expected. 4-yr-olds are a funny breed. Not as threatening as 2-yr-old gremlins, not as noisy as 0-yr-old babes... but still, not quite yet human, if that makes sense.

Had thought that his 2 yr advantage on Nat would make him more intelligent, and therefore easier to deal with. Hadn't bargained on him using such intelligence against me... have so far been up at least 100 times since tucked him up in bed... glass of water... loo... supper... teeth... loo again... biscuit (and therefore teeth, again, naturally)... lost his robot under duvet... more water... found robot...

you get the picture.

Nooooooooo – he's calling me again... no, hang on... that's someone calling me through the front door...

Was Libs!(She's gone now.) Thought it bizarre at 1st coz

1] *she can't stand kids and*
2] *she doesn't even know Mike!*

Turns out she DOES know Mike... didn't just track me down telepathically because of our oh-so-strong friendship, nice as that would have been. She's met Mike at Fusion a couple of times before – thinks he's cool, can't understand why he's into all this God-stuff etc. She came here after her shift at Fusion as she'd seen Mike there this eve... and he told her I was here.

And that's not ALL he told her... he only went and said there was a place going on the Romania trip...

she's only gone and said she'll come!!

Big hmmmmmmms all round. Didn't know what to say when she told me. Really don't want her to come – she won't get on with being surrounded only by foreigners and Cns... she'll embarrass me by acting all non-Cn.

When she saw the look of horror on my face, she began to cry.

Like... real crying, where you sob and bawl and break down in a tearful heap on the sofa.

Then she told me all...
about the abortion.

It was when she was 16.

Kept thinking of stuff to say, like, 'It's OK, it's all in the past,' or, 'You were young – it wasn't your fault.' But words just wouldn't come out.

Held her tight – she held me back, even tighter... and the tears kept coming.

Still not thrilled about her coming on Rom trip, but at least it kinda makes more sense now... she wants to do 'something positive' for some kids who've been abandoned by their parents... no prizes for guessing why...

Am finding it hard to put the 2 together

Libs... and abortion.

Libs = funny/open/fun... abortion = secret/scary/tragic.

She told me the story in depth, but don't feel much like relaying it to you right now, coz

1] *you're a bloke, and*

2] *it sends shivers down my spine... can still hear her sobbing in my head... guess she's still sobbing in her room now.*

Fri 4 Mar

During breakie

Oren's meal this eve. Still haven't told him Bob's not coming.

During *Hollyoaks* She's done it again! Libs just called by. On opening the door, couldn't help but notice that there was a guy attached to her. Soon became clear that it was more a case of her being attached to him... she presented him to me in a way that a hunter might do on catching a large bear...

'Here,' she declared, giving a smile which only Dry B normally brought to her lips.

'He's no gold-belt bungie-jumper, and can barely speak 1 language, let alone 5... but he's a champion liar... oh, and get this... he's called Bob! Don't thank me... no time...'

And off she went, leaving her catch writhing and helpless, looking like he might make a run for it at any time.

Was soooooo embarrassed. Didn't know what to say. Surely this would be taking things too far? The bear then grunted:

'What's in it for me?'

Found myself saying: 'Errrr... you pretend to be my... bloke, just for a couple of hours, at a dinner party thingy... and I'll... I'll buy you a drink after.'

He looked unsure, so added a Big Mac into the deal.

Bear: And a McChicken Sarnie, large fries and Fanta?
Me: Don't push it.
Bear: Look, do you want my services, or not?

Funny how he morphed from bear into professional escort in matter of seconds. Agreed to his demands. Am calling by his room on way to Oren's... he has been briefed on what to say and not to say...

WHAT AM I DOING?!

Post-meal I quit. Quit what? The Rom trip. Being SocSec. Pretending to be a Cn, life in general.

Dear Lydia,
I regret to inform you that I shall no longer be able to serve on the BURP committee in my capacity as social secretary. Please pass the job on to someone who actually cares.

Dear Fax,
Guess what? I'm not a Cn... I'm a big fat fake, who doesn't know one end of Mission Praise *from the other... who has no idea if God exists, and isn't sure if she cares either way.*

Dear Oren,
Stuff Romania. Stuff all your plans to put the world to rights during a 10-day stay in a country that looks like a pigs head. Stuff your pretentious dinner party. Stuff you.

OK – here are the things that were most stressful about the meal, in no particular order...

1] There was no booze to get us all giggly... thanks to Oren's views on alcohol.

2] Oren had adidas watch back on wrist. Means he's seen Libs again in last couple of days.

3] Caz there. They're still all engaged – she was all over him. Is not like I care if she gets hurt, so why does it bug me so that he's been seeing Libs behind her back?

(Libs busy tonight so not at meal, even tho now officially part of the team. Have been trying to persuade her to see counsellor re her... experience, tho not Oscar – someone real. She's not interested tho.)

4] Caz got on my nerves (she shouldn't have been there anyway – she's not going on trip). She started on to Jon about being a vege-burger...

'Tell me something, how come you eat fish? How is it not cruel to kill a fish, but cruel to kill a pig? How come you are fine with eating this trifle, when the main ingredient in the jelly is pork gelatine? Do you think that while cute little Babe the pig was terrified of becoming roast pork, he was all up for ending up as the bottom layer of a trifle?' and so on.

She also said how most lipstick contains fish scales... yuk! Jon made the mistake of saying how they'd recently got into green tea, and off she went again... 'Ahhh – how healthy – all those free radicals killing cancer and all. Thing is Jon, if you drink it while it's too hot, it will scald your throat. Over the years, this could cause oesophagal cancer. You just can't win. I don't know why you bother...'

5] As per our contract, Bob left straight after pud, for a debate he was chairing (the bear thought this bit up himself – he ought to go in for this kinda thing full-time). With him gone, it was just me... and all the couples. You don't know just how much you hate couples until you're stuck at a table full of them (well, 2 of them) when you're single. OK, so Bear/Bob hadn't been genuinely mine, but it was nice to have him by my side, didn't feel like such a... didn't feel so pathetic and unworthy, like I did when he left.

Oren n Caz... Lyd n Jon...
oh, and Jude.
Hate it when couples:

1] *Touch each other.*
2] *Give each other knowing glances or chuckle about jokes only they understand.*
3] *Use pet names.*

I WANT TO BE A COUPLE. Would like to think that when I am, won't make singletons feel like a pile of pants.

Are real male escorts expensive?

Do they do Cn escorts... who act as tho they dote on you, but at the same time as tho they're not sleeping with you, and won't be until you get married?

6] The food. Wasn't stressful in itself – all tasted v good – ate tons. Was me who got stressed, big-time...

My mum makes a smashing coronation chicken. Has been a fave of mine since the beginning of time… hadn't had it since been at uni. Then Oren serves it up as part of 1st course, along with other such salad-type dishes… all v homely and wholesome, but scrummy at the same time.

Everyone was all, 'Oooo Orrrennnn… this is soooooo nice… d'ya make it ya'self?' and it turned out he did. Don't ask me why, but this began to bug me.

He didn't think I was spiritual enough to be on the committee, he noses into my life, he 2-times his fiance, he didn't seem to want Bob to come to the meal (but then spent most of it chatting with him… hmmm) and NOW he's Jamie Oliver with knobs on… HUH!

During post-meal washing up, had to chuck some stuff in the kitchen bin. As did so, spotted an empty packet of 'Chicken delight' or sim in bin. Before stopping to think (like THAT was gonna happen), fished packet out of bin and held it in the air, with a triumphant, 'HA!… nice try Oren, but here's the evidence… you're a fake – bet you couldn't cook if you took a DEGREE in it!'

Everything stopped.

Except my heart, which pounded hard against my ribs (most uncomfortable due to overload of food in stomach). The others were all silently staring at me… me and the manky chicken mix packet… me and my red face… me and my angry red face…

At that moment, realised how much had let everything get to me. Had finally gone insane.

Jon then quietly said that he'd seen Oren make the chicken from scratch, and he'd used no packet mix… and even if he had, who cared?

Caz held Oren that little bit tighter, assumedly in case I attempted to stab him with the bread knife I'd been washing.

I ran.

Some things are too hard to explain. Wasn't sure I COULD explain anyway. All I know is that all this God/no-God stuff has got to me more than I'd thought, and added to the other things stressing me out… madness has arrived, it's official.

Oren's wet Marigolds are sitting on the desk in front of me… hard to storm out in dramatic fashion if have to remove washing-up gloves 1st, so didn't.

Can't sit staring at them any longer, like they're gonna give me some answers or something. Oh, for some answers. For the truth. For freedom, and all that stuff.

Going out now…

Back again Found myself at nearby park, on the swings. Don't remember walking there… have been in bit of a dream since leaving Oren's. Swings are great – make you feel young again. Young and carefree… not young and on edge of breakdown. Wonder if this is how Abby felt when she had her depression after Eve?

Had forgotten Reuben wouldn't be at meal (as he's no longer part of team). Had been looking forward to seeing his reaction to me and Bob… hoped it might push him into really considering me big-time. Haven't seen too much of him recently… rumour has it he's going out with… wait for it… a non-Cn, who's on his course, but am hoping it's based on false information.

If I had Reuben, everything would be OK. If I had God back, everything would be OK. So what do I want more? Hmmmmmm. God, I think. Sussing out God and meaning of life etc… that would be a good starting point. Without this am still lost.

Anyway, odd thing happened… all the above was knocking around in my head, then suddenly noticed there was a guy on swing next to me. It was v late, dark and cold… didn't really expect to have company, esp while on kiddies swings…

He was pretty hot.
He said 'hi' and I hi-ed him back.
His eyes were all deep and wise. He just looked at me for a while, which was kind of flattering… yet it wasn't really that kind of a look, more like he was sussing me out…

Him: Speak to him about it– he'd love that.
Me: Errrrr… who?
Him: God. Just tell him what you're thinking – where you're at… he'll understand.
Me: Urrmmmm… do I know you?
Him: Sort of… well, we've never actually chatted before, but… I've seen you around. Look, don't let things get to you so much. Don't make any rash decisions based on tonight… speak to God first. Got to go now… see ya…

And off he went… it was only as I watched him disappear into the shadows that I noticed how v tall he was – sure I would have remembered him if had seen him at BURP/church before... or was he another of Ethan's cult gang... or another male escort that Libs sent out to comfort me... not that she knew what went on this eve... unless someone told her... but how did any of them know about me making 'rash decisions'?

Kind of felt like if had chance to speak with SwingGuy at length, he'd have all the answers.

Right, am going to take his advice and talk to God, icky as it feels...

Did it. Wasn't so bad. Told him all. Didn't get a reply, but felt bit better. Did he hear? Is he there? Maybe.

Am taking it 1 step at a time from now on... will go on Rom trip, then will consider if want to continue with BURP when come back next semester. Won't make any big confessions to the others quite yet. Kind of want to give God one last chance – a final opportunity to reveal himself... if he fails, will quit him, BURP, church... the whole package. Need to know where I stand... stop being all 'phoney' like people in Catcher in the Rye (v boring book had to do for GCSE English, but making a lot more sense to me just recently).

A Powerpuff Girls send-off

Tues 8 Mar

5 assignments due in on Mon... good job have started them.
Well, 2 of them...

Libs told parents re Rom trip (didn't want to, but I made her) – they sent big cheque. She nearly tore it up, as per usual... but then figured we could use it when get out there, to buy more paint etc.

Oren will be well-chuffed (£100 on paint!). Hope he gives me some credit for encouraging Libs to come on trip...

Libs bizarrely excited re trip... hasn't done much to help 'those in need', says it'll be good for her. Wish I could muster up the same enthusiasm. Just wanna get it over with now. Want to get on with my life, see what direction it's gonna take.

Thur 10 Mar

Hmmmmm. 1 assignment completed, 3 now in progress... 1 remains untouched (is on humanistic-existential therapies).

Lydia just rang – Jon's now got her flu, and can't run Alpha this eve. She wants another Cn there to help her...

she wants me.

Gave all the excuses that were believable, and even some that weren't (think she got suspicious when I said I was working hard on my assignments and couldn't spare an evening off... she knows me too well, darn it).

So, am now an assistant Alpha leader (for an evening) as well as SocSec of the uni CU... why don't we just be done with it and call me 'Archbishop Singleton'... can't anyone SEE I'm faking all this?

Bob, when we are married, I promise I'll share everything with you... even my flu germs.

Post-Alpha Wasn't too bad. Turns out it's held in room above F&Ferret.

Always assumed it was held at church, but this venue much more cosy. All v informal… cool music in background when video not on. LOTS of yumeroonie food – always helps.

Is all v well for the lovely Pippa Gumbel, being married to the Cn equivalent of George Clooney. Now and then he (Nicky, not George) refers to her, v lovingly, and the camera zooms in on her – she's v pretty really, for someone older.

Wish I were her and he were mine (if he was a lot younger).
They met at uni you know…

Does he get his shirt laundered between sessions? Sure have seen other bits of video in the past and his shirt has remained the same. Perhaps he has a load of that particular shirt… or perhaps, being at least ½ divine, he doesn't sweat.

Is that huge bunch of flowers behind him left over from someone's funeral?

Dear Nicky,

You said something about some Cns being like chameleons – adapting to each environment (whether it be with Cns or non-Cns) accordingly. The they're like chameleons on tartan when they're with both Cns and non-Cns… this will be me on my forthcoming trip to Romania. Will anyone notice? Will it hurt?

You also said we ought not to live such double lives. Huh. Easier said than done, Nicky-babe.

Still, you made me think.

What motivates you, eh? How come you're so keen to tell others about God? You must really think he's worth it. Wish I had your faith.

Do you sweat, or just own loads of those shirts?

Please don't think me rude for asking – I'm a student and students are supposed to ask questions… so they tell me.

Have you ever thought about becoming a stand-up chameleon? You crease me up! Particularly loved your gag:

'If all the people who had ever fallen asleep during a church service were laid down end to end…

they'd be a whole lot more comfortable!'

Keep up the good work.

Big hugs and kisses (errrrr… for Pippa, that is),

Jude

Think I meant to say 'stand-up comedian'… sorry, but is v late and brain hurts just typing this.

Sat 12 Mar

Another reason don't want Libs to come to Rom is Oren. How's he gonna lead us all effectively with his mistress in the team, huh? Hope they don't snog between painting sessions.

Libs has finished all but one of her assignments, the cow.

Perhaps am not cut out for doing degree… things sail along OK for a while, but when assignments or exams come alone, just can't cope.

Fax did BURP…

'Right. Scenario. A man bursts into your house with a loaded gun. Says he's gonna shoot your granny. He walks over to her and aims the gun at her head. The intruder has his back to you… you know that you could knock him out with the cricket bat you have in your hand. If you do this though, it might kill him.

What do you do?'

Thought he'd gone bonkers at 1st… what else COULD you do but knock the guy out… then remembered am supposed to be thinking from Cn point of view… and Cns aren't supposed to kill people… are they? Heated debate took place… at one point Lydia asked Duncs if he'd knock the guy out… he replied that he wouldn't as he was a pacifist, as was Jesus (remind me not to be with Duncs when next mugged at gunpoint). Oren was asked the same question, and said,

'No.'

We all gasped… couldn't quite imagine Oren failing to defend the weak. Then he added,

'If you'd known my gran, you'd know she wouldn't need my help… she'd knee him in the goolies while calling the police on her mobile… I'd only get in the way.'

Me and him shared a knowing smile.

Made me miss Maisie tho. Always grin to myself when I think of her, then get sad that she's gone, then feel guilty that I don't think about her enuf. If I died tomorrow, would people still be thinking about me a few months down the line?

As before, Fax gave us no answers… he's gotta stop doing this… gives me 'wonderment' overload.

In between BURP and F&Ferret, Oren asked me if I'd type up our trip itinerary for him, as he's busy doing all the other prep. Great, so he doesn't think me committee material, yet thinks I can handle doing HIS paperwork.

Still, nice to be given some responsibility at last, I guess.

Libs been pestering me frequently to decide what I want from catalogue, so she can claim her money off.

There's too much to do in life.

Really, there is.

Sun 13 Mar

6:34 am

Just rang Abby in total panic… haven't sent Mum a card (is Mother's Day). Soon relaxed when Abby said she'd sent card and flowers from both of us, in anticipation of me forgetting. Phew!

Wouldn't dare ring other pals at this stupid time of am, but kids always get Abby up super-early… when we have kids, they'll be genetically engineered in some way so they never wake up before… say… 10 am.

Sorted.

Post-church Oren asked if I'd done trip itinerary yet… lied – said it was all done, but computer playing up so hadn't emailed it to him yet. He offered to come by and look at computer. He may as well have yelled, 'Liar, liar… pants on fire!' How come he always knows stuff about me?

At coffee, Fax heard Lydia and I stressing over how we're gonna cope in strange country for 10 days with no shower… what about de-hairing ourselves? What about our hair/skin/nails etc? He said,

'Long ago, the people of Nicaragua believed that if they threw beautiful young women into a volcano it would stop erupting'.

An effective convo stopper… but is Nicaragua anywhere near Romania? What's he saying… that we shouldn't be so concerned with our appearance?

That we're gonna get thrown into the nearest volcano on arrival in

Romania?

Do they HAVE volcanoes?

Trip is so near now that seriously getting stressed... is not just plane flight that freaks me out (you ever SEEN that film – *Alive*?) but the fear that wells up inside when think how far away will be from all that I know. We could all get kidnapped/murdered/held for ransom by terrorists etc. Why am I so scared of so much in life?

Reuben all in a state re Nazarene... HE wants them to write their own stuff. THEY want to do worship stuff, and the odd Delirious? cover. No doubt he's heavily talented in the area of songwriting... he ought to do a Robbie Williams, dump those prats and go solo... they're only holding him back.

Kept a look out for SwingGuy (as did at BURP yesterday). No one seems to know of a Cn who fits his description. Shame.

Watched Kilroy with Libs after lunch (she videos it... huh?). Went into bit of a dream... I was presenter on TV, much like Kilroy... but then expanded thinking so that was on GMTV/RI:SE, or even keeping Richard company when Judy wanted a break... or how about my own show... *Jude*? Why stop at presenting? Could move into singing... could sing for Nazarene... no... for Delirious?. They'd ask me to contribute to their latest single... we'd finally make it to No 1 – Delirious? featuring Jude Singleton.

Would be famous... have singing career in style of Cliff (neverending)... would be stinking rich...

Asked Libs if she thought I'd ever be rich and/or famous...

'No, doll, never,' she said.

The truth hurts.

1:24 am Still sweating over assignments... started last one just after Coronation St... deadline is tomorrow.

Tue 15 Mar

Handed all 5 assignments in yesterday. Hope are OK.

Is Rag Wk. Not involved... seems to include students drinking vast amounts of alcohol, parties (with alcohol) and processions (alcohol) and other stuff that am not sure is entirely legal, but is OK, as all for charity.

Oooo... Door...

Was Libs, with my post… Mum's sent some M.O.N.E.Y! (Must be 'Daughter's Day'… if I ever get into parliament, shall propose a notion that this be added to the calendar.) Mum says to buy my fave LP.

Not sure what LP is… will spend it on long skirts for Rom (Oren says we'll need them for church).

Propose a 'notion'?
Or should that be 'motion'?
Do they pass 'motions' in parliament?
Don't they HAVE loos there?

Post-shops Hung out in McDs with Sas for ages… Duncs n Lauren joined us for a bit… all excited about Spring Harvest… v tempted to ask them why spending 5 days in resort jam-packed full of other Cns would be anything to get excited about… 'terrified' is more the word that springs to mind. Still, Minehead's got fab swimming pool… would prob be more at home spending 5 days whizzing down those water slides than 10 days on other side of world (well… sorta).

You know when you're in McDs (or other public loos)… why is it you have to queue for so long? What are they DOING in there? Today there were 4 loos, all occupied for like 3 mins, and still no one coming out.

How hard can it be… go in, pee, come out again. What else goes on in there that I don't know about? Stayed in an extra minute longer, just in case the queue thought, 'She was quick – she didn't do what you're supposed to do.'

Shoppers… huh.

Went to help Lauren get new trainers (trainers are no easy thing for geeks to buy alone). Have decided that, tho we're never gonna be bessie mates (as they say on Brookie) Duncs and Lauren aren't so bad, on their own. It's when they join forces and act all 'couply' that they drive me insane (or, more insane). Saw Fax in shoe shop (our 5th) – he said that before the 1800s there were no separately designed shoes for right and left feet. Is prob a good thing he's not coming to Rom… don't think they're quite ready for him yet.

On purchase of trendy trainers, dragged Lauren around to help me get these long skirts. When trying one on, asked her if it made my bum look too big. 'No, not at all, it looks great,' etc. Then heard, from other side of shop, 'Babe, your arse looks SO fat in that they'll CHARGE you to take it on the plane.'

Was Libs.

Didn't buy it – there are some things about which Libs is always honest…
'bum size' is one of them.

Wed 16 Mar

Just back from yet another yawnyawn lecture. After Fri will have no such
torture for 3 WEEKS! Yip yip skippie doo dar!

In fit of boredom, have spent last 37 mins reading thru some of my letters
to you. Nearly gave myself whiplash as cringed severely a no of times…
whole body kind of lurched backwards in disgust. Some day, will go back
do serious editing. Just the odd tweak here and there… for example,
instead of faffing around with alternative diets, will be down at gym, working on overall body tone/tight abs etc. Instead of spying on unsuspect-
ing/innocent in-laws, will be studying around clock for degree, with intent
of getting a 1st.

Pringles will become rice cakes and *Hollyoaks* become *Panorama*.

If, perchance, you're reading the unedited version… please make
allowances…

Must start to pack. Big job tho – will go see how Libs doing with hers…

Hmmm. She hasn't started packing, but says we can do it together on Thur
eve. Pointed out that we're GOING on Fri eve… she just said to 'chill' and
not get knickers in twist etc.

Ooooh… knickers – must add to list.

Was awkward as Libs had a pal in her room who was reading out this wk's
horoscopes. Never know what to say when people ask me my starsign. If
you say you don't know, they just ask when your b'day is, work it out for
you, and continue to read out your destiny to you… which have always
been taught is v v bad as it's all demonic… blah blah blah. Course, you
could be clever and lie about what sign you are, so that what they read out
isn't really your 'reading' and you can't be influenced/affected by it… but
then lying's a sin too, innit?

Told her was Capricorn…
which am not.

But hey… someone who's poss about to chuck in whole God-package is allowed to choose between her sins, so there.

Thur 17 Mar

Called in on Abby to say goodbye. Is daft as sometimes don't see them for a couple of wks, and will only be gone for 10 days… still, it's a long way to go… seemed like the right thing to do. Always good to see the kids anyway… will miss them loads.

Libs just been here… had thought she'd come to help me pack, but instead she had a go at me for not ordering anything from catalogue yet (she's just discovered that the 'friends' deal is dissolved if it doesn't happen by certain time, and our time's run out).

So am here on my tod, trying to pack. What does one take to a country one knows nowt about, where one will be painting schools/giving aid to the poor etc? Huh?

Hope Libs will be less narked with me by tomorrow… can hardly see how whole thing is my fault anyway.

Friends… who needs 'em?

Fri 18 Mar

What a nightmare.

8:52 am Mum rings – pack insect repellent.
9:42 am Mum again – know how to ask for the nearest police station in Romanian, in case you lose your group.
10:16 am Mum – don't keep your money in a 'dangly bag'… a 'bumbag' won't get snatched.
10:52 am Mum – ring me as soon as you get there.
11:12 am Mum – unless it's too late, in which case ring next morning.
12: 24 pm Mum – remember to take sweets to suck on plane to stop ears popping.
And so on…

The calls got more spread out, but she finally stopped ringing sometime during voting on *Ready, Steady, Cook*, when told her she was stressing me out big-time.

Speaking of stress… am currently staring at my case – it contains 10 pairs of knickers and *Learning to Fly*. The latter ought to go in hand luggage so can read further adventures of Vic Becks on plane.

So, just knickers then…

6:33 pm Am now emailing you this from Oren's laptop… we're in Mike's kitchen, enjoying a stylish send-off (champagne and Marks&Sparks snacks!). Am trying not to let others see what am typing, which is diff as Libs has got them all hyper – they get a full view of screen each time they run round table.

I am NOT hyper… nor am I enjoying myself. Am not part of this merriment.

Feel numb.

Don't care about poor people… don't care about missing tonight's Rag Ball (Duncs, Lauren, Fax and Sas are here – all dressed as Powerpuff Girls).

Keep expecting someone spiritual (like Lydia or Mike) to give me another verse… like that one on truth and freedom… or tell me that God says he really DOES exist etc. When? When's it gonna all fall into place? WHY am I going to Romania? Why am I… oh, we're off to airport… wish me luck/God's blessing (please delete as appropriate)…

Rude monkeys...

Wed 23 Mar

Am writing to you by hand – will type it up when back on British soil. Has all been bit of a blur… will try to recall my thoughts so far…

Plane journey = fear and sadness… decided that, should the *Alive* scenario become a reality, they'd eat either me or Libs 1st, being 2 of chunkiest passengers. Also kept thinking about Maisie and my nan… fought back tears-a-plenty (stopped at services on way to airport – saw hand driers made in Honeypot Lane).

Jon's been studying map of England in the evenings (must be homesick). He spotted a village called Singleton! Is near Blackpool. Perhaps should give up on you Bob, and move there… be a Singleton, IN Singleton, all my days… anyhow – B'pool's cool – all those trams, illuminations, Pepsi Max Big One, donkey rides… wow – my knowledge of B'pool is outstanding… will quit degree and go work for B'pool tourist board, whilst residing in Singleton, ON MY OWN.

Feels freaky to be spending time with both Libs and BURPers (and bunch from Oren's church). Am so used to being 1 person with her, and another with them. Not that have been complete pagan outside of BURP (unless you include the 1 heaving drinking session, cult mtg, getting off with Tate, getting stoned on hash cookies etc).

When Oren told us about this trip he omitted the smallprint…

'It'll be quite cold' = 'Body quickly forgets what it means to sweat.'

'You might find the food a bit different' = 'Grim. Grim grim grim.'

Was offered this stuff called 'Salata De Boeuf' which you'd have thought was beef salad, but looked far more sus than that. Is offensive to Romanians to refuse their food… just thought of Mum's coronation chicken (that it vaguely resembled) and downed it in one. Puke city.

Whilst brightening up the walls of the infant class with a 'zoo scene', Lydia asked if I'd be sending Reuben a postcard… they all sniggered. Turns out they ALL knew about my… feelings, for my love.

Nightmare.

Have they known from the start? Hmmm. Can't think what gave it away… not like have said anything to anyone. If one more person asks me if I want a stamp/pen/postcard/directions to nearest PO… will stick their head in pot of paint until they stop wriggling (don't tell Duncs tho – isn't a v pacifist thing to do).

Think it was the following day when some guys from Oren's church got bored with painting cute monkeys/fluffy penguins… they decided to have huge argument instead.

Intense S&V Cn No 1 said that what we were doing in painting this school etc, was more important than evangelism. Intense S&V Cn No 2 disagreed… strongly. No 2 said we should put down our paintbrushes, go out into the village, doing door-to-door witnessing. No 1 abandoned his monkey to say,

'Imagine a travelling group of unsaved, starving people. The nearest town from this group is 50 miles away, and you are in it. You have a lorry, but only enough petrol to get it to the group once. If they don't have a lorry full of food straight away, they'll die. If they DO get food, they are likely to travel, and become inaccessible. What do you fill the lorry with – Bibles, or food?'

Wondered if he were related to Fax.

Just before someone got hurt, Jon pointed out that the monkeys looked as though they were doing something rather rude… and ought to be completed in an appropriate fashion, lest we pollute the minds of the infant class of Boarta Primary School.

Think would give those villagers food.
As Libs pointed out, in true student fashion…
you can't eat Bibles.

Asked Lydia and Jon re Bibles or food… said they'd think about it… which is cheating.

These 3 (Libs, Lydia and Jon) have been welded together since day 3.

Day 1 saw one of Oren's bunch befriend her… but then launch a fairly violent 'repent or perish' attack on Day 2, putting Libs off, just a tad… surprise surprise. Libs said that listening to her reminded her of *Yoho Ahoy* (kiddies prog, where all they say is 'Yoho ahoy', in a variety of ways) in that she could hear the noise, but it made no sense whatsoever.

So now she's linked up with L&J. Odd – I feel like giant gooseberry if with them for more than a few mins... she seems right at home tho... hope THEY don't try to convert her. She's well-missing her therapeutic pints of Dry B – I won't be held responsible for her behaviour should she get angered.

Would I even WANT Libs to become a Cn? Hmmmm.

Oh, talking of Libs... saw her taking couple of blue pills with her (boiled) water. Drugs?

Nearly finished Vic's book. Is all getting v freaky... Vic's getting hate mail... someone's threatened to kidnap Brooklyn... like, what's HE done?

Yesterday, Oren asked if I was missing Bob. Didn't answer, but asked if he were missing Caroline. He said, 'No, we've split up.' Turns out they finished about a month ago... she wasn't invited to his meal-thing, but turned up anyway, hoping to get back with him. He turned her down. Hmmmmm.

Fri 25 Mar

Only 1 guy from Oren's bunch looks tasty... but he's so yawnyawn. Really can't be bothered. Who needs a bloke anyway, huh?

Chatted with Libs this am – she's NOT on drugs... blue pills are Prozac! Says she's been on it since the day after she told me about the abortion (she'd never told anyone before this). Great – so now am responsible for this too. She says she just needs to sort herself out, and this is part of the process... that it won't be a permanent thing. Know masses of students on the stuff now, and plenty more on stuff a darn sight stronger. Do I need it? OK, so have calmed down a bit since outburst at Oren's meal... but has left big knot inside. Something's gonna burst again soon – only a matter of time. Don't think am medically off trolley, but then again...

We are sleeping in the school – the lads in 1 classroom and lasses in another (the 'zoo' one – those monkeys still look rude, even tho finished). Is no running water, so Oren's bunch have made makeshift 'shower' in play-ground (errr... manky field). Is sim to Big Brother 3 'poor side' one, in that someone has to pour water over you, and you're never quite sure if all your bits are fully hidden from view... v stressful. Is only 2 degrees here – water like ice. Only had 2 'showers' so far – not intending to brave such torture again.

When the locals introduce me to their pals, in Romanian, am sure they're saying,

'This is Jude, from England. Don't get too close... she's a real minger.'

As for the loos... wooden boxes with holes in, that you sit on... deposit what's surplus to requirement... then it just SITS THERE with the rest of the... dung, coz there's NO FLUSH. Urgghhhhhh!!! Come back long queues for McD loos – all is forgiven... at least they're hygenic/humane/don't make you wanna PUKE.

Jon's been in the wars (literally).

Yesterday, he and Lydia were at the school on their own (the rest of us were walking in the hills... think the lovebirds wanted to be on their own). They saw 2 lads fighting in the playground/field. Lydia says the bigger one was really laying into the smaller one, and it looked like he meant business. When Jon saw a knife (come from pocket of big one), he knew it was serious, and the smaller one's life could be in danger. Without thought for himself, Jon launched in direction of big one, who ran off... but not before he'd stabbed Jon in left arm.

He was carted off to hospital (light yrs away – took them 3 hrs apparently). He was in for the night and came back this aft. They did what they could, but he's still in a lot of pain, and will need physio etc, when we get home. He's having trouble moving his arm properly... Dr said there might be long-term damage.

The kid he rescued has attached himself to our group – helped out with the painting today and brought us bread and cheese for lunch... cute.

Have been chatting to Oren a fair bit. He says Maisie's death was one of the hardest things he's ever had to deal with. Feel guilty now – always thought he was so 'in control' and strong... hadn't really occurred to me he might be suffering too. Why am I all so me me ME?

Hate to say it, but he's impressed us all on this trip. He's mastered Romanian since his last trip here 2 yrs ago. He brought a suit to wear in church, which is kinda the done thing for Cn blokes over here. He even cleared up the mess when one of his bunch (who'd obviously MISSED their trip planning mtgs) started dancing (to long slow hymn). Dancing is a sin in eyes of Cns over here. This freak's dancing was a sin to all humanity, worldwide... take it from me – was in style of Popstars/Idol worst rejects.

Oren also has a knack of diverting our host's attention when we're drinking their coffee (thick, strong, black… cold) so we can spit it into nearby bushes. Will never drink coffee again.

This eve, any friendship that may have been developing between me and newly-separated Oren was brought to swift end. Word had got around that he was 'speaking' at Soul Survivor this summer. Joked to the others that he must be leading a seminar called 'How to be the most boring Christian ever' not realising that he was painting just a few metres away from us, around a corner. He came over, all red-faced and angry, saying: 'Actually, it's called "Living with alcoholism",' and stormed off.

Libs then had huge go at me.
In panic, had a go right back at her for sleeping with Oren.

She laughed… a lot, then went off in same direction as Oren. Not the expected response. Will try to avoid them both for remainder of trip. V tempted to tell L&J re Oren's sleeping habits, but won't… he'll expose himself, eventually… perhaps is all part of being an alcoholic (he sure kept that one quiet, huh?).

Bob – please fly on in and whisk me away. Today's confirmed:

1] *Can't trust my friends.*
2] *Can't trust myself.*
3] *Can't trust in 'god' (he's getting a little 'g' coz that's how I feel about things right now).*

This trip is pants.

I hereby officially chuck in my quest for the truth… it wasn't in England and it sure as hell isn't out here.

Things are gonna change when I get back… big-time.

Sun 27 Mar

11:48 pm

Yeah, is v late, but got lots to tell you.

My head is spinning… in a good way. Feel mixture of elation/exhaustion/shock, but again… in a good way!

Right, well, it was the church mtg this eve that really got things cooking. Had spent most of wkd feeling the same as did Fri eve… making plans for handing in notice at BURP, avoiding seeing any of them again… wondering which other friends I should pick to hang out with, and which guy to go for (throw myself at unashamedly)... even practised speech for parents/Abby, whereby I announced and explained my choice to leave 'the church'... for good.

So, church was the last place I wanted to be this eve... but was comforted by the thought that it would be my last ever service.

And then it happened.

The preacher opened with this verse:

Veti cunoaste adevarul si adevarul va va face slobozi.

(Translated = You will know the truth, and the truth will set you free.)

Hard to say what happened next as not entirely sure. Would love to say the sermon that followed was amazing... but don't remember it much. This kind of bizarre feeling of... of joy consumed me. Wondered if it was happening to us all, 'Toronto-blessing' style... but everyone else seemed well-into the sermon – happy perhaps, but not like I was. I also felt warm, which was clearly supernatural as nothing 'warm' about Romanian eves at this time of yr.

Warm inside, like someone had just started a log fire, and was gently stoking it, causing more and more of the wood to catch alight. I felt safe, for 1st time in ages. No longer vulnerable... no longer an easy target. Most of all... I felt God.

Yeah! I did! He was all around me, beside me, in me. God was back (or was it ME that went walkabout?).

Couldn't get king-size grin off my face for rest of service. Caught a few lines of what was being preached... namely some verses from Psalm 139 – all that stuff about how much God loves us and knows us. Like little arrows of fire these verses headed straight for the newly-lit fire within me, causing the flames to lick higher and higher... didn't dare open my mouth in case flames singed hair of old lady sitting in front of me.

Felt like that kid must have felt when Jon rescued him – full of gratitude.

Thought back to all that's happened since JimDream... Tate's abrupt departure during our date, my friendship with Libs, getting involved with BURP, Maisie, my new improved relationship with Abby...

he was there all along.

God.

Who I thought was sleeping/ignoring me/dead. He's let me do certain stuff, but never let things get out of hand. He's provided me with supportive Cn pals, a happening CU, a lively church and a cool chaplain… all to keep me from jumping overboard, so to speak.

When I was little, people used to congratulate my parents on the fact that me and Abby didn't fight. What they didn't realise was that we didn't really TALK at all… I was in awe of her for ages… then skipped straight to resenting her and being uncontrollably jealous.

Perhaps having fights is all part of a relationship… any relationship. If so, everything since JimDream has been my 1st ever row with God. Now we're making up! Is rather like how all that stuff with Abby helped me to get to know the 'real' her, and get closer to her. All I want now is to get closer and closer to God. It sounds all cliched and OTT, but is just how it is…

Anyhow, at end of mtg, opened my eyes (hadn't even realised they were shut!) and spotted bloke a few pews in front that hadn't seen til now. Recognised him tho… v tall and fit… then he turned to face me. Instantly saw it was SwingGuy from the park, the night of Oren's meal. He winked right at me! Not a flirty kind of wink, but one that said, 'See… told ya!'

He wasn't part of Oren's bunch… something told me he wasn't part of anyone's bunch, not in human terms. I turned to face the preacher as he began his closing prayer. The interpreter had given up and just let him go for it. It didn't matter that I couldn't understand each word… he was so clearly and unashamedly in love with God… I cried.

Turned back to look at SwingGuy when prayer over… he was gone. He'd been sitting in middle of pew, with several people on each side. Now there was just a space. No one had left the mtg. Couldn't see him, but knew he wasn't far away.

Figure that if God went to all the trouble to send one of his own to pathetic little me… at least some of Psalm 139 must be a reality, if not all.

Feeling this 'safe' helped me to put to bed my fears… the fear of evil Romanian villagers, who up to this point I'd been convinced would break into our classrooms in the night and attack us/fear of attackers in general/the dark/World War 3… of Satan, who's been so v busy keeping me fearful of life for so many years now.

Sorry – lot's of waffle. Just can't keep it all in tho. Don't want to scare the others with my new-found fire quite yet. Have spoken to one of them tho…

let me expand on that…

After mtg, our lot decided what we'd do. Was on such a high, didn't take note of what was discussed. Sort of 'came round' about ½ an hr later, when found myself walking up huge hill, overlooking village… with Oren! Yeah – just me and him! He could have been the village postman for all I cared… just had to tell someone about what'd happened to me… so did, at length. He didn't say much, but could tell he understood.

It was only THEN that began to question where the others were, and why we were climbing a hill etc. Said to Oren, 'Why are we here?' Turns out the others had voted to stay at the pastor's house for food… Oren had wanted to go walking, and I'd agreed to go with him (so he says).

From a v high up spot, just near some woods, we could see the whole village below us… it looked so quaint (as the Americans say), you'd hardly guess there were families in desperate need of food, clothes, education, hope, God.

Oren said how it was his DAD who was an alcoholic, and not him. He's now in prison… his mum doesn't cope v well. He said how alcohol changes people… sometimes it only took 1 drink for his dad to turn… bad. Said how it was his mum who really showed him what God's love was like – unconditional, eternal etc.

The sun was setting, turning the village of Boarta fantastic shades of red and yellow – quite a sight, like something from a 'Visit the beautiful village of Boarta' brochure, not that there'd ever be such a thing.

Oren then asked if I wanted to go to Soul Survivor with him, to support him with his seminar.

'Go-waaaaaan,' he pleaded (in style of Father Ted's housekeeper), 'you can even drive my car if you want – it'll be good practice for you!'

Couldn't quite work it all out… here I was, chatting to Oren, who's never exactly been my fave person, mainly coz thought he didn't like me… and here HE was, asking ME to come camping with him!

Said I'd go. He smiled. I smiled. The sun smiled one last smile, then popped off for the evening.

He leaned over, took my face in his hands… and kissed me.

We kissed each other.

After a few seconds he pulled away, which panicked me a bit… until he pushed back a few strands of my hair that had sat between our lips, and then we were off again. What can I say? It was pure heaven!

OK, so I'd enjoyed kissing Tate, at 1st... but he didn't know me – didn't appreciate me for who I was. Here was someone who knew me only too well – (zits/glasses/failure in life) but still wanted to be close to me. Now THAT'S the real turn-on!

Was no major snogging session – no stopwatch to hand, but would estimate it lasted 10 secs, post-hair removal. It was quite enough though – enough to feel a whole lot of things I hadn't felt for Oren before, or had I?...

As we sat there, hand-in-hand, he admitted he'd been finding out about me from one of my friends... Libs! Said he'd liked me when he 1st met me, but didn't think I was interested in him. When he hadn't thought me suitable for being on BURP committee, it was because he knew where I was spiritually (nowhere!) and thought it best for ME to be honest with the others.

He and Caroline just sort of happened – she pushed for them to go out. She'd been pushing to get engaged for a while, and when Oren found out I was going out with Bob, he kind of let that happen too. Not long after, he knew he wasn't really in love with Cazzer, the way you have to be to marry them, and told her.

At his meal, he got chatting to Bob (my escort) and soon sussed out what was going on. Huh – rumbled!

He'd seen Libs a couple of times... she'd told him how I always went on about how annoying he was, and how bitchy Caroline was etc. Said there was no doubt I fancied the pants off him, I just wasn't aware of it. It was OREN who'd helped Libs with the 'Jude-jumping-out-of-window-to-pass-test' idea. Libs rang OREN when she saw me go into Mr NextDoor's room, so he could be the one to rescue me.

It was HIM who'd left that monkey keyring outside my door... it was when he thought me and Bob were serious, so didn't want to embarrass himself, but wanted me to have it anyway. Said it'd killed him to see me playing with it all the time – he sooooo wanted me to know it was from him.

You know in corny films, when they say, 'I didn't want the moment to end'? Well, guess what... I didn't want the moment to end!

Life made sense. God was there... and so was Oren.

It did end tho, and here I am, back here, writing to you, in my scrawly handwriting, while everyone else in this classroom sleeps soundly, even the rude monkeys.

Am still in a daze… may it last forever!

Have only got to wake up tomorrow am having lost 1½ stone, all zits, and my hair agreeing to obey me… and life will be perfect!

Serious nose-picking

Wed 30 Mar

Home again.

Well, at parents house… is this still home, or is Bymouth home? Hmmm.

My WWJD band is back where it belongs… on my wrist. And NOT for benefit of parents/Cn pals etc… but for ME – to remind myself of who is now the most important person in my life.

Have been apart from Oren for almost 48 hrs – it's killing me! We've rung/txted lots. He's coming HERE this wkd (Easter), which means he'll meet my parents, pals, church, town… can't wait!

We travelled home on Monday. No one seemed to think it too odd that Oren and I were suddenly an item. Apologised to Libs for accusing her of sleeping with Oren. Told her about Sun eve, and how things were all hunky-dory between me and God now. Kind of freaky, seeing as rarely even mentioned the word 'God' in her presence before. She took it OK. When I asked her if she'd had many interesting chats with Lydia and Jon, she replied, 'Yeah, but don't pop ya cork babe… I'm not you. Rather like my car, I'm just not convertible. Still, Lyd n Jon are cool, and you and Oren are… bearable… so perhaps I'll come to one of your fart things sometime.'

Started to tell her we were actually called BURP, not fart… but what's the use?!

We'd all made some good friends in the village and it was hard to leave (tho not that hard when you began to visualise hot showers and flushing toilets). Mon am the pastor's wife made us 'gogoshi' (pronounced 'go-gosh'), which are doughnuts. They were fab! Couldn't believe they'd made us suffer with such grim food for 9 days… then produced home-made, warm, squidgy, scrumptious DOUGHNUTS on day 10! If I ever go again, will demand them on day 1 (and not ask for levels of calories/fat, that could be higher than is desired to lose weight).

Reuben and Mike were there to collect us at airport (Oren's bunch were staying there for another couple of wks). When I 1st spotted Reuben, he was just coming out of the men's loos, picking his nose. Not just a tactful removal of unsightly bogey, this was something more serious – his finger was shoved waaaaaaaay up left nostril, and showed no sign of coming down 'til it got a decent catch.

WHY did I ever fancy him? Why why why?

We (yes, I am now part of a 'we' – hurrah!) went in Mike's car. We were barely out of the airport when I launched into my Sun-eve-story, which lasted almost all the way to Stonehenge (where my Dad picked me up, as arranged). Going over it all again was helpful for me… realised that yet ANOTHER thing happened Sun night… my guilt re abandoning God/all that with Tate/going my way/lying re faith etc… it all went for a long hike - haven't seen it since!

Mike was well-chuffed, to the extent that am sure could see tears in corner of his eyes. He gave me a word of warning tho – not to think that this would mean things would ALL fall into place pronto. There would still be things I wouldn't 'get' about God/Christianity/life in general… but God would tell me stuff, when I needed to know it, if I stayed close to him. Like he said, none of us is ever gonna know it all. He said something else that I hadn't really thought about, but that really made me grin… that now I know that being a Cn is MY choice, and not just because of my upbringing, or my pals etc.

Reflecting on what he said now (and I am able to 'reflect' on things, being a student and all) am glad that it all happened in the order it did. God started a fire in me… or was the fire God himself? Anyway, this came 1st, THEN I saw an angel (I think) and THEN I bagged myself a (hot) Cn boyfriend. If either of these 2 things had come 1st, would have to question my motive for returning to faith in God.

He's so real to me now… more real than the things I see, touch and hear on a daily basis. He's… oh, phone…

Was Lydia. Jon's arm still bad.
Must send him a card (from me AND my BOYFRIEND, naturally!).

Hmmmm. Guess when it comes to sacrifice, Jon sees eye to eye with Jesus.

Fri 1 April

9:32 am

Paannicccccccc!! Oren just rang, said he'd realised how busy he is over Easter and won't be able to come.

Can't BELIEVE this… is this his way of letting me down gently? He seemed so keen til now. Is so TYPICAL that this should happen to me… will NEVER be able to get myself a decent bloke who actually likes me and… hang on, phone…

10:14 am Was Oren, with 'April Fool'!

Will forgive him, but only coz I love him…

Huh?
Who said that?
Do I?
That's a bit freaky, but quite possible.

We chatted about his dad and stuff. Oren says he knows he goes a bit OTT when BURPers have been drinking… to him, all alcohol is bad news, because of what it did to his dad. He admitted it's not the only thing he can get intense about… said he wants ME to help him get the right balance! Ahhhhhh – bless.

Told him that some of my bitterness toward him was perhaps due to fact that knew he WAS right to be concerned about certain things… it just made me feel guilty as it showed up my apathy.

Felt good to be honest with someone, for a change.

Strange, but he says that it was my LACK of faith that attracted him to me (oh, and the fact he thinks am piece of hot totty!). He could see that I was lost, but intent on discovering the truth. He knew that, when I rediscovered it/God, my faith would be so much stronger. I'd be someone who'd really want to live for God 100% because I worked it out for myself… it wasn't handed to me on a plate.

Bit freaky – does he assume am going to morph into super, S&V-style Cn?!

Still, he's right… do want to go for God 100% now, as I know he does also. His faith is so rock-steady… why he ever waited around for me to get my faith all sorted will never know. Wonder if

Sorry, had to break for phone. Was Libs. She's still on about this catalogue thing – how she's so pee-ed off that she left it too late to get the voucher. In a flash a thought came to me (not something that happens often/ever). Told her it was a bit like that with God. He's made an offer… is up to her to respond, but there is a deadline – either when she dies, or when he comes back, either of which could happen tomorrow. There was a long pause at her end when had said this… then she said, 'Hmmm… yeah, thanks for that, hon.'

Don't THINK this means have converted her, but hey – it's a start!

S'pose God must have put that thought in my head. More proof that him and me are pals again (no way I would have said that to her otherwise).

3:16 pm Managed to put ON 3 lbs in Romania… v bad. Blame all those gogoshi. Have asked parents for money equivalent of E Egg instead of egg itself. Told Abby same thing (she usually gets me a whopper!). Oh yeah, Abby and co are coming home tomorrow too… so house will be chocka. Mum dashing round like some psychotic house cleaner from Stephen King novel, like she's gonna attack/drown in bleach anyone who DARES leave a rim round bath. Bless. Dear God – please DON'T let me be like her when am a mum.

Back to all-important subject of E Eggs tho – Oren says he's gonna get me a choccie one anyway, coz

1| *I love choccie, and*
2| *he loves me just the way I am*!!

Oh… he also says I shouldn't stress about my gifting – he reckons I'm jam-packed full of giftings… I just need time to 'release' them!

Think have found the perfect bloke…

4:47 pm Oooooooohhh… that's a bit harsh!

Am listening to Chris Moyles interview with so-called 'guest'… could he BE any bitchier? Still, is v funny guy – has grown on me.

Wish I could be so quick with my jokes.
Wish I HAD jokes to be quick with!

Often hear his show when in Lib's room… think will switch to Radio 1 when go back to uni. My homesickness packed up and left shortly before Rom trip. Having a boyfriend's gonna help too. There's only so much of T Wogan a girl can take!

Looking back over these 1st 2 semesters, feel like have grown (not just in size). Have learnt more about myself, and finally learnt the truth – God is real, understands me more than I do, is looking out for me, is OK if we go at my pace (slowly)… is crazy for me!

Have made many pals, most of whom have surprised me by turning out to be a different person than had 1st assumed. People are so complicated… studying psychology only makes it worse!

Some things still don't know tho:

1] *Why all the trees on campus have numbers on them?*
2] *Why no one told me I could've done a degree on 'Madonna' instead?*
3] *Why my curtains are waterproof?*

Still, there's time. Wonder if is poss to switch over to Madonna course next semester... wonder if there'll ever be a Vic Becks degree... Finished her book last night – is all OK in the end – Brooklyn remains unharmed... but you'll NEVER guess who it was who'd been threatening them, it was... no, you read it ya-self ya lazy slob!

9:28pm Just got email from Mike. Was scan of article in Bymouth Times...

'Five students of Bymouth university have recently returned from Romania, after a 100-day trip.
This was no holiday though – their work mainly involved panting. They panted the interior of a village school, working with locals from the church.
Oben, the leader of the group, said, 'It's been a worthwhile tip... we've enjoyed ourselves whilst giving a helping hang to the Romanians.'
university Chaplain Mork says: 'They have taken God's love to Romania... I feel privileged to be working alongside such students. If anyone wants any further information, please don't contact me via the Chaplaincy office'.

Hmmmmmmm. If degree thing too hard next semester, will take up job at Bymouth Times as proofreader.

Sat 2 Apr

Note for when go back: return sex books to Oscar.
Don't want 'Oben' finding them, getting the wrong idea!

He should be here in 43 ½ mins (Oren, not Oscar).
Hmmmmm. Should I act cool, or keen?
Studenty jeans, or lady-like skirt?
Cover-up, or au natural (zit city)?
Oooohhhh... wonderment invasion...

Perhaps will just read *heat* to pass time...

Dear Bob is Annie's first book. She is married to Mark, and has two children – Tilly and Fraser. She works as a learning support assistant at her local primary school, as well as studying for a theology degree by distance learning. She loves tiramisu... but gets queasy at the very sight of cucumber.

Visit the Dear Bob website: www.dearbob.com